THE PARTY GUEST

AMANDA ROBSON

Published by AVON
A division of HarperCollins*Publishers* Ltd
1 London Bridge Street
London SE1 9GF

www.harpercollins.co.uk

HarperCollins*Publishers*
1st Floor, Watermarque Building, Ringsend Road
Dublin 4, Ireland

A Paperback Original 2022

First published in Great Britain by HarperCollins*Publishers* 2022

A catalogue copy of this book is available from the British Library.

ISBN: 9780008430627

Typeset in Bembo by Palimpsest Book Production Ltd, Falkirk, Stirlingshire.
Printed and bound in the UK using
100% Renewable Electricity at CPI Group (UK) Ltd

This book is produced from independently certified FSC™ paper to ensure responsible forest management.
For more information visit: www.harpercollins.co.uk/green

To my friends in the Cayman Islands

Prologue

Hatred, envy and resentment live inside me, as acidic as bile. My mood swings, beyond my control, as quickly as a tsunami rises and bares the evil eye of my soul.

1
Ralph

I'm not in a good mood. I'll be forty-five in three days' time. Five years past middle age. Halfway to ninety. It wouldn't be so bad if my life was full of happiness and contentment but, as a matter of fact, it stinks.

As I sit in the taxi on the way from Naples airport to Villa Panorama just outside Praiano, with my girlfriend and what's left of my family, I resent how much money this birthday trip is costing me. Why did I dream up the idea in the first place? So pleased you had agreed to join whatever birthday jaunt I suggested, it was to impress you, Sarah, my – unfortunately – *ex*-wife. Why did you walk out on us eight years ago, leaving me and our children, who were then only nine and twelve? You said you wanted to live your life alone. You hadn't even run off with someone else. I'm still in love with you, you know that, don't you? And you play upon it sometimes.

But we've managed to continue to bring up our family together, and remained good friends. And from time to time we've even hooked up. So . . . so . . . when I spent thousands of pounds booking this villa for a whole fortnight, in the romantic place where we spent our honeymoon, I was full of hope and expectation.

But you crushed me a few weeks ago when you announced you were bringing a partner. A partner. After all these years! And so now I have invited my on-off girlfriend, Gemma, to join us on this jaunt. To try and make you jealous by showing you that I too can easily find someone else. I'm not proud of myself for using her to save face. Gemma's body is great, but she's not easy to talk to. And the truth is, despite her obvious hopes, I don't want to commit. I don't want to spend a lifetime sitting across from her in awkward silence. I wish I could appreciate my girlfriend the way a pretty thirty-something-year-old deserves to be appreciated. But I know we'll split up soon and I'll use a corny line like *it's not you it's me.*

'Such a long journey, such a drag,' our daughter Janice complains as the taxi pulls up the cliff above Sorrento, the sea below us spangled with diamond crusts of sunshine.

For a second I want to snap back at her. But I take a deep breath and remind myself of how bitter she is, because of the way you left us. Janice is full of angst, unlike her brother, Patrick, who seems to have coped well with our divorce.

A special holiday. After working ninety-hour weeks for so long, two weeks off should be a real treat. But I'm stuck in a taxi with my girlfriend, Gemma, my seventeen-year-old daughter, Janice, my twenty-year-old son, Patrick, and his girlfriend, Anna, while you, Sarah, the love of my life, are about to arrive at the villa I've paid for, with your new lover. Whoop de dooh. Fucking fabulous forty-fifth birthday. Congratulations, Ralph Kensington. Let's crack open the Louis Roederer as soon as we arrive.

2

Sarah

I'm sitting on the Alitalia flight from Heathrow to Naples holding your hand, knowing I should be looking forward to celebrating my doting ex-husband's birthday. Knowing I should be looking forward to seeing my offspring. But I'm not. It's crunch time for you and me, Jack. We need to tell my family the truth about our relationship.

If I could have married you eight years ago, when I left my husband, I would have. We've been together, secretly, ever since then. But I couldn't come clean until now. I love Ralph as a friend, I really do. Just not in the way I love you, Jack. The way I love you is on another level.

I squeeze your hand. You squeeze back. You lean across and kiss me. You pull away.

'Are you nervous?' you ask.

'Not when you kiss me like that.'

3

Ralph

The Mediterranean sun beats down on us as we stumble out of the taxi. I pay the driver. He bangs our suitcases onto the pavement, grunting and inhaling, and lights a cigarette. The bright daylight presses into my eyes like a knife. I fumble in my bag for my sunglasses.

'Where do we go?' Janice demands, hands on her hips.

'Over the road. Down the steps by the church,' I reply.

'With these heavy bags?'

I sigh inside and nod my head.

'Isn't there a lift?' Gemma pipes up. 'I'm not sure I can manage,' she says, rubbing her back.

'We'll just have to. It'll be worth it when we get there.' I step towards her. 'Here, let me help.'

I drag her bag and mine, plastic wheels grinding across melting tarmac, as we cross the road.

'How much further?' Janice asks.

I stop and pull the map the travel company sent us from my pocket. 'We need to go down to the piazza by the church, walk across it, down another set of steps, and the villa is about two hundred yards after that.' I pause. 'It's not far and the view will be well worth it.'

We thump our cases down the marble steps that lead to the piazza. Sighs. Grunts. Groans. Eyes rising to the sky.

'It's your own fault for bringing too much luggage,' I snap.

As we slide our cases across the stone and marble piazza that fronts the church, the world opens out. The bay stretches out beneath us; a turquoise shimmer of ocean, dotted with boats, caressed by a horseshoe of pink and grey cliffs, topped with pine and cypress. Even more beautiful than I remember when you and I came here for our honeymoon, Sarah, over twenty years ago now.

The Amalfi Coast. The most romantic coast in the world when you're young and in love. Everything about it is lyrical. Soft sunrises and colourful sunsets that spread behind a glittering sea. The breathtaking intensity of the cliffs rising from the water like battlements. Houses clinging to the steep land, like brightly coloured limpets, holding on for life itself, surrounded by bougainvillea, rock roses, iris and geranium. Cypress, stone pines, oak, hornbeam, ash and poplar.

Soft light, hot evenings of love and lust. Why couldn't I have pressed a button and stayed here with you, Sarah, young and in love?

'Come on, Dad. Stop daydreaming. Let's get to the villa.' Janice's voice pulls me away from my contemplation of happiness and beauty.

'OK, OK. Just coming.'

I continue to drag mine and Gemma's suitcases along the edge of the piazza, my entourage following me. Down more steps. Along a narrow passageway, past entrances to villas marked with pottery decorations. At last. A sign to Villa Panorama, pointing down another hundred steps.

'They should have warned you about this in the brochure,' Gemma says with a sigh.

My stomach knots. I bite my tongue. Does she have any idea how much this is costing me? We arrive at Villa Panorama. Panorama indeed. The view is a closer but parallel one to the view from the piazza. Exasperation melts and fragments.

'Wow, Dad, this is amazing,' Patrick says.

The young people find prosecco and beer in the kitchen, and gravitate towards the terrace. By the time I have decided which rooms to allocate them, the cover is off the swimming pool. Anna and Patrick have found their swimming costumes and are canoodling in the water, drinks in hand.

'It's beautiful,' Gemma announces. 'But it's a bit of a walk back to the village.'

'Well I'm sure you'll manage,' I reply. I put my arm around her. 'Let me show you to our room.'

I steer her away from the pool and the terrace, through the ground floor of the villa with its bright porcelain-tiled floor decorated with sunflowers, up into the master bedroom, the largest bedroom on the first floor.

'They like heavy furniture, don't they,' she says frowning at the mahogany wardrobe and matching dresser.

'I suppose so,' I reply, shrugging my shoulders.

I open the door to our private balcony. 'Do step outside.'

The balcony contains two sun loungers and a sun umbrella surrounded by pots of patio flowers; iris, lilies, bougainvillea, clematis, jasmine and honeysuckle. The view from the patio, as the cliffs shelve into the sea, is sharp and carved and magnificent.

She takes my hand in hers. 'Thanks for bringing me,' she says.

She turns to me, puts her arms around me and kisses me. I pull away.

'I'm glad you're pleased you came,' I say, voice dry and churlish.

A sad, slow smile. 'That sounds edgy. Why are you so sensitive at the moment?'

'It's just that being here brings back memories.'

4

Gemma

I try to kiss you again, but you back away. I know you are thinking about Sarah. Always thinking about Sarah. I need you. But before I can have you, I need to make you forget about her.

5

Sarah

Ralph opens the door.

'Welcome,' he says with a flourish of his arms.

We drag our suitcases into the hallway. Whitewashed walls. Porcelain floor tiles glazed in yellow and blue. Ralph looks so pleased to see me that even after all these years guilt stumbles inside me. He holds my body too tightly against his in greeting.

'You're wearing Rive Gauche, your old favourite,' he announces as he releases me.

He takes your hand, Jack, and shakes it vigorously.

'Lovely to meet you,' he bellows at you, far too loudly, and I know he is on edge. You give him a guarded smile. His mouth stretches into a line. 'Looking forward to getting to know you,' he continues, voice like lead.

Janice steps into the hallway. 'Hey, Mum.'

'Janice, this is Jack.'

You smile and nod your head. My daughter, Janice, doesn't smile back. My son, Patrick, is here, hugging me. He steps back and a young woman appears by his side. She has a neat, slim figure and a pert face. Pale chestnut hair falls like a helmet down to her earlobes.

'Hey, Mum, this is my girlfriend, Anna.'

'Lovely to meet you,' I say. 'I've heard so much about you. You met on the medical course, didn't you?'

'Yes, during the body dissection,' Anna says.

'Romantic,' I reply laughing.

She stiffens. 'I like to think our relationship is pretty romantic,' she replies, eyes darkening.

I watch her stretch her arm out to hold Patrick's hand, as if for protection. I've said the wrong thing. She's wary of me already. Another young woman steps into the hallway. A friend of the children, presumably. She is curvy and wearing what looks to be an expensive designer dress, clinging to her figure in all the right places.

'Hi. I'm Ralph's girlfriend, Gemma.'

Girlfriend? So young. No wonder he hadn't mentioned her. I'm pleased for him. Now he's met someone, maybe he'll stop fawning over me.

'Let me show you two to your room,' Ralph says.

'Thank you,' I reply.

He leads us up a spiral staircase from the hallway onto the first floor, and then into a double bedroom with a large balcony. Heavy yellow silk curtains and matching counterpane. A mahogany bedhead, and mahogany furniture; characterful and old, giving gravitas to the room.

'It's beautiful, Ralph. Thank you.'

He looks at me wistfully. 'At least somebody is grateful.'

'Surely everybody is. This is such a beautiful place.'

He seems so low. So dispirited. For a second I want to hug him, hold him, tell him everything is all right. But I cannot. Even now after all these years, I'm always having to push him away. He's all over me at the slightest opportunity. He needs to accept I'm with someone else.

'Come on, Ralph, we're going to have a lovely time for your birthday.'

'I hope so,' he replies wistfully.

'Thank you so much for inviting us both. What are we doing on the actual day?' you ask.

'We're off to a restaurant in the mountains,' I watch Ralph reply, looking through you as though you are invisible. Getting to know my family will take some navigating. We have been so secretive about our relationship. They are so used to having me to themselves.

Ralph turns towards me and pushes his eyes into mine. 'Forty-five years old. I can't believe it. Where did all that time go?'

His eyes pool with tears. He steps back and widens his shoulders. He gives us both a bright, forced smile. 'I'll leave you two to unpack.' He pauses. 'Champagne on the terrace in half an hour.' He sidles away, closing the door behind him. Melancholy hovers in the air he leaves behind.

'He's not in a good place, is he? It's all because of me,' I say.

You pull me towards you, and hug me. 'I'm sure they'll all understand, when we explain. I expect Ralph will have moved on more than you think.'

'I hope so.' I sigh. 'I'll tell him first. As soon as I get an opportunity to speak to him in private. I want to give him chance to get his head around this before his actual birthday celebrations begin.'

6

Ralph

I leave you in your bedroom with your new lover. An attractive silver fox, a few years older than us, with sleek metallic hair. He has a resonant television voice, smacking of public school and Oxbridge. Of intellect and success. A superhead. An adviser to Boris Johnson. He has been asked to chair an educational report for the government. You told me all this, over the phone, when I asked what your boyfriend did. You made it sound as if he'll soon breeze his way to a knighthood.

I step into the kitchen and pour myself a brandy. I take a sip and savour the taste as it burns the back of my throat. I down the rest of the glass in one.

7
Janice

I knock on your bedroom door, Mother. You open it and stand in front of me, stone cold beautiful. Flowing blonde locks. Thin pale face. Finely balanced nose. There is something ethereal about you. A look of Galadriel from *Lord of the Rings*.

'Lovely to see you, Janice. Do come in.'

I step into the bedroom you are sharing with your lover, who's unpacking his suitcase. The room is twice as big as the box room Dad has allocated to me. I envy you your sea-view balcony. Jack looks up and pushes his hair from his face.

'Hi, Janice,' he says with a smile.

He looks a bit like Dad, only older. What's wrong with you, Mother? Most women of your age would fancy a younger model. And even though Jack is rather dashing, surely you can see that Dad is just as good-looking? Dad has rock-star good looks. Quite a few of my friends fancy him, in fact. Resentment festers inside me.

'I need to speak with you in private,' I say.

Your lover shrugs, and his smile widens. 'OK. Sure, I'll go for a walk. I'd like to stretch my legs after the journey.'

He crosses the room and stands in front of you. You move your lips towards his. They meet, and I watch you kiss. A slow, passionate, Hollywood kiss that makes me feel sick.

'Don't forget, champagne on the main terrace in about twenty minutes,' you remind him.

His eyes twinkle into yours. 'How could I forget?' He kisses you again and leaves.

'Come and join me on the balcony,' you say, voice happy and resonant.

We sit opposite one another at a small circular table, surrounded by pots of brightly coloured flowers; orchids, lilies, bougainvillea. As I look at you, your complacency and your beauty, my stomach tightens.

'Such a caring mother, aren't you? I can't believe you brought someone with you. This is Dad's celebration, not yours.'

You look at me as if you don't know what to say, mouth slightly open, like a guppy. I raise my arms in the air and widen my shoulders. 'And I want you to know I will never recover from your abandonment.'

'Please, Janice, don't bring this up again. How can you still say that after all the time I have spent with you and Patrick?'

I raise my eyes to the sky. I know what's coming next – the *I love you so much* routine.

Your eyes soften. You smile at me. 'I love you so much, Janice. I didn't abandon you, I just divorced your father. I will never abandon you. Surely you must know by now that I'm always here for you?'

'But you weren't. You could have stayed with Dad for our sake. Surely children should always come first?'

You shake your head. 'I couldn't stay with your dad, Janice, you know that. We've talked about it before.'

I swallow to stop myself from crying. 'But . . . but . . . why? If you loved Patrick and me, you would have.'

'Of course I love you both. Just because a marriage dies doesn't mean you stop loving your children.'

'You always say that, but clearly you just didn't love us enough.'

You shake your head. 'How much is enough? I would die for you.'

'You didn't need to die. All you needed to do was honour your commitment and stay with the man you married.'

I stand up to leave. You stand up and place your hands on my shoulders. I stiffen and step away from you. Your eyes fill with tears. Good. You have made me cry for so many years. It's your turn now.

'Try to understand, Janice. I love you more than anything. If I had taken you both with me, it would have totally crushed your father. I tried, but he was so distressed. I just couldn't do that to him.'

Anger rises inside me. I breathe deeply to stop myself from hurting you. I am not sure how much longer I can contain the evil eye inside me.

8
Sarah

Janice slams the bedroom door. As always, after one of our altercations, part of me dies inside. Our conversations always follow the same pattern. She blames me for abandoning her. Later on, when she has calmed down from her tirade, I suggest counselling. She refuses. It's a vicious circle that needs breaking. One day she will listen. One day we will manage to get her the help she needs.

I hear voices from the terrace below. Anna and Patrick. I strain my ears.

'Your mother was rude to me. She dissed me.'

'Whatever do you mean?' Patrick asks.

'She implied meeting me over the dissection wasn't romantic.'

A pause. 'She was trying to be friendly. Just making a joke,' he says, voice clipped.

'People often use humour as an excuse for rudeness.' Her voice sounds rigid and tense.

'Oh, Anna, please don't take against my mother when you've only just met. I so want this time together to work.'

There is a pause. 'I'm sorry. I just can't tell you how nervous I am about meeting your family. You and I have been getting on so well. I don't want anything to spoil it. I really want "us" to work.'

The conversation stops. I look over the balcony. They are wrapped in each other's arms, snogging. And I thought it was just going to be Ralph that was difficult on this trip.

Ralph. Always so busy with his job that he never had any time for me and the children. A good provider, earning enough money to keep us all in the lap of luxury, but I felt like a wealthy single parent, bringing the children up alone. I didn't need to teach for the money. I continued because, even though it was hard work, I loved it. Sharing my passion for literature with others kept me sane. The staff room became my adult company.

Ralph never understood why I left him. He has begged me to come back so often. Maybe if I could have told him the truth earlier, he might have found it easier to accept. I stand on the balcony in the evening heat of Amalfi and think back. A trip to a play in the West End. *Skylight* by David Hare. A star-studded cast; Bill Nighy and Carey Mulligan. Champagne in the bar beforehand. Expensive seats right at the front. Ralph spent most of the first half checking emails on his iPhone while I sat engrossed.

At the interval, in the bar, cradling a double G&T, 'What a load of 1970s left-wing trollop,' he said, with a toss of his head.

I sipped my Chablis. 'I loved it. David Hare's brilliant.'

'The play's dated. No one thinks like that anymore.'

'Well I do, actually. And so do most of my friends. That's why I am finding it refreshing.'

One mismatched trip to the theatre didn't matter. We didn't need to agree on everything. It was just that as time went on, we didn't seem to agree on anything. And then I met you, Jack, and we understood one another.

9
Jack

Champagne on the terrace. Ralph's girlfriend Gemma is a sycophant, hanging on your every word and smiling. Ralph can't take his eyes off you either. His attention towards you annoys me. When will his life move on? Perhaps he should dump Gemma and find himself an age-appropriate girlfriend. Maybe communicating with a contemporary would give him more contentment.

And now Janice, a younger version of you, with smaller eyes, is walking towards me, body stiff with resentment. For your sake, I must try and befriend her.

Janice comes to stand next to me and smiles a wolfish smile. 'So, Jack, what do you do for a living?'

'I'm in teaching,' I reply.

A short, sharp laugh. 'Come on, come on. Be more specific.'

'I'm actually the head of Twickenham School in Whitton.'

'The same school as Mother? The big comprehensive that looks so ugly from the A316?'

'That's the one, except it is rather state of the art if you step inside. We have every modern facility. In fact, I'm very proud to be its head. I can show you round, if you like?'

She tosses her head and her long blonde hair gyrates around her shoulders. 'I'm quite happy at Waldegrave School, thanks.' She pauses. 'Are you new? Is that how you met Mother?'

'You'll explain how we met soon, won't you, Sarah?'

Sarah looks across at Janice. 'Yes, of course I will. But let's just enjoy the meal first.'

'That's typical of you, Mother – withholding information,' Janice replies, leaving her champagne flute on the glass patio table, and rushing away across the terrace.

You glance across at me, eyes laced with pain. I know how hard you try with her, my love. You have discussed her problems with me so many times.

'She seems very distressed. Do you think one of us should go after her, Ralph?' you ask.

He shakes his head. 'She'll soon calm down, as long as we leave her alone.' He laughs, a slow artificial laugh, and raises his glass. 'Come on. Let's have a toast. To love and laughter on the Amalfi Coast.'

10
Sarah

After champagne on the terrace, the guests sidle off one by one to change for supper, until Ralph and I are the only ones left. This is it. This is my opportunity.

I take a deep breath. 'Ralph, can we go for a walk?'

His face lights up. He beams at me, pleased that I've asked for his company. 'Anything for you, Sarah, as long as we are back in time for supper.'

We leave the villa and set out along the passageway. Away from the open terrace, the hot dusky evening wraps around us like a blanket. We climb the steps to the church and the piazza. The piazza is buzzing. Teenagers and families promenading, a group of boys playing football. Gnarled old women sitting on the benches, heads together, chatting.

'Do you fancy another drink?' I ask. 'I know we've had champers but I'm up for a chilled bottle of white.'

He nods his head. 'Let's try the café that looks out over the piazza. I thought it looked nice when we arrived,' he suggests.

We settle at a table by the window and order a bottle of pinot grigio. We sit in what for now seems to be companionable silence, sipping white wine and watching fingers of orange melt across the skyline as the sun sets. They melt into the sea with a flash of green.

'I'm worried about Janice,' I start. 'She came to our room and had her usual tirade. She was so angry I didn't manage to broach counselling.'

He shakes his head and smiles. He takes my hand and squeezes it. A platonic hand of friendship while we discuss our offspring. 'You mustn't worry. She'll soften. I'll talk to her again when we get back home.'

'I'm concerned about Patrick too,' I say. 'Anna seems very sensitive.'

'Anna's OK,' Ralph replies, and takes a large gulp of wine. 'You worry too much. Always have. Always will.'

'I suppose they'll find their own way.' I pull my hand away and shrug my shoulders. 'Let's move on from the children. Ralph, I need to tell you something.' I pause. 'I need to talk to you about Jack and me.'

Ralph's eyes flatten and his body stiffens.

'He seems smooth and creamy. Impressive,' he says, voice sharp. 'A teacher, isn't he?'

'Well, yes. And a bit more than that.'

'So you mentioned on the phone. Proud of him, are you?' he almost growls.

I don't reply.

'When did you meet him?' he asks.

I take a deep breath and meet Ralph's gaze. 'That's the thing. I've actually known him a while.'

Ralph's eyes darken. 'Oh?'

'I want you to know the truth, but this is difficult.' I hesitate. 'I met him before I left you. At that point we were not "together", but I'd already fallen in love with him.'

Ralph shakes his head slowly, in disbelief. 'What do you mean?'

'I fell in love with him, but I couldn't be with him properly.'

'Everyone has a wandering eye occasionally. It doesn't need to mean anything. I would have forgiven you.'

Insides like lead, I open my mouth to speak. 'It wasn't just a wandering eye. As I said, I was in love with him; still am. I had to let you go, for your own good. I wanted you to have the freedom to move on.'

Silence falls between us as Ralph sits trying to digest what I have said. I watch him sink another glass of wine.

His face darkens. 'Why didn't you tell me the truth?' he asks with a bitter snarl. 'You left me for another man and you didn't tell me.'

'It was because of his wife.'

'So you didn't want to hurt her, but you didn't mind hurting me,' he spits.

'She had MS. He needed to care for her. We spent a lot of time together, just as friends. We only became more than that later on.'

Ralph clenches his right fist and bangs it on the table. 'Later on? You mean you tried not to shag for as long as possible?'

'You make it sound so crude when we love each other so much. I never meant to hurt you, Ralph.'

He leans towards me, eyes blazing. 'You never meant to, but you have. More than you can possibly imagine. This whole time I thought you weren't with anyone, I kept hoping.'

His voice cuts into me. I feel wretched.

'Why are you telling me this now?' he asks.

'Because . . . because . . .' I splutter. 'Jack and I are engaged. We're getting married. Soon.'

He shakes his head in disbelief. 'Where's your engagement ring? I don't see one.'

'It's at home. I didn't want to wear it until I'd told everyone.'

'How considerate,' he replies. His voice is flat, defeated.

I put my hand on his arm. 'I'm so sorry.' I pause. 'But I need you to understand that my relationship with Jack is forever.'

11
Ralph

I look out across the piazza and see a family stepping across it. A family like we once were. A mum and dad and two toddlers. A sharp pain, like the blade of a knife, twists inside me, and moves through my belly. I look beyond the family, beyond the piazza, out to the cliffs and the inky sea. Oh Sarah, I cannot manage without you.

You have tears in your eyes. It is hard to believe that you really mean this. That you are doing the right thing, and you don't regret leaving me. I smell your scent. Your Rive Gauche. I think of the first time we made love. Bodies melting together on the bed, in your compact room in your beehive hall of residence. Our coupling seemed so natural. So perfect. So right. Memories rotate and run into the physical bond that remained for a while when you first left our marital home – falling back into our double bed with comfortable familiarity. Slipping into effortless ecstasy.

It meant so much to me that you still wanted me, even after your choice to leave. But now that you have explained what was happening at the time, I guess it was just a physical release for you, because you hadn't consummated your physical relationship with *him*. The pain of that thought stabs into my heart.

'Please, Sarah, how am I supposed to cope with this?' I beg.

12

Gemma

The sun has set and you have disappeared. In half an hour we are all supposed to be gathering for supper. I was hoping to talk to you alone before that. I ring your mobile. No reply. I text you. Same answer. I skulk around the villa but there is no sight nor sound of you. You are not in the pool. You are not in the kitchen. I think I will punish you by going for a long walk and not bothering to come back at the right time. Two can play unavailable and obtuse. I step out of the villa and walk along the passageway, thinking about the evening we met at The Grand nightclub in London. About how much things have deteriorated since then.

I was dancing with a girlfriend, jumping up and down to the beat. You were there with a group of male friends. We caught one another's eye and smiled. My girlfriend went back to our group; your friends evaporated into the crowd. We spent the rest of the evening together. We danced and danced. We made numerous trips to the cocktail bar, and flirted and laughed. I found out that you were an investment banker.

At the end of the evening, by which time we were both rather squiffy, I went back to your place in an Uber. We made love and I enjoyed it. It was rather vanilla. But then, what's wrong with that? The next morning when I awoke lying in bed next to you, and your face came into focus, I saw very clearly, at close quarters, what a dish I had picked up. Much older than me but slim and handsome with big brown eyes. A slightly hooked nose; sexy and masculine. I looked around your central London Mayfair crash pad as we ate breakfast delivered from the Ritz, and I fell in love with your deep crunchy voice, your laugh, your smile. Your lifestyle . . .

Unfortunately you are unreliable. Sometimes I see you every night for a week. Sometimes you don't contact me for a month. Men do not like clingy women, I know that, but I find being cool difficult because I think I am in love with you. It's worth persevering because when you hold me against you for a slow dance at a party, I feel electricity. The room moves away as if there is no one else in it. Time with you invigorates me.

But, Ralph, why did you invite me to your birthday celebration when all you want to do is spend time with her?

I close my eyes and wish she was dead.

13

Sarah

Back into our bedroom. You are lying on the bed reading *Atlas Shrugged*. You look up and close it as I enter. You give me your wide breezy smile, and as usual, my stomach melts.

'How did you get on?' you ask.

I take a deep breath. 'I've finally told him the truth.'

'How did it go?'

I shake my head. 'Not well. He was very distressed. Perhaps we shouldn't have come.'

'He begged you to.'

'I know, but even so, I should have used my common sense. At least I should have left you at home.'

Your face crumples. 'I'll fly back today, if it'll make things easier?'

I step towards you and slide next to you on the bed. We cling to one another and kiss.

'No. Don't go. I never want you to leave me, ever. We'll deal with this. We'll get through this together.'

14

Ralph

I'm numb with the pain of your loss. This is as painful as the first time you left, because for many years it has felt as if you hadn't really gone. I still had you to myself. Or so I thought.

I managed to hold it together after our conversation in the café, as we walked back from the piazza, along the narrow, walled pathway. But now back in the villa, you have gone to join your superstar in your bedroom, and grief engulfs me in waves. I slip into the kitchen to fetch the brandy bottle. Alcohol will help me escape.

The kitchen is hot and steamy; the housekeeper who comes with the villa is bustling and busy. A line of pizzas topped with tomato, fresh oregano, mozzarella, salami and olives wait in a line to go in the oven. She's chopping up salad.

'Supper will be served on the balcony at nine p.m.,' she informs me as I reach for the brandy bottle and a glass from the cupboard above her head. She beams at me and continues, 'You'll love my tiramisu. It is the best.'

I force a smile and nod my head. I leave her in peace and escape to the terrace. I drag a chair to the right-hand rear corner, where I hope no one will find me, and pour out a large slug of my favourite spirit. The night is so hot that sweat pools at the base of my spine and the back of my legs. The heat feels solid and presses against me. Oh Sarah. Why did you abandon me? We were happy, weren't we? What more did you want? I down a tot of brandy in one and let the memories come.

The first time we met was the end of my second year at Bristol University. On a hot summer night, at a party on the roof balcony of a friend's penthouse flat. Overlooking the waterways and the SS *Great Britain*. You walked towards me, your long flowing hair curling around your face like that of a Botticelli angel. Your perfect face pulled me in immediately. You smiled at me and my heart rotated. I didn't know what to say to you. Where to start.

'What are you doing here? Who do you know?' I asked, rather clumsily.

'Everyone. I'm studying English and I want to be a teacher so I need to be friendly with the whole world or I'll never cope. And you? Let me ask the same question of you?' you said sipping from a can of cider.

'I only know James, the guy who's holding the party. I'm studying economics, so I only understand graphs and numbers. I need someone like you to help me hone my people skills.'

You laughed.

I looked at your beauty and took a deep breath. 'I expect you get asked this all the time, but what's your favourite book?' My question sounded so wooden, I winced inside. And I hardly ever read novels, so I expected the conversation to go nowhere after that.

You sighed as you considered, a slight frown rippling across your forehead. 'Right now I suppose it's *Moon Tiger* by Penelope Lively.'

My eyes widened in surprise. 'That's a coincidence, I've read that. And I don't often read novels.'

'Did you enjoy it?'

I nodded my head as enthusiastically as I could muster.

'I love the way the main character is so interesting and intelligent.' You paused for breath. 'Yet at the start the nurse is about to dismiss her mentally because of her age,' you continued. 'It made me really think about judging anyone because of age or disability.'

'That's why our English teacher insisted we studied it,' I replied, lying through my teeth. I had no recollection of the novel's content. It had made no lasting impression on me. But then novels never do. I prefer facts and reality.

'I love the way the ideas are intertwined and entangled. The interwoven themes and ideas of her clever mind fascinate me,' you said with a lightbulb smile.

Despite our different interests, I felt so comfortable with you right from the start that I always expected we would have a long, stable marriage, not a sudden, painful divorce. How could you not appreciate everything we had together? All the money I earned? Everything that I gave you? What about the birth of our children? Patrick in 1999, Janice in 2002. Our minds, and our genetics, blended together. I look back and I can still see the ecstasy on your face as you held each newborn to your chest.

Do you remember Patrick's fifth birthday when we took the children to Disneyland Paris for a surprise? We didn't tell them in advance in case I couldn't take the time off. They thought we were going to the cinema in London, but when our train arrived at Waterloo we whisked them down the escalator to the Eurostar terminal. When we told them where they were going they jumped up and down like spring lambs in excitement. We had a perfect life.

Crying inside, I take another slug of brandy. Footsteps across terracotta. I look up. Gemma is standing in front of me, hands on her hips.

'Why are you still out here?' she asks. 'Are you ready for this evening?'

I sigh inside. 'I'm drinking and thinking.'

'About?'

'Happy times. The past.'

'Did you have a nice time on your walk?' she asks, voice sharp.

I shrug. 'As a matter of fact, it was depressing,' I replied as I topped up my glass.

Supper time. Alcohol has softened my mind and blurred the edges of my pain. And now I know I need to stick to beer. The ground is undulating a little, like a ship at sea, and people's faces are moving in and out of focus. I see you looking at me across the table from time to time. Through guilt? Through concern? Looking more beautiful than ever, face illuminated by candlelight as you pick at Parma ham and melon.

15

Gemma

I lean towards Jack, showing as much cleavage as possible. I know my generous breasts are my best feature. And despite your inattention, Ralph, I am confident enough to know that the rest of me isn't bad either. I arrange myself in my well-practised selfie position. If you are going to take too much notice of Sarah, I'm going to take too much notice of Jack. Let's see how you feel about that.

Jack's eyes glance down at my boobs.

Bingo.

Sarah, you over-confident, self-contained bitch. Let's see how you like your man's attention on me.

I put my hand on his arm. 'Later, I wonder whether we can escape from the others to have a chat in private. I need some educational advice and I hear you're an expert?'

I give him my best smile. The one that always turned on my ex. The one I like to rehearse in the mirror, every morning.

16

Jack

Gemma leans towards me. She is too close. So close I can smell her vanilla perfume. So close I can taste her breath. Her eyes shine into mine. I look down at her curvaceous figure and for a second I think, you lucky man, Ralph. But I stop in my tracks. What a stupid thought.

She's not much of a conversationalist, is she? And Ralph never seems to take much notice of her. Maybe he is bored of her. I suppose she is a bit of a 'type'. Painted-on eyebrows. Spider's leg eyelashes. Brightly coloured, figure-hugging dress. She looks like a *Love Island* date; plastic eye candy that I suppose many a middle-aged man would appreciate.

Now she is stroking my arm. 'I do hope we can snatch a moment on our own together later. I need your advice.'

'What about?' I ask, pulling away to pour myself a glass of water. I take a sip.

'You know. The Tony Blair thing. Education. Education. Education.' She puts her head back and laughs. I frown, not sure what is so funny. 'And you are such an expert, aren't you?' she continues, eyes sparkling into mine. 'I need some advice.'

Is she coming on to me? It seems as if she is and I have to admit that part of me is flattered. I look across at Sarah. She catches my eye and smiles, her Julia Roberts smile. She looks beautiful tonight. She always does. Here I am, about to announce my engagement to the woman I love, wanting to make a good impression on her family, and now, oh my god, Gemma has put her hand on my thigh. I place my hand on hers and lift it away.

17

Sarah

Jack, I admire your Robert Redford good looks as I look across at you. Gemma has her hand on your arm and is bubbling with effervescence. Now her hands are under the table and she is leaning towards you. She looks so animated; as if you are making her feel special. You have that effect on people, don't you? I think the way you radiate interest in others has helped you in your career.

My stomach tightens as I watch you being so friendly with a much younger woman. You were unfaithful to Susan for six years. But then I pinch myself. You love me. Ralph is right, I worry too much. I trust you completely. I will trust you until the end of time.

18
Jack

I take a deep breath. Sure, I'll make some time for Gemma later if she needs my advice. But just now, I'm concerned people will think I'm flirting if I'm seen talking to Gemma too much; especially Sarah's children. I'm desperate to make a good impression. Sarah trusts me with her life. I want it to stay that way.

I scan the room and sigh inside with relief. Everyone else is chatting. No one is looking this way. And Gemma is busy talking to Patrick now, hanging on his every word, wide-eyed.

I look across at the birthday boy. He is drunk. Red faced and sweating. He seemed a bit out of it even before we began to eat. Sarah, you told me earlier that he hasn't taken our news well, so I suspect that is why he has hit the bottle. I feel so sorry for him, losing you.

I don't think my wife, Susan, would have taken it well either, had I been honest and brave enough to tell her. I didn't want her to go through any more distress than her illness was already causing. I considered honesty would have been tantamount to cruelty. So I spared her the pain of knowing about my new relationship. At the time, I thought I was doing the right thing, but now the enormity of my behaviour is biting back, causing me anguish every time I contemplate the past.

After suffering from multiple sclerosis for many years, Susan died of pneumonia, just four months ago. When she first started to use a wheelchair, she had requested to be put on DNR, so antibiotics were denied.

What happened to my wife was such a tragedy. She was so athletic in her early days, an excellent dancer – I met her at salsa class. Always so giving and kind. I sit here looking across the table at you, Sarah, my love, remembering Susan's generosity.

I see her in her wheelchair in the kitchen, by the dishwasher, stretching her arms to lift dirty plates from the counter and then leaning down painfully to load it. I entered the room and stood watching her, sunlight pouring in through the window behind her and dancing on her strong chestnut hair. Her body was weak and withered, but her face remained the same. I watched her slot the final plate into place. I didn't offer to help. Constant assistance hurt her pride and made her feel useless. She turned to me and smiled.

'When I'm gone, promise me you will find somebody else. Life is no fun on your own.'

I bent down and took her hands in mine. 'If I do, they won't compare.'

My stomach churns now as I re-live my lie. I had already met you, Sarah, and I was deeply in love. I loved and respected her too, of course. But I needed you more than life itself, and I couldn't manage without you.

You met once, didn't you? You knew, but she didn't. It was her last Christmas. She had been in the home for six months. You were helping our music teacher, singing in his choir; performing carols in all the local care homes. Your choir was gathered around the Christmas tree in the residential lounge of Susan's home, banging loudly through all the old favourites; 'Oh Little Town of Bethlehem', 'Good King Wenceslas', 'Hark the Herald Angels Sing'. Susan was sitting in a recliner very close to you. You knew it was her because I had shown you a photo. You said she looked happy; she was trying to sing, and she was smiling. Loving the carols. When the concert was over you went over to say hello. You touched her hands and told her she looked beautiful. Because she did, apparently; shiny golden-brown hair, smooth and silky, curling at the ends. Nut-brown eyes bursting with enthusiasm and kindness. You squeezed her hands, but she couldn't squeeze back. She could no longer move her fingers. The staff had to do everything for her by then. She had no freedom. No privacy.

'If you have a man you love, treasure him. I have always treasured mine,' she said in her strange, slurred voice. A few days later she could no longer speak.

You left the home feeling guilty and refused to see me for several weeks. You really wanted to wait until she died, before seeing me again, but I begged you and cajoled you. Despite the pain Susan's words had caused me, I could no longer manage without you. I was holding you in my arms when I received the phone call from one of her carers, telling me that she had gone. The warmth of your body and the smell of your scent on such a sad day wrapped around me and comforted me. I should have felt guilty at the time, but I didn't. I couldn't. I needed you so much. You did everything to help me, helped me organise her funeral – a service at the church we attended, a burial in the churchyard followed by wine, cake and sandwiches back at our house. You made the food and helped to serve it. I think my friends just thought you were the caterer.

And now, four months later, we are secretly planning our wedding. Another low-key affair. We do not want to draw attention to the length of our relationship. Now Susan has been dead a while, and we are actually getting married at last, after hiding our relationship for so long, instead of unbridled joy I am starting to feel a deep-seated guilt. Memories of Susan and how we deceived her keep haunting me.

I watch Ralph, swaying and waving his lager glass in front of him. Standing up to propose a toast. Ralph now knows the truth and can't cope with it. My heart turns to lead. Susan wouldn't have coped either, if she had known.

19

Ralph

'Thank you all so much for coming to help me celebrate over the next fortnight. As you all know, the formal celebration will be held on my actual birthday, on Monday, at a restaurant up in the hills. Wait until you see it. It's fantastic. The best pizza and pasta in the whole of Italy. The most stunning view. But tonight, I just want to propose a toast to you, my ex-wife, Sarah. The love of my life. I want you all to know that despite our decision to go our separate ways, I wouldn't change a moment of the time we had together. I'm so grateful you are the woman I have had my children with.' I pause to push my lager glass up in front of my face. 'To Sarah. May she always be happy.' I pause. 'Congratulations, my darling, on your engagement. To Sarah and Jack, everybody.'

I raise my glass again before I slip back into my chair and the room begins to spin around me.

20
Gemma

She's engaged. Jack and Sarah are engaged. This should be good news, for me. But that is what's bugging you, isn't it, you insensitive man? The 'love of your life' marrying another. How dare you refer to her as that in front of me?

What do you see in her? She is thin, pointy and flat chested. Like most skinny women of forty plus, her face is a spider's web of fine lines, particularly around the eyes. She has furrow lines beginning to form on either side of her mouth. I've seen photographs of her when she was young. Now she is older, her eyes have shrunk too.

You're only forty-five, for heaven's sake. You need to pull yourself together. You need to get engaged yourself.

21

Sarah

The meal is over. It was delicious. Melon and Parma ham, followed by freshly baked pizza topped with fresh basil and oregano, mozzarella, olives and salami. Herb salad. My favourite pudding, tiramisu. But Ralph is so drunk he has spoilt the evening. His eulogy to me was beyond embarrassing. The way he announced our engagement when I had asked him not to say anything yet, because I wanted to tell everyone individually. The look his girlfriend gave me during his outpouring of slurred words was pure vitriol. And I don't blame her. I would feel the same about my presence, if I were her. And Janice looked acidic too. Even more acidic than usual.

He is still sitting at the head of the table gulping down lager. I watch him bang his glass onto the table, stand up and walk towards me.

He arrives and bends on one knee, at my side. 'Come with me for a romantic moonlit walk.'

I look across at you, Jack. I raise my eyes and shake my head to let you know I'm sorry about the behaviour of my ex. You leave your chair and come across to speak to me.

'I think it will help if you go for a walk and talk to him. You need to make sure he fully understands the strength of our relationship,' you whisper in my ear. 'Good luck. Be careful. Ring me if you need me.'

We kiss softly on the lips. A hand pulls at my back. I turn around. Ralph is tugging at my dress. 'Break it up, Jack,' he slurs. 'Come on, Sarah. Let's go for that walk. You're mine for the rest of the evening.'

I stiffen inside. But I know I must tear myself away from you and try to appease him.

22

Patrick

Good for her. Mum has found happiness at last.

'As congratulations are in order, what about a glass of champers, everybody?'

I might as well ply everyone with more booze to try and lighten the atmosphere. Not everyone seems to be as pleased for Mum as I am. Janice looks as if she has eaten a wasp. Anna just hasn't settled in the company of my family, and Gemma's face was like thunder as Dad made his speech.

'That's good with me,' Jack replies.

'Yes, please,' the others chorus.

I see Jack's arm brush gently across Gemma's back for a second as he guides her across the terrace, towards the sumptuous patio furniture. She turns to look at him and smiles. Anna and Janice stand up and join them.

I step into the kitchen, fetch a bottle of Louis Roederer, and five glasses. When I return to the terrace, Gemma is trying to snuggle up against Jack on the oversized patio sofa. He is leaning as far away from her as possible. I watch her attempt to place her hand on his thigh and see him brush it away. What is she doing when Mum and Jack have just got engaged? I think she just does whatever she can to try and make Dad jealous. But she doesn't need to do that. Surely Dad realises how attractive she is.

I open the bottle with a resounding pop, and pour us each a glass.

'Congratulations, Jack,' I say, raising my glass in the air. He smiles from cheek to cheek and sidles further away from Gemma.

'Congratulations,' everyone repeats.

'How long have you known our mum?' Janice asks.

'Well, it's been a long time, but we've taken our relationship very slowly, because we didn't want to hurt anyone.'

A deep-rooted silence bores into the night, camouflaged by the oppressive hiss of the cicadas. We sit sipping our champagne. Janice's face is pinched and drawn.

'What about you, Gemma, how long have you known our dad?' she asks.

Gemma finishes her champagne and places her glass on the table. 'Quite the opposite. Not long. About a year.'

Janice narrows her eyes. 'That's a long time for him. He's had so many girlfriends. They never seem to last.'

I look across at Janice and shake my head in warning.

She shrugs. 'What's wrong with stating facts? I'm only being honest.'

'Only being honest. Only joking. Lame expressions used to cover up rudeness,' Anna interjects.

I look across at Janice. She is tight lipped.

Gemma smiles. 'It's fine with me. I've had a lot of relationships too.' She pauses. 'But I'm bushed after the journey and everything. Jack, please will you walk me to my room? As I said at dinner, I need a bit of urgent advice on an educational matter. It's about a course I'm thinking of applying for.'

Anna, Janice and I exchange glances as we watch Gemma and Jack walk across the terrace together. Gemma stumbles a little and laces her arm through his to steady herself.

23
Sarah

Ralph and I step into the passageway. He is unsteady on his feet, leaning on me as we struggle along.

'Come on, this is ridiculous, let's turn back,' I snap.

'Nonsense, nonsense,' you reply. 'The night is yet young. We're off to the piazza, again.'

I sigh. I must have been mad to agree to this. But . . . but . . . I tell myself, I really do need to try to get through to him. He really, really, needs to forget about me and move on. Every time he trips and stumbles, I support him with my arms. Every time I suggest we turn back, he refuses.

At last, the piazza opens out in front of us. Away from the narrow passageway the night seems brighter. The full moon is luminescent. Stars shine down on us like halogens. We sit on a bench by the church.

'What did you want to talk to me about, Ralph?' I ask.

'This is last chance saloon,' he slurs. 'I'm offering you the opportunity to come back to me, before you dig your heels in any further with that chap.' He puts his arm around me, breathing alcohol fumes across my face. 'I have so much money now. So much more than when you left. You'll never want for anything. I'm a much better bet than him.'

I sidle away from him to escape his breath. 'Jack and I have as much money as we need, thank you – money isn't everything. In fact, it isn't anything if you're unhappy.'

He puts his head back and laughs. 'Of course money is everything. If you are unhappy, you can be unhappy in comfort.'

'Some of the wealthiest people I know are the most miserable.'

'Like who?'

I stir uncomfortably on the bench. 'Well, you, for example.'

'That's only because you left. If you came back my life would be perfect.' There is a pause. 'I want you, Sarah. Nothing compares to you.'

He puts his head back and begins to sing Sinead O'Connor's 'Nothing Compares 2 U'. He is tone deaf, and doesn't have the voice for it. After a while he falls silent.

'Someone will have to compare to me,' I tell you. 'You need to find someone new, too.'

His head collapses onto my shoulder and he falls asleep, snoring gently. I can't put up with any more of this. I text you. *Please come to the piazza to help*.

As I sit waiting for you to arrive, which feels as if it takes forever, I look up at the stars and will the size of the universe to make my worries diminish to the point of insignificance. But the more I ponder, the more I worry. Ralph is deeply unhappy. I haven't been honest. I should have told him the truth, years ago, that nothing can match the raw passion I feel for you, Jack.

Why did I think coming for a walk with him would help? Why did I think coming on his birthday trip was appropriate, when I'd just got engaged to be married? All I am doing is causing him more grief. Leaving my engagement ring at home was hardly going to appease anyone. I should at least have had the tact to come alone, without Jack *or* my ring.

I hear rushing footsteps pulsating across the piazza. You are approaching, at last; red faced and puffing, as if despite the time you have taken, you have been in a mad rush.

'Hi there, having fun?' you ask.

'Not exactly,' I grimace.

'OK, OK. Let's take one side each and guide him back.'

He stirs and opens his eyes. 'Hey, mate, what are you doing here?' he asks with a snarl.

'I've come to help get you back to the villa.'

He drags himself up to standing, pulls his arm back, clenches his fist and punches you in the face.

'That's for stealing my fucking wife.'

24

Ralph

Jack's face moves in and out of focus in front of me. Despite the firmness of my punch, I don't seem to have broken his nose or drawn blood. The piazza begins spinning like a roundabout. Faster and faster. I feel sick. I try to swallow my nausea back, but it rises inside me. I bend over and vomit spouts from my mouth in a torrent, regurgitated tomato and cheese splashing across the pretty marble tiles of the piazza. The acidic stench pushes into my nostrils and makes me vomit again. I need to get back to the villa. I need to get away from here.

I black out, and the next thing I know you are both leading me down the passageway, supporting me, arms around my waist, your shoulders bolstering up mine. We are staggering along together like a six-legged monster. Jack is a school head. A bossy type who likes to be in control. I don't need a prat like this to help me home. I take a deep breath, puff up my shoulders and swerve so that he bangs into the wall.

'Be careful, Ralph,' he warns.

'I'll bang you into the wall whenever I want, you wife stealer.'

'Calm down. You're very drunk. Please don't be aggressive.'

'You're very unpleasant. Please don't be sanctimonious.'

Sarah, my love, you stop walking, detach yourself from our human chain and stand in front of us both. You look so beautiful, in the shadowy moonlight. Like a sylph, or a fairy. I could stand here in this passageway and look at you forever. I feel myself wobbling. I lean forward and balance myself by putting my hands on your shoulders.

You put your head on one side, and grimace. 'It's very late. We're all very tired. Please don't be argumentative. We just need to get home safely.'

You reattach yourself to my side and our six-legged monster continues moving. Slowly.

We reach Villa Panorama, at last.

'Hey,' you say, 'let's get you into bed.'

I put my head back and laugh. 'Oh how I wish.'

'Cut the crude innuendos,' snaps the silver fox who is probably too old to get it up.

'Come on. Upstairs,' you insist.

Together, you support me as I climb the stairs. My legs keep falling away from the ground. I feel as if I am flying as you swing me along between you. At last we are standing outside my bedroom door.

'Goodnight, Ralph. Sleep it off,' you say, and kiss me on the cheek.

'Night, mate,' Jack says, slapping me on the back.

Mate? He's not my mate. I feel like popping him one again, but I sense I don't quite have the co-ordination for it. They leave me standing by the door of the master bedroom.

'Goodnight and thank you,' I manage; sharp and sarcastic, despite the fug in my head.

25

Gemma

I escape to our bedroom relieved to undress and collapse into the king-size bed alone; Egyptian cotton sheets crisp and cool against my skin. I sob and sob. I cry and cry. I cannot believe what has happened to me tonight. I need to get my own back. I need to take control of my life.

I lie here restless and wakeful, surrounded by heavy mahogany furniture and silence. After the pain of my experience with Jack, I have a plan. He won't get away with the way he has treated me. I'm determined to sort him out tomorrow.

But what should I do about my relationship with you, Ralph? After I have dealt with your ex-wife's fiancé, should I up the ante to win you over? Surely youth and beauty will dominate the cosy familiarity of a middle-aged ex-wife? You certainly are dishy with your chocolate-brown eyes, your finely curved nose. Your hard body honed by frequent trips to the gym. When you're not drinking too much and fawning over her, you are charming, eloquent and good fun. And you have money. I admire the way you rake it in, with your successful career in the City.

You need companionship. A fresh start. A new wife. Another child. I need a man; a good provider. I'm thirty and I want to start a family straight away. I would like a first child at thirty-one, a second at thirty-three. That would be perfect. I have no intentions of being a geriatric mother. I need to win you round. I need to obliterate Sarah. From your life. From your mind. I'm strong. I'm determined. I always get what I want.

My deliberations are interrupted by the sound of voices from the other side of the bedroom door.

'Goodnight.'

'Thank you. Sarah. Jack.'

26

Ralph

I fumble with the door handle and take a while to turn it. I push the door open and stumble into the room. The light snaps on and Gemma is sitting in our bed, bolt upright. I cannot see her face clearly; it blurs in front of me.

'Where have you been?' she asks.

'I went for a walk to the piazza,' I reply as I flop onto the bed.

The bed smells heavily of the lavender oil she rubs on pillows to help her drop off to sleep.

'Again?' There is a pause. 'With the love of your life, I gather.'

I put my arms around her. 'No, Gemma, it's not like that.'

27
Gemma

You reek of alcohol. The stale acidic scent springs from your breath. It oozes from your pores.

I move across the bed towards you and hold your eyes in mine. 'What is it like, Ralph?'

You put your arms around me and pull me towards you. Now I can smell the sharp acrid scent of vomit as well as alcohol. You begin to kiss me with breath like the air in a brewery. After everything that has happened this evening, I'm not in the mood for a drunken advance from you, but I force myself to put my tongue in your mouth and respond. Frigidity and rejection won't win you over. Only passion will do that. Anyway, you probably won't be able to manage, so I might as well play along. You'll be asleep in five minutes. I undress you and throw your clothes onto the floor. Much to my surprise, you are erect. I hold your body close against mine, run my hands up and down your back and then move towards your crotch. Here goes. I take a deep breath. This will help my plan along.

28
Jack

We slip into bed and our bodies melt together. It never felt like this with Susan. Even before she was ill, when she was at the peak of her health and energy. She never had your drive. Your passion.

Your muscles clench tightly around me and nothing has ever seemed so right. You do this to me every time. We climax in unison.

29

Ralph

Gemma smells of lavender. She is stroking my back and kissing me. She is stroking my penis, but she isn't holding it right. Lying so still next to me. She doesn't really want me. Her body is heavy with sleep. Heavy with disinterest. Rubbing my penis like an automaton. Clasping it tightly. Too fast. Too tight. It doesn't feel comfortable. Masturbation would be more interesting. My erection falters. I roll over and drift off to sleep.

30

Gemma

However much I try you won't stay hard.

'I'm sorry,' you mutter, rolling away from me, into your sleeping position. Your chest rises and falls heavily, and you begin to snore. My plan to woo you already failing, disappointment simmers inside me. This won't do. I run my fingers up and down your spine. I kiss the back of your neck.

'Ralph, please wake up. I want to talk.'

'Let's talk in the morning. I'm very tired.'

'Please, my darling, communication is so important.'

No response. You are out for the count, snoring volume increasing.

I snap on the light and climb on top of you, naked, legs astride your chest. I shake you gently and plant a kiss on your forehead. 'I can't wait until the morning.'

You open your eyes and blink.

'What are you doing? I've already been sick this evening. Do you want me to retch all over you?'

I give you half a smile and shake my head. 'Of course not. I've already told you I just want to talk to you.'

Your body stiffens. You let out a long, slow sigh. 'And what you want you always get, do you?' Another sigh. 'Get off me then, so that I can sit up.'

I slide off you, back to my side of the bed. You sit up and yawn. You stretch your arms above your head.

'Come on then, fire away.'

'What's going on with you and Sarah? Why did you call her the love of your life in front of everyone?'

You shake your head. 'Nothing is going on.' You shrug. 'We just have a good friendship. We need to be friends to bring up the children together.'

'Friendship?' I splutter. 'And they're hardly children anymore. They're independent young adults. Why did you end the evening by ignoring everyone else and going for a walk with her?'

'I needed fresh air.'

'You were already outside on the terrace.' I pause. 'A normal person goes for a walk with his girlfriend, not his ex.'

You smile a lop-sided smile. 'I was squiffy. Not thinking properly. I'll make it up to you tomorrow. Please, Gemma, let's make friends. We're lovers, not enemies.' You peck me on the cheek, blasting the scent of stale alcohol across my face, snuggle down beneath the duvet, roll over and fall asleep again.

Wide awake, I lie down next to you, holding on to your sleeping body, feeling every rise and fall of your chest, savouring your warmth. At least you said we were lovers. Not the love of your life, but your lover. That's a start.

31

Ralph

I lie next to Gemma, pretending to be asleep. Feeling her generous breasts pressed against my back. Her legs entwined with mine. Thinking about how hot she is to shag when I'm up for it. I'll make it up to her in the morning. By then the room should have stopped spinning. By then I should have stopped feeling sick.

32
Jack

Usually after we make love I sleep like a baby, but tonight I feel restless. My brain is wired, the past firing like electricity across my mind.

I see Susan as I first met her, so sweet, so doe eyed, so innocent. Her body crumbles in front of me and is replaced by your slender strength and beauty. I see you on the day you walked into my study.

'Do sit down, Mrs Kensington,' I said, holding my breath, for except on a movie screen, I had never seen anyone so beautiful. Wondering why, with looks like yours, you were teaching English at my school, and not filming in Hollywood. You reminded me of Cate Blanchett or Liv Tyler.

You followed my instruction and sat in the low fabric armchair in front of my desk. I leant forwards to continue looking at you. The balance between the fragility and strength of your looks was confounding and magnificent. It was summer term. You were wearing a duck-egg blue dress that caressed your slender figure.

'How can I help you?' I asked.

'I want to ask your permission to direct a play, next term. It's a version of *Romeo and Juliet* that I've abridged. I thought it would be rather moving to perform it with teenagers as young as Romeo and Juliet actually were. Most professional actors are too old to play them.'

Your eyes danced with anxiety as you spoke. I was new. The previous head was into sport, not music and drama. I'd always been an avid proponent of all three.

'That sounds a great idea,' I replied. Your voluptuous lips widened and a dimple showed to the left of your cheek. And then you smiled. You smiled and the room turned red. My life was on fire.

My wife, Susan, had just been diagnosed with multiple sclerosis. It was a terrible shock to us. At that time, she was coping bravely and cheerfully, at least in front of me. And I loved her. I had no intention of being unfaithful.

The next term you produced the play, having rehearsals after school for an hour every night. Susan's weakness was already increasing. Now, no longer cheerful, she had become quiet and sullen. Some evenings I would slip into the back of the school theatre before I drove home. To observe. To take an interest in the school activities. Your voice, your every movement intrigued me. I had never met anyone like you before. One evening, as I was driving home, I saw you, laden down with a heavy bag of books, walking home along the main road. I stopped the car and wound the window down.

'Can I offer you a lift?' I asked.

You smiled. Fireworks exploded in my mind.

'Yes, please. My car's broken down in the school car park. I'm going to have to sort it out at the weekend, because I've got a lot of marking to get through for tomorrow.'

I leant across and opened the passenger door. You sank into the seat gratefully.

'Where do you live?' I asked.

'Lebanon Park.'

'I know it. It's just around the corner from me.'

With you sitting next to me, the air felt electric. A weird, heightened sensation of energy and light. I could hardly think. I could hardly breathe. What was going to happen? Nothing. Nothing could ever happen. We were colleagues. Both married. Nothing could ever happen.

But it did; eventually. Two years after we met we finally succumbed to the electricity between us. We fell into each other's arms at your house one day, when I had popped around to talk about the next school play. I suppose it was a ruse. We could have talked about it at school. Your children were with Ralph. We were totally alone. The temptation was too much.

Susan, poor Susan, finally died peacefully in her sleep oblivious to our relationship, four months ago. And now Ralph is left angry and bereft. Watching him is showing me the sense of betrayal Susan would have experienced if she had known. What can I do to help him? To calm him? Nothing. What's done is done. We can't wind back our lives. But when I think of the pain we have caused him, the pain I would have caused Susan, I feel wracked with shame.

33
Ralph

The morning after the night before arrives. As soon as I wake up, I fall into Gemma's arms. This time I'm on fire. I roll on top of her. She opens her eyes and smiles. I kiss her on the lips. I kiss her all over her body, until she is ready, until she is ripe for me. She seems to enjoy it. I don't think she is faking. When we have finished, I leave her sleeping, lying on her back, replete. I tiptoe from our bedroom, pad through the villa and step out onto the terrace.

Feeling exhilarated after a surfeit of good sex, I breakfast with you, Sarah, and your fiancé, on the terrace. You are the only ones up early enough to join me. Pastries and coffee. Sun low in the sky. A gentle heat haze softening the silky blue horizon.

But my heightened mood doesn't last. An awkward silence hovers over the patio table. Should I apologise for getting wasted last night and punching Jack? Or should you apologise, Sarah, for ruining my life? Or should Jack apologise for stealing my wife? I catch my reflection in a side window of the villa, smile at it and run my fingers through my hair, surprised that I do not look anywhere near as bad as I feel. Surely my looks are OK? As good as his? Better, I think. Being five years younger than him makes all the difference.

I pull my eyes away from my reflection and frown across at my guests. You are sipping coffee, eyes locked with your fiancé, pastry untouched on your plate. A smile simmers across your lips, a smile that lights up your face. My insides tighten. I want to hit Jack again for taking you away from me. I have never been a violent person. Never. I never got into a fight at school. Never raised my hand to anyone. Until last night. And now, I just want to shake him and hit him again, with more precision, more bite.

You finally tear your eyes away from his gaze and turn to me.

'How are you feeling today, Ralph?' you ask, a little too pointedly.

'Fine,' I snap. 'Why wouldn't I be?'

You raise your eyebrows. 'Fine?' you push.

'Fine considering the situation. Life's such a blast.'

You put your head on one side in an attempt to look sympathetic. 'Life can be very difficult. But even in our lowest moments one can try to find light and beauty.'

'Is that the sort of thing you say to your students?' I ask.

'Sometimes.' Your eyes hold mine and my stomach rotates.

Your fiancé leans forwards. 'Ralph, let's go for a walk together after breakfast. Clear the air. Get to know one another.'

I do not want to get to know this woman stealer. I'd prefer it if I never had to see him again. But you are looking across at me, speaking to me with your eyes. They are whispering into mine – *don't be churlish, do this for me, do this for your children.* Whispering, softly, silently, gently with a glance and a sigh.

'OK. Good idea,' I reply.

34

Gemma

I wake up in the villa bedroom, hot, sweaty and panicked. I dreamt about what happened, reliving it in minute detail.

He grabbed me from behind, just as I was leaving, turned my body to face him and pushed me to the floor. The floor was solid marble. It was cold and hard. He lay on top of me. I tried to push him away, but he grabbed my arms and held them above my head with his right hand. His left hand tore away my knickers – I was only wearing a flimsy G-string so that part was easy for him. He seemed to know exactly what he was doing, not that I thought about that until afterwards; the bastard must have done this to someone before.

I rush to the bathroom and splash cold water on my face, hoping to push the memory away.

35

Jack

Ralph and I are ambling along the cliff path. I inhale the view; the scent of pine and bougainvillea, the memory of your body in my arms last night. We walk for ten minutes until we reach the tip of the promontory at the edge of the bay, where an empty bench beckons us to rest. We sit down. The sea shimmers beneath us like an iridescent cloth of silk. Jet skis play like plastic dolphins at the base of the cliff. A motor boat cuts through the distance, leaving a lacy wake. The butterfly wings of distant sail boats flutter on the horizon.

I know I need to connect with him. For your sake, Sarah, for the sake of this family. He has too high an opinion of himself to understand why you left him. And I will never tell him the truth; he is already hurting enough. If I try and explain to him how tempting, how beautiful you were, and still are, how much I couldn't resist you, it will only provoke him. If I try and explain that you were unhappy with him, it will cut into him like a knife. If he knew how mundane you found his company, and how much when we are together our life rises to another level, he would be devastated. He is so different to you, Sarah. You and I love reading novels and poetry. We love the theatre; in a different life we would have danced across a stage together. He is a money man. Making money has always been his focus. You told me he reads two non-fiction books a year, about technology or war. We devour novels in our sleep; two a week.

I turn to look at him. He is staring into the bay, eyes distant. 'Look, mate, I'm sorry about what's happened,' I say.

'There's no point in saying sorry,' he replies. 'Sorry doesn't change the situation. It doesn't make me feel any better if that is what you are trying to do. The only way I will feel all right is if we could reverse time.'

I do not know how to reply. Silence hangs between us and solidifies. After a while I cut through it. 'We didn't fall in love on purpose.'

He turns to me, brown eyes darkening to black. 'How could you do it to *your* wife?' he asks.

And the feeling of guilt that I am trying to suppress tightens across my head like a band. It moves down my body, across my chest, my stomach. I clench my jaw. I expand my chest, then I take a deep breath and wait for it to snap. I punch my fist into my hand to relieve my tension. I've never hated myself more.

36

Gemma

Standing in the bathroom, the cold water on my face has not helped. I feel him one again, pushing my legs apart with his knee. He spat on his hand and used his spittle as lubricant. But it didn't help. His penis ripped into me with a burning intensity that made me yelp. He thrust into me and pumped. It didn't take long. He came quickly with a final explosive grunt in my ear and a crescendo of pain.

I am a strong woman. Proud of my sexuality. I won't let this crush me.

37
Jack

Ralph and I have talked long enough. I put my hand on his arm.

'Thanks for the chat, mate,' I say. 'I'd better go. I'm off to the village to get a present for Sarah. I'll see you back at the villa.'

38
Gemma

I need to get back to the villa. I walk along the cliff path trembling and crying; tears streaming down my face, stepping back through the villa onto the terrace. I console myself that no one will ever know the truth. If you tell a lie often enough, the lie becomes the truth in your mind.

I return to our bedroom. Relieved you are not here to see what a state I'm in. I change into clean shorts and a crisp white lacy blouse. I put on my high-heeled sandals. The truth in my mind is that I have been in our bedroom all morning, reading a book.

I step out from our room, onto the balcony. I stand and look down at the main villa terrace below. At the potted plants; geraniums, orchids, hibiscus, olive and lemon. The housekeeper is setting the table for lunch, humming as she works. Beef carpaccio, caprese salad. Bottles of San Pellegrino. Rosé wine.

Two hands appear, in the corner of the balustrade, gripping the stone edge. A flash of dark hair. A head. Your head. The housekeeper is oblivious, head down, folding linen napkins. You pull yourself up. You lift your right leg over the balustrade first. I notice you are wearing your new espadrilles. You jump down, landing in a heap on the patio. You scramble up to standing, look around and then brush yourself off. You run your fingers through your hair, widen your shoulders and stroll across the patio nonchalantly.

And then Sarah steps onto the patio from inside the villa, dressed in a floaty Indian print dress. Your eyes meet. You smile. You have arrived at the same time from different directions and now you are standing gazing at each other lovingly. What are you both covering up?

39
Sarah

Ralph is walking towards me, looking as dapper as ever in his seersucker shorts and bright red pumps. His looks were never the problem.

'Hey, Ralph, what time did you get back? Where's Jack? I haven't seen him since breakfast.'

'I've been back a while. We walked for about an hour, then he said he wanted to walk into the village to buy you a present. So we parted ways and I went down to the beach. I wanted a bit of time to sit and think.'

'How did your conversation go?'

A clipped smile. 'Fine. Great. He's a nice bloke.'

'Did you see Anna, and Patrick? That's where they were heading. I'm not sure where Janice went. She left a bit later.'

He shakes his head. 'Didn't see the young lovers. But I didn't go to the first beach. I went to the small cove a bit further on. It's not as good for swimming so it's far quieter. I really fancied a bit of peace.'

'Jack's not picking up his phone. It's totally dead. I thought the reception was quite good around here.'

Ralph smiles a mocking smile. 'You always were a worrier, weren't you? Whatever I did, I couldn't cure you of it.'

I bite my tongue. He is just hurting after our announcement. But actually, because of my teaching persona, I have always been far calmer than him.

'Come on, have a glass of rosé. Relax.'

He walks across to the patio dining table, picks up a glass and pours me a large slug. I accept the drink planning not to down it. Drinking alcohol at lunchtime goes straight to my head.

'I'm sure he will be back for lunch,' Ralph says.

'OK then. Well I'll take your advice and relax in the sun until everyone returns.'

My good intentions slip. I take a sip of wine as I flop onto the sun lounger. Maybe Ralph is right. I am too much of a worrier. Of course you will soon be back, Jack. Instead of fussing, I am going to lie in silence and think about our wedding. We are planning a simple ceremony in one of the offices in York House, Twickenham, the day after we return. Just us and two witnesses, both friends of yours. Followed by photographs in the gardens, by the pond and the willow tree. By the summer border of the sunken garden. The four of us will then have lunch at Petersham Nurseries. We will have a big party later, when everyone around us has got used to the idea of our relationship.

My pink silk dress is pressed and ready, hanging in our wardrobe. My engagement ring, a diamond cluster centred with a large sapphire, locked safely in our safe. Soon I will be Mrs Sarah Rutherford. An honour that I will be proud of. You are a lovely man, off to buy me a present when I already have everything I want. I picture you eyeing up trinkets in the tourist shops that line the main road. Brightly painted blue and yellow pottery. Pretty bottles of limoncello decorated with yellow ribbons. Cheap silver bracelets. Homemade soap.

I hear voices. The young people are back, chatting and laughing. All three of them. Janice must have been with Patrick and Anna, then, this morning. I'm pleased they are having fun. By the time I open my eyes they are already sitting at the table.

'Come on, Mum, time to eat,' Patrick says, gesticulating for me to come over. 'This looks delicious,' he tells the housekeeper.

I walk towards the table and realise that you are still not here. I leave the terrace and step into our room to check whether you have dozed off there, after your long walk in the heat. No. The room is empty. Untouched since we last left it. I try your mobile again. No reception. Straight to voicemail. But . . . nothing can have happened to you. You've only walked to a few shops a few hundred yards from here.

I join the lunch table, next to your empty place.

'What have you done to Jack, Mummy? Where is he?' Janice asks.

'Popped into the village to get me a present, apparently.'

'He knew we were all having lunch together, didn't he? Perhaps he's realised how selfish you are and done a runner,' she replies, hard eyed and sullen.

Charming, Janice. Thanks for your support, I think but don't say.

Ralph offers me some caprese salad.

My throat is too dry to eat. I shake my head. 'No thanks.'

40

Ralph

You sit staring into space, sipping rosé wine, not a touch of food entering your mouth. You need to calm down. He's only gone to get you a present. He told me that. And I told you. Why are you so worried?

41
Gemma

Have you even noticed me today, Ralph? You did graze the side of my cheek in an excuse for a kiss, before you sat down next to Sarah for lunch. I watch you looking distracted, necking rosé wine as if there were no tomorrow. Are you an alcoholic? Is that your problem, or is there something else to explain why you run so hot and cold with me?

I take a bite of the salad. It is delicious – smooth creamy mozzarella, the sharpness of fresh tomato, the resonant tang of fresh basil that I love. I try to tell myself to calm down and just enjoy being here, whatever happens between us. I'm on a freebie on the Amalfi Coast, for God's sake. But then I look across at you again and see your handsome craggy face, your slim elegance, and my heart lurches. What can I do to make you want me?

'What's everyone doing this afternoon?' Patrick asks.

As I turn my head towards him, I realise he does look a bit like you. I suppose he is rather attractive too.

'Anyone up for a touch of beach volleyball?' he asks, looking straight at me and smiling.

'You're coming shopping with me in Amalfi,' Anna insists, 'I need a new handbag. The leather here is fabulous.'

'Do you need anything in that department?' Patrick asks me.

I smile inside. I would so like to say yes, and go and flirt with him, just to see how he would respond, to try and annoy you,

Ralph. But I tried so hard to rile you last night and it all went wrong. So very wrong. So no more flirting for me.

'No, thanks,' I say to Patrick, avoiding his gaze.

'Any other takers?'

'I'm going to stay here and wait for Jack to come back,' Sarah says.

'I can stay here and do that if you want to go off,' Ralph replies.

Sarah grimaces. 'I'm quite happy to wait for him, thanks. Why do you think he's taking so long? Did he tell you what he was getting for me? Maybe he needed to take the bus to Amalfi, not just walk to the village?'

Ralph shrugs his shoulders. 'Yeah. Maybe. He said he was going to the village, but perhaps he couldn't find what he wanted there.'

I picture Ralph climbing back onto the terrace earlier. Why was he doing that?

42
Janice

I agree to join Patrick and Anna on their shopping trip, it will distract me. Help calm me down.

'Come on. Come on. Meet you by the front door in five minutes and then we'll go and catch the bus,' Patrick insists.

The bus journey from Praiano to Amalfi winds along cliffs which cascade into a turquoise velvet sea. The sharpness of the drop is breathtaking. The colour of the sea is invigorating. No wonder my father loves it here. I must show him more gratitude for bringing us. But then I think about the bimbo he is cavorting with and my good intentions stall.

We step off the bus and stand admiring the broad sweep of Amalfi harbour, pastel buildings clinging to the mountain as it rises majestically above the town. Into the town. Standing looking across the piazza at the cathedral. I walk to the bottom of the majestic stone steps that lead to it and look up. Its quirky mixture of styles fascinates me. I'm glad I came. This is much more interesting than lying on the beach. To the left of the main body of the cathedral there are wedding cake turrets; clock towers, square upon square and round upon round. The main structure is tiled and arched, topped with a cross, and ornate gold filigree. I stand and try to drink the memory of its beauty in. I do not want to go home and forget it.

'Come on, Patrick,' Anna snaps. 'We came here to look at handbags.'

I turn to look at her. She is standing, pert and pretty in pink, impatient hands resting on impatient hips. She raises her shoulders and sighs. 'Are you coming, or shall we just meet you for a drink later?'

'Later is fine with me. Text me when you've finished shopping. Let me know where to meet.'

Anna and Patrick stroll off, hand in hand, heads together, chatting. I climb the wide stone steps, cover my head with a scarf and enter the cathedral. I take a sharp intake of breath as I am stung by its beauty. Its ornate painted ceilings. Its elegant stone arches. After paying my respects to the relics of St Andrew, I turn around too quickly and bump into a mother cradling a baby in her arms, so protectively. So adoringly. A familiar wave of desperation sweeps over me. Oh, Mother, how could you ever have left us? I bite my lip to suppress tears. I shiver inside. It's cold inside the cathedral. I rush to leave. I step outside, but even the heat of Amalfi does not warm me now.

43
Sarah

Lunch is over and you're still not here. Patrick, Anna and Janice have gone shopping. Gemma and Ralph are sunbathing on the terrace. I pad away from the patio and return to the privacy of our room. The shirt you wore last night is strewn across the wicker chair in the corner. I pick it up, bury my face in it, and inhale your scent. The muskiness of your body. The sharp fresh tang of your lemon aftershave.

I fling myself onto the bed. Where are you? Why don't you ring? Have you tripped and twisted your ankle somewhere with no phone reception? Has someone stolen your phone? Or has it just run out of battery? To make sure you are all right I resolve to phone the Carabinieri at four p.m. The housekeeper told me their number. I look at my watch. It is three now. One hour to go.

After an hour that feels like a lifetime, I dial the number of the Italian police. A deep male voice answers and, even though I have tried to learn a little Italian on holiday over the years, my mind goes blank.

'Do you speak English?' is all I manage to ask.

'A leetle, yes.'

'My fiancé went on a cliff walk this morning. He was expected back at our holiday accommodation for lunch and hasn't returned. There is no reply from his mobile. Can you try to find him?'

'I do not understand.'

I sigh inside and repeat myself.

'I no understand. I get my colleague, Luca.'

The line goes silent for a while.

'Luca Rosetti, here. How can I help?'

I explain the situation for the third time.

'Maybe he's still shopping. Maybe he is choosing something special for himself. A grown man is free to roam wherever he wants,' Luca replies, voice smooth and complacent.

'But . . . but . . . he may be injured. He may need help. It is not like him to disappear.'

'Many men go off for a while. To visit their children, their mistresses. They just need a break from their wives.'

Indignation swells inside me. 'My fiancé, Jack, isn't like that. Please, please, help me.'

'I'm sorry, madam, I have many more pressing issues to deal with today. Give him time. Ring back if he hasn't returned by tomorrow morning. *Arrivederci.*'

The phone line dies.

44
Gemma

This afternoon you are fast asleep on a sun lounger on the terrace; exhausted after whatever you were up to this morning. I lie next to you, listening to R&B music on my iPhone. No one else is around. This is it. This is my opportunity. I pick up your espadrilles from the side of the sun lounger. I carry them through the silence of the villa, to the privacy of our room.

I turn them over and lay them on our bed. As I thought, they have debris from the scrubland ingrained in their soles; little stones. Soil. Tiny fragments of leaves. I take a photograph of them. You bought them at the local beach shop yesterday. I watched you cut the labels off before you wore them and toss the receipt into the waste paper basket.

I rummage through discarded tissues, empty packets of new holiday toiletries. I find the receipt lying beneath an empty blister pack of paracetamol. I lay it on the bed and photograph it too. I wrap your soiled shoes in a plastic bag and hide them behind the wardrobe. Ralph, you can't deny you avoided walking back along the cliff path this morning and crossed the scrubland instead. This is my insurance policy. You have plenty of money, so it won't be a problem to treat yourself to a new pair of espadrilles when you realise you have lost them.

Job done, I step out onto our balcony and breathe deeply to relax. The scent of bougainvillea and jasmine envelops me. The sun caresses my skin. Voices rise towards me from the terrace. I look over the balustrade and see Anna and Patrick standing just below me, staring at one another earnestly. I strain my ears to listen.

'You're so disapproving of me at the moment,' Anna says.

'I just mentioned the fact that buying two new handbags is rather excessive. I need to be able to say what I think from time to time,' Patrick replies. 'You only need one handbag.'

'How would you know? You're not into handbags.' She pauses. 'I bought you a man-bag and you never use it.' Another pause, longer this time. 'Just don't tell me what to do.'

I stand on the balcony looking down at Anna, and my stomach knots. I would not put up with rubbish like that. If a man tries to control me, he ends up suffering.

45

Janice

I'm in my bedroom, about to shower before dinner, when it starts. It follows the usual pattern. My heart races in overdrive. Blood pumps against my eardrums. Pain rises like fire between my breasts. Shooting pains radiate from my chest, stabbing down my left arm. I lie on the bed and concentrate on my breathing. In and out. In. Out. Breathe. Breathe. In and count to five. Breathe in through my nose. Out through my mouth. One, two, three, four, five.

Everything is going to be all right. I can cope with my life.

46
Gemma

Dinner tonight. Sitting around the large dining table on the terrace with Ralph, Patrick and Anna, wearing my pink Chiara Bono dress; matching lips and nails by Dior. Jack still hasn't returned, so everyone is really worried now. And Sarah hasn't left her room since lunchtime. The housekeeper took her a light supper, but she just waved her away, apparently.

The night is too hot, the food too filling, and due to current circumstances I can't think of anything to say. Neither can anyone else. The only sound is the scraping of cutlery across plates and the hum of the cicadas.

'Anyone up for clubbing later?' Patrick suggests, breaking through the silence as he looks across at me, eyes twinkling. 'We can't all sit around here moping all night. I'm sure Jack will make an appearance soon.'

'I love dancing. I'd like to do that,' I reply with a smile. Thank God for Patrick. Someone needs to lighten up this trip.

'I thought we were having "us time" this evening?' Anna pouts. 'I thought we were going for a starlit walk on the beach later – *à deux*?'

Patrick looks across at Anna and his eyes soften. 'OK then. But perhaps we could all go clubbing another night?'

Anna grimaces. 'That depends whether you just want to let loose on this holiday or whether you want to stimulate your brain; personally, I would rather keep my energy for looking at the local antiquities. We're near Pompeii, aren't we? I would like to go there instead.'

I bite my lip to stop myself frowning. What's wrong with her? Clubbing and visiting Pompeii aren't mutually exclusive. Patrick meets my eyes across the table. The dark intensity of his gaze is interesting. He definitely is a dish like his father. For a second I imagine being at the nightclub alone with him, strobe lights flashing, music pumping. But no. I pinch myself. I prefer older men. Men with stability and money. His father is a much better bet.

I look across at you, finishing off your cannelloni, and necking your glass of local red wine. Tonight is going to be another long, long night, tolerating your mismatched family. Tolerating your drinking. But it'll be worth it in the end; when I claim my prize.

47
Sarah

The morning finally arrives. Hands trembling, I telephone the police again.

'Luca Rosetti, please.'

'Speaking. How can I help?'

'It's Sarah Kensington here; I rang yesterday because my fiancé is missing. He still hasn't come home.'

Luca is here, dressed in the black military uniform of the Carabinieri. He is about forty years old, with a slight figure. He has a hooked nose, and almond-shaped eyes. His assistant, Matteo, is with him, wearing the same funereal outfit. Matteo is taller, like a beanpole or a wooden toy soldier, with a seemingly permanent frown, and small, beady black eyes. He hasn't spoken a word since he arrived. I suppose he doesn't speak English.

Ralph is sitting next to me on the basket-weave patio sofa. The police are in two armchairs opposite us.

'So when did you last see your fiancé?' Luca asks.

'Yesterday morning at breakfast.'

'What time was that?'

'Around ten.'

'And was everything all right between you?'

'Yes, very much so.'

The housekeeper scuffles towards us and hands out small cups of espresso.

'*Grazie mille*,' Luca says as he bends his head to take a sip. 'As far as you know, where did he go, after breakfast?' he asks me.

'On a cliff walk with Ralph, as the men wanted to get to know one another, before Jack and I get married.'

'Ex-husband befriending husband-to-be.' His eyebrows rise a little. 'Interesting.' He pauses. 'Was there any antagonism between them?' Luca asks, looking straight at me.

I shake my head. 'No. Not more than you might expect.'

He leans towards me and folds his arms. 'What does that mean?' he asks.

I turn towards Ralph. 'I think you were a little surprised by our relationship, weren't you?'

'Oh, yes, I was. And I had been a bit upset and got rather drunk the night before, when I first found out about it. But when we were on the walk we made peace. All I have ever wanted is for you to be happy, Sarah.'

Ralph looks across at Luca as he continues.

'He said he was going into town to buy Sarah a present. We parted in friendship on the cliff mid-morning. As far as I know, no one else in our party has seen him since. But somebody somewhere must have; on the cliff tops or at the shops or something.'

Luca slaps his thighs and stands up. 'Come on, Matteo. Let's go and find him. Now.' Matteo doesn't jump up immediately. '*Pronto*. *Pronto*,' Luca says snapping his fingers.

They leave, taking away the reassurance of their military presence, and panic begins to bubble inside me once more.

TWENTY-FOUR HOURS LATER

48
Sarah

Since you went missing, minutes run together, and every second of every day is all the same to me. After another wakeful night, wading through time as heavy as mercury, morning eventually arrives. I sit on the main terrace and watch the sun rise. It casts fingers of pink across the horizon. Oh, Jack, are you somewhere near, watching it, injured and alive? Can you see its beauty? Wherever you are, will it give you hope we will find you? Sunset, sunrise, and fireworks have always inspired you. Wherever you are, hold on until the police find you, my love.

Two more hours drag. The doorbell rings. I open the front door. Luca and Matteo stand in front of me, again.

'*Boungiorno*,' Luca says.

'*Boungiorno*,' Matteo echoes.

I invite them in and they follow me onto the terrace. We settle on the outdoor lounge suite. The others haven't appeared for breakfast yet, so I sit facing the police alone, trembling with dread. Their faces are like marble and I know that nothing good is coming.

Luca clears his throat. 'So far, despite helicopter and power boat searches all along the coastline, we have not found any sign of your fiancé.' My stomach churns. 'Sarah, we need to find out as much as possible about what was going on between you. Please, be honest. Did you and Jack have an argument?'

I sigh. 'No. We're very much in love. Enjoying planning our wedding, which is in two weeks. There was no disagreement of any kind.'

Luca's eyes darken and he hesitates. 'And to your knowledge, has Jack ever been suicidal?'

I shake my head vehemently. 'No. No way. Jack is always full of enthusiasm for life.'

He leans forwards. 'And now he's not here, what about Ralph? Did Ralph and Jack really get on? Was there any animosity between them?'

I take a deep breath. 'They'd only just met. Ralph was shocked I had a partner, but he was coming to terms with it. Like we said, he invited Jack for a walk so that they could get to know one another.'

'Is there anything else you need to tell us about your relationship with either man?'

Aware of what he is trying to imply, I bristle inside. 'Ralph was my first husband. We're still friends. Jack is my new partner who I'm marrying very, very soon. That's it,' I insist.

49
Ralph

Luca is sitting opposite me, in the formal dining room of the villa. As in our bedroom, the furniture in here is heavy and dark. The mahogany clock on the dresser ticks loudly. The air tastes stale. He folds his arms, places them on the table and leans towards me. He pushes his eyes into mine. Too hard. Too vehemently.

'You were jealous of him because your ex-wife was in love with him, weren't you? Because she had just got engaged and was about to re-marry?'

I pull my eyes away from his. 'Of course not. Sarah and I split up years ago. I mean, I was surprised at first that she had a partner. They have been together a while and only just told us. But surprised is surprised. It isn't jealousy or envy.'

He smiles a slow, wry smile. 'So no reason for you to push him off the cliff then?'

I stiffen. How dare he talk to me like this? And they haven't even found Jack's body. For all they know he may be alive.

'Absolutely no reason,' I say, voice strong and indignant.

'If he's fallen from the cliff, he must have jumped or slipped after I said goodbye. We were on good terms when we parted.'

'Despite the fact you still have passion for your ex-wife? I've seen the way you look at her. You still desire her, don't you?'

'Sarah and I are friends.' I pause. 'Have you met my stunning girlfriend, Gemma?'

A slight shrug. 'I'm aware who she is. I'm interviewing her next.' He pauses. 'You implied that he might have killed himself. Do you know of any reason why he might have done that?'

I nod my head. 'Well, he cheated on his wife who has just died tragically of MS. Maybe guilt overwhelmed him. He's a kind person. A teaching type with high moral standards, which he failed to adhere to. It just wouldn't surprise me if he couldn't cope with the way he has behaved, and jumped.'

50
Gemma

Luca, the little detective, sits in front of me in the dark windowless dining room in the middle of the villa. A room people seldom use in this summer kingdom of outside space and sunshine. He is like a cartoon caricature with his jerky movements and snappy uniform. The fact he wants to interview me is really worrying. Did someone see me coming back from the cliff path? Will they blame me for Jack's disappearance?

'Have you any reason to be suspicious of your boyfriend Ralph's intentions towards Jack?'

A sigh of relief. At least it's not me he's suspicious of. But then my stomach tightens. I do not want a shadow cast over Ralph, either. I want him to propose marriage, not custody visits.

I take a deep breath. 'No. I can assure you that Ralph had no bad intentions towards Jack. Ralph is a gentle man. Kind to everyone. He paid for this whole trip for us all, you know.'

'And does he ever give you the impression that he is still interested in his ex-wife?'

'He's in love with me. We have a very passionate relationship.'

He stares at me thoughtfully, and leans back in his chair.

'Can you think of anything else that might be helpful to us?'

I shrug and pause thoughtfully. 'I just wonder how stable Jack was, after treating his wife so badly. Grief does funny things to people, you know. Pushes them to the edge.'

'Are you implying that you think he might have taken his own life?'

I look around the room, thinking hard. 'Yes. I think it's possible.'

51
Sarah

It's Sunday evening, two days since you went missing and I'm feeling sick to my stomach. Tomorrow at first light the Carabinieri are sending out a motor boat rescue crew and a helicopter to search the coastline again. It must be to look for your dead body. They can hardly be expecting to find you alive now.

The others are having supper, but I cannot bear to eat. I take my clothes off and slip into bed. I can't face spending time with anyone this evening. Jack, how can this have happened? How can you be missing? We have so much to look forward to. You're about to advise the government on educational policy. Rumour has it you're likely to be knighted. We plan to travel; to Australia, New Zealand, Thailand, Cambodia. Later, when you retire, you're going to learn to sail. Something you have always wanted to have time to do. And we want to cross the Atlantic in luxury on the *Royal Clipper*. To get an Alsatian puppy; the dog you have always craved, and call him Alfie.

This can't be happening. Please, please, come back, Jack.

52
Janice

This holiday is a nightmare. I'd rather be at home, working in the local art gallery, hanging with my friends in the park, smoking cannabis and having a laugh. Using fake ID to go to the pub by the river, to go to the local nightclub. I tried to get out of coming away with the older generation, but Dad insisted. He bribed me with extra pocket money to help me through the rest of the school summer holiday, otherwise I wouldn't have come. And now Jack is dead and it's all my fault.

I think about Chris Tomkins, and shiver. Chris Tomkins, a tall, blond, gangly guy in my year at school. The sort of person who seemed to be all elbows and knees. I'd always been top of the class in French, English and History. And not far off the top in everything else. I worked so hard because I wanted to get A stars in everything. I wanted to be picked out as an Oxbridge candidate. I fancied to go to Clare College, Cambridge. Or Girton, maybe. But when the summer exams came, I bottled it. When I turned the exam papers over to read the questions, I was so nervous, the words floated in front of me, contorted and blurred. I took deep breaths and tried to do the best I could, but my brain felt as if it was in a fug. My results were OK. But Mr Average, Chris Tomkins, took everyone by surprise by getting eleven A stars. He was picked by the teachers to apply to Oxbridge and I wasn't. I was so jealous, emotion rose from the pit of my stomach.

I made sure his life didn't work out. I tampered with his father's car. His father was killed instantly in a head-on collision on the local A road, a few days after the exam results came out. It was thought to be an accident. No one found out. My hatred and envy are energies that I can't control.

The walls between my compact room and Patrick and Anna's are cardboard thin. At first all I can hear is the murmur of their voices. But now they are shouting, the paper wall is shaking, and I can hear their words clearly.

'Stop criticising me. I'm finding it difficult enough being here; without you adding to the problem,' Anna shouts.

'Do you think I'm finding it easy? I've never been so close to such worry and pain before. You should support me; not complain about me all the time.'

And then silence falls. Followed by groans of pleasure. I die a little inside. Not again. I heard it all last night. So clearly, so graphically. And sure enough, all too soon Anna's screams sound loud and clear, like the screams in a porno video. I've never made love, but I guess those videos are over-egged and artificial, no human being would make a noise like that naturally. At least I hope I never sound so uncouth.

Hearing my brother and his girlfriend at it is too close to home, too embarrassing. The thought of my brother pumping and grinding makes me feel sick. I groan inside and reach for the earphones Dad treated me to at the airport on the way over. I pump up the volume of my playlist and pull my pillowcase over my head. But I can still hear the distant rumpus of their love making.

I turn my mind in on itself and try to think happy thoughts. If I don't, I believe something really, really bad will happen to the whole mismatched bunch I'm on holiday with. The truth is the only person I don't resent on this trip is my father. And even he annoys me at times. Everyone needs to watch out.

53
Ralph

I wake up and open my eyes. It takes a few seconds for my mind to come into focus, and then I realise it's Monday morning. My forty-fifth birthday. Fucking fantastic. Happy birthday. Happy fucking birthday, Ralph. Forty-five today. How can we celebrate when Sarah's fiancé is still missing? Tonight was the night we were pulling out all the stops, hiring a minibus to take us to the best restaurant on the Amalfi Coast, tucked high up in the hills. We were going to look down on the lights of the bay below and relish a banquet. There would have been speeches and champagne. But no. Fuck. Fuck. Fuck. Instead, I am about to ring up and cancel.

I sit up in bed and find Gemma is sitting up next to me, fully made-up, wearing a black silk negligee.

'Happy birthday,' she says and pushes her lips against mine and snogs me.

The scent of her Kenzo perfume wraps around me. She thrusts her tongue into my mouth and reaches for my crotch. I wriggle away.

'I've got too much on my mind for that sort of thing today.'

She pouts a little and reaches for an envelope on her bedside table. She hands it to me and I rip it open. A fancy voucher for a trip in a hot air balloon, just outside Bristol, when we get back home. Doesn't she know I'm afraid of heights? I'm not sure I will be able to bear to do it. But I do not tell her that.

I lean across and kiss her. 'Thank you very much.' She pushes her lips against mine again. As soon as I can, I pull away. I slip out of bed and pull on my shorts and a T-shirt.

'I'm off to the kitchen to get some coffee. Would you like a cup?'

'Yes, please.'

I leave our bedroom, closing the door behind me, and step into the silence of the villa. None of my family seem to be up yet. I find the housekeeper already bustling about in the kitchen. Emptying the dishwasher. Wiping the counters. An enormous birthday cake dominates the antique pine table in the middle of the cooking area. Three round layers covered in white icing, edged with blue piping. 'Happy Birthday Ralph' is written across the top layer, in thick blue marzipan. Two large wax candles, a four and a five, stand next to the letters, waiting to be lit when appropriate. What a way to spend the day, waiting for the police to find a missing person. Missing presumed dead. Not much hope of any other outcome.

'Please take that cake away,' I instruct the housekeeper, voice clipped.

She shakes her head. 'I do not understand.'

'Take that cake away. I do not want it.' I click my fingers in her face. '*Pronto, pronto, pronto.*'

She puts it back into the white cardboard box from the bakery, lifts it up, and scuttles away.

54

Sarah

I open my eyes and, despite the solid slowness of time I am passing through, I realise that it's Monday morning. The morning of Ralph's birthday. Before my eyes begin to fully focus I hear a knock on my bedroom door.

'It's Ralph, can I come in?'

'Yes, please do,' I manage to reply.

He steps into my room, the skin beneath his eyes paper thin and dark. His unbrushed hair sticks up in clumps. Eyes darting. Transferring his weight from foot to foot.

'Happy birthday,' I say.

'My birthday is cancelled. The police are here, asking to see you.'

Is this it? The news I have been dreading? My stomach rotates. My legs go weak. My heart thumps against my ribcage.

'I need to get dressed. Give me a few minutes.'

'I'll wait for you outside.'

I slip out of bed, clean my teeth and throw a tracksuit on. I push my feet into my slippers and run my fingers through my hair. No time for my contact lenses. No time for make-up. Whatever I look like, I do not care.

I leave the bedroom to find Ralph waiting patiently in the corridor, looking at an old print of Praiano, hanging on the wall opposite my door. He turns to me and smiles awkwardly. I don't smile back, my stomach is churning. He takes my arm. We pad along the corridor towards the sitting room. Our heads are so close together that I can inhale his breath, I inhale his strength. Despite our differences, the old flatness between us, right now I am glad that he is here. We enter the room. Luca and Matteo are sitting like royalty, in their over-smart military uniforms, black and funereal. Their heads are high and shoulders back. They look imperial, as if they own the place. Luca has knitted his eyebrows together, making him look more sinister than ever. He folds his arms and leans them on the table in front of him. Matteo looks complacent. But then as he speaks no English, all he ever seems to need to do is to observe the situation.

'Please, sit down, Ms Kensington,' Luca says.

I sink into the red velvet sofa that has long since become threadbare and requires replacing. Ralph sits next to me and takes my hand in his. I stiffen. Why is he so sympathetic? Does he already know what has happened? I brace myself.

'Ms Kensington, I'm very sorry to have to tell you this, but we have found what we suspect to be your fiancé's body, five miles out at sea, towards Positano. We have taken it to the mortuary and we need you to come and identify it, please.'

I feel numb, as if I am looking down on the scene from a distance, hearing his words through thick fog. At least they have found your body, my darling, my love. At least I can say goodbye to you properly.

Ralph squeezes my hand. 'Should I come with you?' he asks.

'No, thanks,' I whisper, tears beginning to stream down my face.

I manage to pull myself up to standing, the room swaying gently around me. The blood rushes from my head. I fear I am going to faint. Luca puts his hand on my arm, ready to lead me away. I lean into him and cling on to his arm to steady myself. He smells sweet. Too sweet. He is wearing Brut, the aftershave that my dad used to wear. But he has put too much on, and its scent claws into my nostrils, making me feel sick. But I cannot move away from him. If I do not hold on to him, I am afraid I will fall.

'The car is parked across from the piazza,' he says as we begin to walk through the villa.

I turn my head to say goodbye to Ralph. He waves his fingers at me and mouths, 'Good luck.'

Oh, Ralph, I think, as if luck will help me and Jack now. Fate has already played its card. Holding on to Luca, stepping through the villa. Closing my mind to his scent. Past heavy antique furniture and local prints, everything blurred. Outside into the stinging morning heat. Walking along, mouth dry, sweat already plastering my T-shirt against my skin.

The walk to the police car seems to take forever. I do not feel real as I force myself to move along, concentrating on the ground, concentrating on putting one foot in front of the other. Even movement is an achievement.

Along the passageway, across the piazza, I am vaguely aware of a group of elderly men, standing in a group, eyes darting towards us as we pass. Up the steps, gasping for breath. Onto the pavement of the main road.

The police car is parked outside the café and *gelataria*. Tourists are sitting on the terrace, guarding their suitcases, eating croissants and sipping coffee. Waiting for their transfers presumably. Oh my god, I wish that was you and me, waiting to go home. Why did I bring you here? Why didn't I let you go when you suggested it? Why did I just pull you towards me, kiss you and tell you I never wanted you to leave me ever? I kissed you, like Judas, when I should have just sent you home.

Matteo left before us. He is sitting in the driver's seat of the shiny black car, drumming his fingers on the steering wheel in time to music. As soon as he sees us, he leans forwards. I guess he is switching the radio off. He jumps out and opens the doors for us, bowing his head respectfully. Luca sits next to him. I am shown into the back.

As we drive along the coast road, I close my eyes. I cannot bear to look at the sea. The sea that took you away from me. But closing my eyes gives me no relief. My mind is full of dark water pulling you further and further away from me. I try to hold my arm out to save you, but I stretch and stretch and I cannot reach.

Someone has their hand on my shoulder. Someone is shaking me gently. So gently. I open my eyes. It is Luca.

'We're here. Are you all right?' he asks.

My stomach knots. What a stupid question. How can I possibly be all right? But I swallow. I push my dread into the corners of my mind. I force my nausea down into the pit of my stomach.

I nod my head with as much bravery as I can muster. 'Yes.'

I step out of the car and take Luca's arm. Once again, the scent of his aftershave engulfs me. But now I am getting used to it and it simply reminds me of the past, of my father, and it comforts me a little. He leads me to a small modern building. We step through a rotating glass door into a compact reception area and waiting room with a line of plastic chairs. He signs us in, producing his identity badge, and a wad of paperwork.

'The mortuary attendant will come and get us in a few minutes, we need to sit and wait,' Luca explains.

We sit together on hard plastic chairs looking out onto the car park. Footsteps across linoleum. I look up. A woman in a lab coat is walking towards us. Skinny. Long black hair, thick and dull as straw, scraped back from her face. She stands in front of us. Her forehead is furrowed with lines etched into her face. She says something quietly in Italian.

'They're ready for you now,' Luca translates.

We stand up. Arm in arm, we follow her through a swing door to the right of reception. Into a white nondescript corridor.

She stops outside a metal door and unlocks it with a key held on a chain around her neck. We step into the mortuary. I have only ever seen mortuaries on TV. I have never been inside one before. It is cold. The walls are covered with steel doors that look like the doors of catering freezers. She stands in front of one and pulls it open like a drawer, wheeling a trolley out. A trolley with a body covered by a white sheet on it. She turns to look at me. The lines in her forehead contorting together.

'*Siete pronti?*' she asks.

I look across at Luca. 'Are you ready?' he translates. His brown eyes are soft with concern as he asks.

In a thousand years I will never be ready for this. I do not reply. He puts his hand on my back.

'Come on,' he says. 'Brace yourself. Get it over with.'

'OK, OK.'

'Do you want us to go?' he asks.

'Yes, please,' I mutter, nodding my head.

He gesticulates towards the door with his head to the furrowed woman. I hear their footsteps pad to the door as they leave.

I stand transfixed, staring at the sheet that covers you. Silence presses against me, ringing in my ears; silence so loud I want to run away from it. But there is no alternative. I am your next of kin. No one else who really knows you is here. I have to do this. I step towards you. Slowly, slowly, hands trembling, I pull back the sheet.

You, but not you. Bloody, bashed, swollen. Contorted. I see your tiny scar just above your right eyebrow. The one you got when you crashed your bike and flew over the handlebars, landing on the road. I cannot bear to investigate further, to check the ones on your elbow and knee. I would have to pull the sheet down further. I simply cannot let myself see any more injury to your beautiful body. Oh, Jack. This is the worst day of my life.

55
Ralph

A birthday treat. A formal interview at the police station. Sitting in a windowless room across a plastic table from Luca and Matteo. Goodness know why Matteo is even here; he doesn't speak a word of English. He doesn't contribute in any way, except to press a button to start recording my interview. And to frown and frown. Luca is a different matter. His chestnut eyes dart around the room, observing every detail.

Despite the cold stone walls of the interview room, sweat is dripping off me. I struggle against the desire to wipe it off my forehead as I do not want to draw any attention to it.

Luca leans back in his chair, face unreadable; immobile. 'As you know, your ex-wife, Sarah Kensington, has identified her fiancé's body, and it has been sent for autopsy, so the full information about how he died will soon be available. In the meantime, we just need your carefully considered statement, as you were the last person to see him alive.'

'I've already told you everything I know.'

He shakes his head. 'Now he has been found dead we need a more detailed description. Your contact with him has now become invaluable.'

Luca asks me all the same questions he asked me before. I give him the same answers. The difference is he's recording it this time.

56

Gemma

'Ms Richardson, tell me what happened the day Jack went missing,' Luca instructs.

I give him a short, clipped smile.

'Nothing in particular. It was the first day of the holiday. I slept in late. When I got up it was almost lunchtime. Jack and Ralph went for a walk together, and then after that Jack popped into the village to buy Sarah a present – a tourist gift; limoncello or something.'

'How did you know that?' Luca asks, leaning forwards.

'Ralph told everyone.'

'And you believed him?'

'Why wouldn't I?'

'That is what I need to find out. What is the truth and what is hearsay.'

'I'm not sure how I can help – why would I expect my partner to be lying?'

He smiles a smile that is so stiff it is almost a grimace. 'And where were you on Friday morning?'

I try not to stir uncomfortably in my chair. I reply with my best smile. 'Why are you asking me?'

His brow crinkles into an exasperated frown. 'We have found a body. It is a serious issue. We will be asking everyone in your party in the hope someone might have some information about what happened. I can assure you, madam, this is normal police procedure.'

However reassuring he is trying to be, I don't want him to know about my walk along the cliff. I don't want anyone to know about that.

I take a deep breath. 'I was in my room reading a book.'

'All morning?'

'Yes.'

57
Ralph

Sarah, you haven't left your bedroom since you returned from identifying Jack's body. You returned from the mortuary a broken person. You could hardly speak, you could hardly walk.

What can I do to help you? What can I do to make you feel better?

I knock on the bedroom door.

'Who is it?' a faint voice calls.

'Ralph.'

'Again?' There is a pause. 'I've already told you I'm fine.'

'I heard you sobbing. Of course you're not fine.' I wait a few moments. 'Sarah, I'm coming in.'

I open the door slowly and step inside. The curtains are drawn. I can't see anything at first. As my eyes grow accustomed to the dark, I blink and your bedroom begins to come into focus. As I noticed when I stepped inside earlier, it looks as if it has been ransacked. Drawers and wardrobe open. Clothes and shoes flung across the floor.

'I was looking for clues as to where he was, before we got the dreadful news,' you tell me as you watch me eyeing up the devastation. You start to sob.

Daylight is curling around the curtain edges. I look across at you, sitting up in bed, holding a sheet over your chest to cover your breasts; eyes red and swollen from crying.

'Crying is good. It's cathartic,' I say.

'How would you know? Have you ever lost anyone you love this much?'

It doesn't seem the right time to remind you that I lost you.

'Is there anything I can do to help?' I ask. My words hang limply in the air.

You do not reply and disappear beneath the covers. You begin to sob, your cries rising to a high-pitched feral wail. The sound of your pain pierces into my mind. I can't bear it a second longer. I need to leave you to cope with your grief alone. I tiptoe towards the door.

'Ralph, please don't go.'

I turn around and sit at the end of your bed. 'I'm here if you need me.'

Time seems to stand still.

After a while: 'Are you sure there's nothing I can do to help?' I ask.

'Of course not,' you sob. 'No one can bring Jack back. I can't even take his body home to bury it until we get the autopsy result.'

'When did you last eat?'

Slowly, slowly, you appear and pull yourself up to sitting again, wrapped in your sheet.

'I don't remember,' you answer, snivelling into a large cotton handkerchief.

'Would you like some chicken soup?' I ask.

You shake your head vehemently. 'I know you mean well but I don't need a nursemaid. I just want my fiancé back.'

I lean across, put my hand on your leg and pat it. 'I know you don't need a nursemaid. But I just want you to know that I can help you in any way you need. I can help you arrange to ship his body back to the UK. I can help you arrange the funeral. I am here for you. As long as you know that.'

Your eyes fill with tears again. Your lower lip trembles. 'I know you have always been around for me.' You begin to sob. 'But it isn't you that I want.'

58

Sarah

I bury myself in my bed covers and cry. I sob. I screech. I wail. I splutter, I panic, I fight for breath. I see your face moving towards me to kiss me goodbye, just before you set off on the cliff walk with Ralph. Your kindly, handsome face. So expressive. So animated. Your simmering hazel eyes. I remember standing on the patio when your lips touched mine, and once again I feel the gentle electricity that I always felt when we kissed.

And then I see your stone-cold, bruised head in the mortuary. No longer you, Jack, but an alabaster impression of the man I love. Dead eyes staring at the ceiling. Dead eyes that I can't push from my mind.

59
Ralph

I move through the silence of the villa. Through the sitting room, the windowless dining room and the kitchen. I do not know where Anna, Patrick and Janice are. Perhaps they have gone to the beach to get out of the house. I know Gemma will be lying in wait in our bedroom, wanting something, no doubt. A serious chat about our relationship. To woo me with her sexual skills. To nag me into buying her an expensive gift; she has a penchant for Chanel perfume, designer clothes and ostentatious jewellery. I slip into the kitchen relieved to see that the birthday cake is gone and the prying eyes of the housekeeper are nowhere to be seen. I have asked her to leave. We all need some privacy.

I pour myself a stiff G&T with ice and lemon, and step out onto the terrace. Past the pots of bougainvillea and geraniums.I stand knocking back my drink, leaning across the balustrade, looking at the view. Our life has stopped. I'm walking on eggshells. Meanwhile the world moves on all around us, unaware, nonchalant – uncaring of our difficulties. People are sunbathing on the beach. Swimming in the bay. Balancing on paddleboards as they skim elegantly across the water. Jet skis bash and thrust into the waves. Sail boats race before the wind, motor boats tormenting them with their wake. It's windy today and kite surfers play. Their world is a party gilded with sunshine. But in our villa we are all walking a tightrope of emotion.

A tap on the shoulder. I turn around. It's Janice, standing in front of me, a younger version of you, Sarah, long flowing blonde locks, and the face of an angel, showing off her tan in a white bikini.

'Are you all right, Dad?' she asks.

I sigh. 'Not exactly. This wasn't how I envisaged my birthday celebration. And I've cancelled the restaurant, as I'm sure you've guessed.'

'It was a stupid, crass question. I shouldn't have asked you whether you were all right.' Her face crumples. She bursts into tears. 'I'm so sorry, Dad. It's all my fault. It's my fault that Jack died.'

I shake my head. 'It can't be. Don't be ridiculous.'

I take a deep breath, step towards her, and pull her towards me. I hug her. She clings to me like a limpet to a rock.

'I'm frightened, Dad. Frightened as hell.'

'Stop it Janice. This is nothing to do with you.'

60
Gemma

I'm lying on a sun lounger on our balcony, hoping for a chat with Ralph. He'll have to return here sooner or later, to change into his swimming trunks, or to fetch his wallet, or something. I want to know when he thinks we should use the birthday present I gave him. After this upsetting news, in some ways now hardly seems like the right moment to plan a treat, but I think having something to look forward to might cheer him up. Even in times of trouble we all need things to look forward to. I want to see him. I want to hug him. To hold him. To comfort him.

My eyes are tightly closed, trying to relax after the tragedy that has occurred in our midst. It is dreadful news that Jack's body has been found. I was hoping mystery would continue to surround his whereabouts. Slowly, slowly, inhale, exhale, breathe, breathe, I tell myself. Inhaling the scent of the jasmine that is climbing up the wall beneath me. The salty freshness of the faint sea breeze. Listening to the clock in the piazza chiming in the distance, thinking about Jack. But I am not relaxing. I am angry. About the way he treated me. About the way he deserved what happened to him.

Ralph, I want you to cling to me, to wrap yourself around me. To surround me with commitment and make me feel safe. Right now I would love to feel safe. All I want to do is to think of happier times. I close my eyes and step back to our first date. Dining with you at Skylon restaurant on the South Bank. You were such a dish in comparison to the men I usually dated. Such a dish that my heart was fluttering. Dressed in chinos and a pink, slim-fit Ralph Lauren shirt that clung to your abs. I was wearing my favourite dress from Reiss. And a generous douse of Chanel No.5 perfume. We raised a glass of bubbly. I proposed a toast.

'To us. To our relationship,' I said, worrying that that was a bit pushy.

'Personal,' you said, eyes meeting mine and sparkling with enthusiasm. 'Or business?' You paused and sipped your favourite champagne, Louis Roederer.

'What about both?' I replied.

'Well then, let's start with business. Can I interest you in a digital marketing contract with my investment bank?'

'Yes, please. I would love to help you market your company's business. Can you expand upon your needs?'

'My needs are not that business-like right now.' You leant across the table and kissed me. My heart was on fire.

I am woken from my daydream by the sound of our bedroom door clicking open. I slip off the sun lounger, step through the patio doors and walk towards you. You are standing in the middle of our bedroom, staring into space like a haunted creature.

'Are you OK?'

You jump at the sound of my voice and turn towards me, eyes darting nervously from side to side now.

'How are you feeling?' I ask.

'How do you think? Dreadful,' you snap.

'What about Sarah?'

You flop down onto the bed and sigh. 'Worse than I could ever have imagined.' You put your head in your hands. 'We're all moving through a living hell. It is impossible to imagine how something as awful as this could have happened.'

My stomach twists inside. I sit next to you on the bed and put my arm around you. You stiffen almost imperceptibly. I rub your back gently to try and relax your muscles, but you shrug me off and edge away like a sulky teenager.

'Gemma, look, I'm sorry, I'm not feeling very touchy feely right now,' you mutter into your hands. 'I need to be alone to figure out how I can help Sarah.'

Sarah, Sarah, Sarah. Whatever I say, whatever I do, she is all you think about. I sit in silence next to you, staring at the old print of fishermen on the Amalfi Coast that is framed on the wall in front of me. The painting shows long thin open boats that remind me of Viking ships, with fishermen aboard wearing hats that look like turbans. Waves curl over the bow of the ship.

The picture turns my mind to Jack. The way he slipped off the cliff. I see his body tumbling into the water. I feel scared. So scared. I place my hand on yours and squeeze it. It remains limp in mine. I need to divert attention away from myself.

'You've been caught in the middle of a tragic situation that isn't your fault,' I say. 'It's bound to be hard on you. No wonder you're worried about Sarah, but I'm worried about you too. Can't I try and help you?'

You shake your head. 'I don't see how you can.'

'I suspect we all need counselling. I'm pretty devastated. Until now, I'd never spent time with someone just before they died.'

You sigh. You look up. You push your dark and angry eyes into mine. 'You seem intent on making this all about yourself.'

Anger builds inside me. I push it down, deep inside me. I was trying to do the opposite. Nothing I ever seem to say or do to consolidate my relationship with you seems to work, Ralph. It will be so much easier when Sarah has gone.

61

Sarah

A distant whisper reminds me that I ordered Ralph a birthday present, handmade silver cufflinks from a craftsman in the village. I groan inside. I haven't the energy to get out of bed and go to collect them. I cannot possibly walk across town. I feel so sick I haven't been able to eat. When I stand up, blood rushes from my head and I fear I'm about to faint. I need to get Janice to help. I text her.

Janice, I'm in my room. Please come and see me.

I drift into a fitful sleep, tossing and turning and tangling myself in my sheet. I wake and check my phone. No reply from Janice. Why hasn't she checked her messages? Why hasn't she come to see whether I'm all right? Patrick and Anna haven't either. Ralph did, but I wasn't in the mood to see him. From reading articles about grief in the past, I know that even though I feel desperate right now in these early days, I am still anaesthetised to his death, to the pain. My mood will only dip. I'll have to force myself to leave my room and go and find her. I want to make sure I've got Ralph's birthday present before I become too depressed to think about it.

I fight my nausea and twist my body to place my feet on the floor. I cling on to the side of the bed and pull myself to standing. Blood drains swiftly from my head again and I am sure I am about to collapse. But just when I think I am about to lose consciousness, my head clears and the room stands steady in front of me. I manage to get dressed. Picking up my bra from on the basket-weave chair in the corner, clean pants from my bedside drawer. I pull on a T-shirt and a pair of shorts, and run a brush through my hair. Make-up, perfume, contact lenses all a step too much.

I open the bedroom door and step into the world beyond. The oppressive silence of the villa. Through the dining room, through the sitting room. Down the stairs through the kitchen onto the large balcony. Janice is lying on a sun lounger in her white faux-leather bikini, reading a Penguin Classic. A keen student of A-level English, as I once was.

I stand by the sun lounger and stroke her arm to get her attention. She opens her cornflower-blue eyes, a mirror reflection of mine. She sits up.

'Hey, Mum, are you OK? How are you coping?'

My stomach knots. I do not know how to begin to reply.

'Janice, did you get my text?'

She shakes her head and her long blonde silken hair swishes across her shoulders.

'I need you to do me a favour. I need you to go and collect the birthday present I've bought for your father.'

'What have you got him?' she asks.

'Some handmade silver cufflinks from the local jewellers. I ordered them months ago.'

She frowns. 'Does buying an expensive birthday present for Dad help, when you were in love with someone else?'

It's the past tense that does it. I lose it. I lean forwards, draw my arm back, move forwards and slap her hard on her right cheek. She winces and clasps her hand across her face.

'You bitch,' she retorts.

'Bitch? You think I'm a bitch?' I screech. 'I've just lost my partner. Have you no compassion?'

She stands up, red faced, eyes spitting with anger. 'You slapped me. You started it. I'll go and collect Dad's birthday present. For his sake, not yours.'

62
Janice

Mother, when people don't know us well, they guess you are my soulmate, because we look so physically similar. You, in fact, are quite the opposite. You stand in front of me riddled with indignation; body stiff, feet wide apart, breathing deeply as if you are about to have a panic attack. How can you be so indignant when you just slapped me in the face?

You are so foolish to cross me. You will die next. Don't you realise what I have done? Don't you realise how dangerous I am? I'm always asking for help. I'm always trying to tell you and Dad. But neither of you believe me. You minimise what I say. But one day it will happen. The police will discover the truth about me. And you'll end up in a grave.

63
Gemma

Monday evening. Ralph's birthday. Or should I say un-birthday. We're not on an extravagant trip up the mountain to the best restaurant on the Amalfi Coast. The birthday cake has been given away to a local children's home. The stash of vintage champagne remains unopened. The housekeeper is too intrusive and has been dismissed. A heavily grieving Sarah is hibernating in her room. At least she is out of my hair, out of my face – for now. It would have been easier for me if she had died with Jack. Two flies in the ointment removed in one go. Jack was a real bastard, that's for sure.

Instead of our flash dinner out, I have cooked for everyone. Patrick, Anna, Janice, Ralph and I sit on the terrace, eating pasta carbonara, in silence. An evening silence more oppressive than the daytime heat.

'Why don't some of us just fly home?' I suggest as I clear away the plates.

'Good idea,' Anna pipes up brightly. 'We can't relax. We don't all need to sit around and wait for the autopsy results.'

'The police have asked us all to stay in the vicinity,' Ralph replies, mouth in a line. 'I'm sorry, but we're all stuck here for the time being.'

Anna walks to the edge of the stone balustrade and looks out across the inky sea. She lifts her chin to inhale the distance. And then she puts her head in her hands and sobs. Patrick walks over to her and hugs her from behind to calm her. She turns around and melts into him. Janice raises her eyes to the sky.

'Such a drama queen,' she mutters.

'Maybe,' I reply. 'But I know how she feels.'

Janice glowers at me. I pile up the plates and begin to load the dishwasher. Patrick extricates himself from Anna to help. Ralph, Janice and Anna settle on the outdoor sofa with a bottle of brandy and a bottle of limoncello.

We clear the meal away. The kitchen now smells of cleaning liquid; dishwasher buzzing softly. Patrick and I stand in the middle of the kitchen, feeling virtuous. Moonlight floats through the curtainless window. Lights twinkle in the bay beneath us. The night is yet young, but we will all be feeling too low to go anywhere.

'How's it going with Dad?' he asks, hanging the tea towels to dry on the hooks by the oven.

I bite my lip. I feel like crying, but I just shrug my shoulders. 'I'm not sure really. It's hard to tell how anything is going right now, with a dead body in the mix.'

He smiles at me. 'I agree. It's most distressing, isn't it? I never imagined in my wildest dreams I would find myself in a situation like this.' He pauses. 'Just so you know, I think he's lucky to have you.' He puts his hand on my shoulder. I look up into his eyes.

'Thank you.' I pause. 'And you and Anna? How's that?'

He smiles a slow, sad smile. 'Don't ask. Let's put it this way, it's not going as well as usual.'

'She doesn't like me, does she? I can see things are a bit tricky.'

He winces a little, a slight frown between his eyes. 'Is it really that obvious?'

'Yes.' I shake my head. 'No.' I pause. 'What I mean is, your relationship is none of my business.'

He laughs, a dry half-hearted laugh. 'Yes. No. That clarifies that, then.'

We look at each other and giggle.

'Come on, time to brace ourselves and join the others. Let's hit the brandy and limoncello,' I reply.

His hand brushes across my back as we leave the kitchen. We join our party on the terrace. They are jovial now, after plying themselves with copious amounts of alcohol. Too jovial given the circumstances. Singing a cheesy version of 'Life is Life' by Opus. A hit from the mid-eighties that the older generation always seem to sing at parties. Le-la, la, la-la. Too loud. Totally inappropriate. Ralph, you are really in the groove, shouting along at the top of your voice, as you definitely can't sing.

As soon as Patrick sees what is going on, his face stiffens. His jawline freezes. He marches across to you and puts his hands firmly on both your shoulders. 'Dad, be quiet.'

You continue shouting.

Patrick's voice rises above the cacophony. 'Stop right now. This is inappropriate.'

The noise stops.

'I know. I'm sorry. It's just all so awful,' you say, lip trembling. 'I was trying to pretend to be cheerful.'

You stand up, cling on to Patrick, and hug him. He hugs you back. My heart is breaking to see you like this. Right now, I wish it was me you were clinging to. I wish it was me you needed. I always want to be here for you, Ralph. To be needed. Patrick holds you tight, until you step back and release him.

You flop back onto the sofa, tears in your eyes.

'Come on, you two, join us, have a brandy,' you say, looking across at me, swallowing back your tears.

At least you are taking notice of me tonight, despite the state you're in. You reach for two glasses from the coffee table in front of you and pour each of us a stiff one. I take a sip. Its molten taste burns my tongue and I wince.

Anna yawns and stretches. 'I'm off to bed,' she announces, standing up.

Patrick's eyes are glued to her sashaying hips as he stands up.

'I'll say goodnight too.'

He follows her. I snuggle up to you, hold your hand and squeeze it. You squeeze back, and put your arm around me. I inhale your closeness, the scent of brandy on your breath and enjoy the moment.

But no. I look up at the sound of footsteps. Sarah is walking across the patio, wearing a long cotton nightdress, silken blonde hair billowing behind her in the soft evening breeze. Moving slowly as if she is in a trance, as if she is playing a part in a Shakespearean tragedy. Looking like Ophelia from *Hamlet*. She stands in front of us, eerie and ghost-like. So, of course, you untangle yourself from me and stand in front of her, transfixed.

'It's not quite midnight yet, so it's still your birthday. I had to rouse myself from my misery to come and give you your present.'

Tears dry, you smile now as if the world is perfect. She hands you a black leather box trimmed with gold. I see your eyes glistening beneath the patio lights. You open the box. I stand up and crane my neck to look, without intruding by moving any closer. Cufflinks. You take a sharp breath. They must be hand engraved or something.

'They're beautiful, Sarah, thank you.'

You stand looking at her in a way you never look at me. She really needs to join her fiancé.

64
Ralph

My beleaguered birthday is over. The morning after the disappointing night before, I escape from the villa and walk to the beach. I intend to have some peace, lying on a sun lounger, listening to the sound of the waves folding into the beach. Away from Gemma. Away from Sarah and her grief. The pathologist is carrying out Jack's autopsy today. My stomach churns as I picture him on the examination table, his long, slim, elegant body laid out like a putty model. Penis curled and limp like a giant sea slug; useless to pleasure you now. Head bruised and battered. Almost unrecognisable. The pathologist cutting him open like a piece of meat; slicing through muscle, revealing his guts. I tremble inside as I imagine the damage the pathologist will find. Pathology. What a dreadful career.

I push the stench of death from my mind as I walk along Via Umberta towards the beach. Past the whitewashed apartments and villas that hug the cliff, gleaming like whitened teeth in the sharp morning sunlight. It's a breezy day and wind fluffs the waves in the bay into pretty tufts of lace. A day like any other summer day to the locals as they prepare to use their talents to make money from the tourists. Pizza ovens hot and ready. Café fridges full of cold iced drinks. Sun loungers on the beach scrubbed clean and ready for today's recumbents.

I stroll towards the beach, hiding my worry deep inside me,

like a jack-in-a-box hides beneath its lid, on top of its spring. I wind down the cliff path towards the small stony beach, formed in a small indentation in the cliff. I hire one of the waiting sun loungers. It's early in the day. There is hardly anyone else here. A young couple tangled together. A middle-aged man with a heart-attack belly and a big bushy beard. A couple with bulky rucksacks sit on towels at the edge of the beach. Backpackers, I guess, who cannot afford the hefty ten euros for a sun lounger.

I try to settle down, but I can't relax. Every muscle in my body feels stiff, so I decide to go for a swim. I peel off my clothes, down to my trunks, slip my beach shoes on and stumble across the hot stony ground towards the sea.

The water must be very warm at this time of year, but because I've been roasting on the sun lounger, in contrast, every millimetre of my body feels cold as I slip into the sea. When the water reaches waist height, I take the plunge and launch myself forward in a cautious breaststroke. For the first few minutes I shudder at the coolness of the water, but then it begins to pass across my body like warm liquid silk. The movement eases my muscles. They begin to work together, smoothly and effortlessly. I exhale in relief. That's better.

I see a large motor boat traversing the edge of the cove. Its wake pushes towards me like a maelstrom. I duck my head, but I can't stop it. Water cascades over me and forces me under. I can't think. I can't breathe. And when finally my head emerges, I am gasping for breath. Is this what it was like for Jack when he landed in the water? I pinch myself and tell myself not to be stupid. Of course not. He must have already been dead by the time he hit the water. His head would have already hit the cliff several times. My stomach churns and I rush out of the water.

I navigate the stones and move back towards my sun lounger. Someone is lying on the sun lounger next to mine. Rammed next to it. Ready to invade my body space. It's Gemma, wearing a bright yellow bikini, greasing herself in sun oil. If she was a potato she would fry. As soon as she sees me, she waves and smiles.

'Surprise. I decided to join you.'

My stomach knots, but I keep smiling. I need space. I want to be alone.

'How thoughtful of you. Can I get you anything? An ice-cream? A cold drink?'

She beams back at me. 'No. Your company will do just fine.'

'About that. I can't stay here long. I've just had an email from work,' I lie. 'I've got to go back to the villa and sit in front of my computer. I need to check on some investments for a major client.'

Her face falls. She pouts a little. For a second she looks a bit like a gargoyle.

'But . . . but . . .' she splutters. 'I've just paid for the sun lounger. It was expensive.'

'Well stay and enjoy it. I'll be back before you know it,' I say as I begin to gather my clothing together.

She reaches across and grabs my arm. 'Please. Let's just have a quick talk before you go.'

I sigh inside. 'You are a one, aren't you, Gemma? There's no escaping you,' I reply and follow my words with what I hope is a friendly laugh.

'You manage often enough.'

Not very effectively, I think but don't say.

'You found me here.'

She leans towards me, eyes sparkling intensely. I think she is attempting to flirt. 'You wanted me to. You told me where you were going.'

Oh, did I? That was a mistake. I didn't tell her on purpose. I told Janice over a croissant and coffee at breakfast. Maybe she overheard me. Then she gets that look on her face. The one where she wants me to discuss my feelings. The sugar-saccharin lovey-dovey look that drives me insane.

'I need to know where I stand. You still seem to be obsessed with Sarah. I find it most insulting. It denigrates me. It is only fair that you tell me the truth.'

How can I tell her the truth, right here and now? She'll go ape-shit. God knows what will happen. I take her hands in mine.

'Gemma, you are my future, Sarah is my past,' I reply, taking a deep breath and mentally crossing my fingers behind my back.

She looks at me, narrow eyed. A hint of gargoyle again.

65
Sarah

It's Thursday morning. In a few hours it will be a whole week since we arrived on this hellhole of a holiday. By some miracle I have forced myself to get dressed and leave my bedroom, but now I am exhausted and wilting in the searing heat. The temperature is ramping up; each day hotter than the last. Surely the weather will break soon, and a storm will come? But there is no sign of that. I look up at the sky; a saturated peacock blue, not a cloud in sight.

We are sitting on the terrace, all of our group – Patrick, Anna, Janice, Gemma, Ralph and me, eating a late mid-morning breakfast. Anna and Janice are nibbling fruit. All I can manage is coffee. Gemma, Patrick and Ralph are demolishing chocolate croissants from the bakery. Even the sight of them eating so normally when I can hardly eat a thing is making me feel sick. The doorbell rings. Ralph pads to answer it.

He returns with Luca and Matteo. They stand on the terrace in front of our dining table.

'Good morning,' Luca says. 'We wish to speak to Sarah, alone.'

My stomach tightens. 'OK,' I reply. 'Follow me. We can go to my balcony.'

As I walk through the villa my body feels empty, not like a natural part of me, as I try to anticipate what is coming now. I hear their footsteps following me. Feel and sense their movement in the air behind me. Through the kitchen, through the dark dank dining room. Up the stairs, along the landing, into my bedroom.

'Sorry, it's a bit untidy,' I say as we weave through the discarded clothes on my bedroom floor.

We step out onto my balcony, and sit around the small wrought iron table. Matteo's face is as stiff and expressionless as usual. Luca's eyes pierce into mine. 'We have received the autopsy report,' he announces.

My heart pounds in overdrive.

He straightens his back and pushes his fringe from his eyes. 'The pathologist has concluded that your fiancé, Jack, committed suicide.'

This can't be real. My hand grips my chair tightly, and metal presses against me. I *am* on the balcony of my room with Luca and Matteo. This is happening.

'No,' I exclaim. 'He wouldn't. He didn't. I don't believe it. It must have been an accident.'

Luca sits looking at me, wide eyed with sympathy. 'It is what the pathologist has concluded from the evidence.'

We sit in silence as Luca allows me to digest the information. I hear the cicadas buzzing. I look out across the bay and see a small sail boat playing in the distance. After a while, he continues.

'No one else seems to have been involved. We did not find any other DNA. His injuries are consistent with jumping off the cliff. There are no injuries on his body to indicate he slipped accidentally.'

'But . . . but . . . how accurate is an autopsy on someone who has spent days in the sea?'

Luca's frown draws his brows closer together. His eyes darken. 'Are you questioning our competency?' he asks.

'Of course not. No.' I feel tears welling. 'It's just so distressing to hear, when I thought we were both so happy.'

Luca's face softens and crumples. 'I am sorry to have been the bearer of such sad news. I will go and tell the others. *Vieni via*, Matteo.' There is a pause. 'Any questions, let me know. If there is anything I can do to help, please call. You have my number.' He puts his hand on my shoulder and squeezes as he leaves.

I sit on the balcony filled with emptiness and dread. Knots in my chest. Knots in my stomach. In my head. Hard, contorted knots that solidify inside me and whip up into anger. You can't have done this. I know you can't.

I step away from the balcony, into my bedroom and flop onto the bed. The walls of my room move towards me as I fight for breath. I need to get away from here. I need to force myself to look over the cliff edge and confront what happened. I wait for my breathing to calm and leave the villa.

I dash along the passageway and stumble along the cliff path. The sun, searing and majestic, in the cloudless sky above, burns into me. I can hardly bear to look down at the ever-changing movement of the sea that claimed your body, my love. But I make myself. I stop at a place where the path runs close to the cliff edge. Where the cliff is sheer. I stand and look down. You could have slipped here. You could have slipped anywhere. I stand between two small sharp, craggy rocks and imagine it was here. I look down. The sea swells and falls, crusted with ripples of sunlight glinting like diamonds, many hundreds of feet beneath me. The height, the distance, makes me feel dizzy. I step back from the edge.

I have never been religious, but I cannot believe your energy is truly gone. I just cannot accept it. There must be a god somewhere taking care of your soul. Your soul was too precious to have been randomly destroyed. I kneel down, close my eyes and press my hands together like we did at school when I was a child. Jack, I pray for you. I thank a higher being for the joy we had.

Did your guilt about loving me, when Susan was still alive, finally overcome you? In the end, was it all too much?

66
Ralph

Luca and Matteo are back from their conversation with Sarah, stepping out onto the terrace, flat eyed and serious. Dark harbingers of doom. The silence that had already descended on our group after they arrived deepens. Silence humming through my mind, insidious and oppressive. I long for normality. Happy, irrelevant chatter. Music. Traffic. A dog barking in the park. Children playing in the distance.

Luca and Matteo stand before us. Luca has his hands behind his back, shoulders wide, feet apart. Matteo stands to his right, body position mimicking his master. Luca moves his arms and holds them by his side. Matteo copies him.

'The autopsy report has concluded that Jack committed suicide,' Luca announces.

The news reverberates across the terrace. In whispers. In sharp intakes of breath. Sideways glances. Shuffling feet. Strange grimaces.

Suicide is heart-breaking. Suicide is tragic. But it conveniently releases you back to me, Sarah. I make sure I look painfully distressed, by holding my head low, and looking at the floor.

'How awful,' I mutter. 'Are you sure?'

'Are you wanting to criticise our autopsy procedure in Italy?' Luca replies, voice harsh.

'So it wasn't an accident then?' Gemma asks, voice high pitched.

'It would appear not, from the autopsy, but we need to continue gathering facts. We have to file a report on the circumstantial evidence before the case can be closed,' Luca replies. 'In fact, we need to question you all again, one at a time. Perhaps we could start with you, madam? Shall we go to the dining room where we can have some privacy?'

67
Gemma

Sitting in the passageway of a dining room that we never use except for police interviews, I look at the strange collection of ornaments on the dresser. A cheap vase filled with dusty flowers. A pottery pig. A bowl of painted egg shells. A Toby Jug pirate. A Toby Jug fisherman. Thank goodness this is the only part of the villa that is tacky. It is a shame we have had to spend so much time in here being questioned by the men in black.

Luca is sitting opposite me, giving me a strange half smile, friendly but not friendly. Is it supposed to be intimidating? He twiddles the pen he is holding between his fingers. Matteo is beady eyed and frowning as usual. What a pair. Policemen glued at the hip, who look as if they could both be Mafia gangsters.

Luca takes a deep breath. 'Gemma, please tell me any impression you had of Jack's state of mind on Friday night, and Saturday morning, before he went missing,' he says.

My mind slips. I am back on the first night of our trip, sitting next to him. Talking to him, getting him to flirt with me. Watching him start to respond, eyes sparkling with lust.

'Gemma, please,' Luca says.

I pull my thoughts away from Jack. I look across at Luca, pen poised, waiting for me to speak. I take a deep breath and brace myself to lie.

'He did seem rather flat.'

68
Janice

'Thank you for your time, we do appreciate it,' Luca says, narrowing his eyes. 'I can assure you we won't keep you very long. As we explained on the terrace, we are asking all of you a few questions about Jack, just so that we can draw a line under what has happened.' Luca leans forwards in his chair. 'Is there anything you think we need to know that might help?'

Now that the autopsy report has concluded suicide, I have a chance of getting away with this. I want to laugh out loud, but I stop myself.

'He seemed very low,' I begin. 'Very withdrawn and quiet. I'd only just met him, so I can't tell you whether he always behaved like that, but he certainly seemed very depressed to me.'

'Your mother is adamant that he was very happy and positive. That he had too much to live for to have committed suicide.'

I give him a clipped smile. 'She just won't want to admit she wasn't enough for him.'

69
Patrick

Luca and Matteo. The creepy dining room. I sigh inside. I wish I could just lie next to Anna on the beach and forget about all this. Hold her hand. Listen to music. Soak up the sun. Poor Mum. Losing her fiancé. Poor Dad, having his much looked forward to birthday ruined. Grief upon grief. Depression. Misery.

Luca is sitting at the dining table opposite me, pen in hand. Notebook in front of him. He's a bit old fashioned. Why doesn't he just record what I am saying on his phone?

'So how did your father feel when he met your mother's fiancé?' he asks.

'He was a bit surprised. He didn't even know Mum was in a relationship until recently, and then on the first night of the holiday she told him they were getting married.'

'Surely that caused major ructions?' he asks.

'We were all a bit surprised.'

Luca raises his eyebrows. 'Bit surprised?' He pauses. 'Was that your father's only reaction?'

'Well, I'm not really the best person to ask. I was busy looking after my girlfriend, Anna. It was the first time she'd met my family, so I spent most of the time talking to her; making sure she felt comfortable.'

Luca leans forwards and fixes my eyes in his. 'Patrick, I am not interested in how much time you spent making a fuss of your girlfriend. Please focus on my question. Tell me what you made of your father's reaction to your mother's news.'

'He seemed OK. He had too much to drink on the first night of the holiday, which is normal for him. He's a heavy drinker. At the end of the meal he stood up and proposed a toast to Mum and Jack's happiness.' I pause. 'He seemed fine. He has a beautiful girlfriend, Gemma. So why would he mind?' Luca nods. He scribbles some notes in his pad. He looks up. 'And now, tell me how Jack was on Thursday evening?'

'I'm a medical student. I've just finished a project on suicide. It's common for suicidal people to keep their depression well hidden from those around them. He seemed fine, but I'm not sure anyone's impression of his state of mind counts for anything.'

Luca's lips quiver in annoyance. 'I'll be the judge of that.'

70

Anna

Patrick's family are nothing but trouble. I can hardly believe what is happening all around me, drunkenness, death. Gemma trying to flirt with my boyfriend. And even though we're not allowed to leave yet, I'm not sure how much longer I can cope with being here.

I look into Luca's large chocolate-brown eyes. 'I'm sorry. I've nothing more to tell you. I hardly talked to Jack or Ralph on Thursday evening. As I said, I saw Gemma flirting with Jack; but then that is normal for her – she flirts with everybody. And Ralph was very pissed. But after a certain hour in the evening, that seems to be normal for him, too.'

71

Ralph

'Previously you mentioned you thought Jack might have jumped, because he was overwhelmed by guilt for cheating on his wife,' Luca says; eyeballing me. 'Did he actually admit to feeling guilty to you?'

'In a roundabout way.'

He leans towards me. 'Please, explain.'

'When we were on the cliff walk together, I did ask him about the timing of his relationship with my wife.' I pause and lean back in the uncomfortable dining chair I'm sitting in. 'It was clear from what he said that it began before his wife, Susan, had died.'

Luca is scribbling in his pad. He looks up. 'How did you react?'

'I asked him how he could have done that to his wife – and *he* reacted very badly.'

Luca frowns. 'What happened?'

'He began breathing heavily, stiffening his fist and punching it into his other hand repeatedly, as if he was stopping himself from punching me. He did seem in a terrible state.' I pause. Luca is writing frantically now.

Luca's eyes darken. 'Why did you not tell us this last time we interviewed you? You said you parted best of friends.'

'Well, I mean, we did. In the end. I was sitting with him on the bench, at the view point. When he calmed down, we had a nice chat. Then he said he was going to the shops to look for a present for Sarah, so I left him to his own devices and came back to the villa.' I pause and sigh. 'I wish I hadn't left him now. If I had stayed, I might have been able to save him.'

Luca finishes writing and looks up. 'Perhaps you could take us for a walk along the cliff, show us where this was precisely?'

Not a question. An instruction. 'Of course, I'll show you. Anything to help.'

'And was that the last time you saw him?'

'Yes.'

We leave Villa Panorama and head for the cliff path. I take the lead. Luca and Matteo tromping behind me. Every time I turn around to check where they are, they are not looking at the view. I suppose they have grown up with it and take it for granted. They are both sweating heavily in their black suits. I walk confidently towards the view point, trying not to look into the ocean, trying not to dwell on what happened to Jack.

I round two more bends and stop to turn around. Luca and Mattteo almost bump into me, damp pools in their armpits, beads of perspiration decorating their brows.

'It's here,' I announce. 'I said goodbye to him right here.' I pause. Almost in tears, I shake my head. 'As I said, if only I'd known what he was about to do, I'd have done everything I could to try to stop him.'

72

Sarah

I'm sitting on the sofa of the terrace next to Ralph, drinking a G&T, and watching the sun softening across the surface of the sea like liquid gold, remembering how much you loved to watch the sunset. Ralph's shoulder is touching mine and despite my despair, his familiarity comforts me.

'Suicide is impossible. The autopsy must be wrong. He must have slipped,' I insist.

Ralph sighs and his shoulder pushes against mine more closely. 'Maybe in the end he felt too guilty about Susan.'

'But . . . but . . . he'd been living with that for years,' I splutter.

Ralph finishes his gin and puts the glass on the table in front of us. 'Maybe his imminent happiness with you pushed his guilt over the edge.'

His words cut into me like electricity. My body stiffens.

Ralph pulls me towards him and holds me tight. I inhale the scent of the sandalwood aftershave he always wears.

'Sarah, my darling, I'd give anything to make this right for you.' A tear runs slowly down my left cheek. Ralph brushes it away with his finger. He leans forwards and softly, gently kisses its pathway.

'I wish my kisses could blow all your tears away.'

I let him kiss me, but his touch stings my skin. It breaks my heart in two. I wish it was you who was here to kiss me, Jack. I will never get over you.

73
Ralph

I kiss her on the cheek and she clings on to me so tight, as if I am the most important man in the world. Time is now. It doesn't matter if there is no tomorrow. I'm getting what I want, at last.

74
Gemma

I step onto the terrace in search of some company and a drink. Oh my god, Ralph and Sarah, you are entwined together like ivy around a tree. This must end. I will prise you apart.

75

Sarah

Ralph is a dull shadow of you, but it is nice to have him here, consoling me. His familiarity is a comfort. Footsteps across the patio. I turn my head to see who it is. Gemma. Dressed up to the nines in a long floral dress with a top so low cut it only just covers her areola. A chunky fake diamond necklace breaks up the large expanse of bare skin. Her black eyelashes stick together in clumps. She stands in front of us, with a wry smile on her face.

Ralph jumps up. 'Good to see you, Gemma. Can I get you a drink? I was just about to top us up.'

She puts her head on one side and her smile increases. 'I'd love some white wine, please.'

'And you, Sarah?'

'The same. Thank you.'

Ralph steps away towards the kitchen. Gemma sits down next to me, taking Ralph's place. She is wearing perfume with over-powering hints of vanilla and rose. Her legs brush against mine. She leans across and takes my hand. She pushes her face too close to my eyes. My stomach knots. Does everyone think they can invade my body space just because I'm bereft?

'How are you doing?' she asks. Too sympathetically. I do not want to be an object of pity. The muscles in my neck tighten and I tell myself to relax. This woman is Ralph's partner. He provides some stability in my life. She means well. I must stop being ageist and bitchy. Unkindness never helps.

'Thanks for asking.' I pause. 'I'm all over the place.' I take a deep breath. 'I'm finding it very hard to accept he committed suicide. It hurts too much.' I swallow to stop myself bursting into tears. 'I can't believe I'll ever get over it.'

'Suicide is such a difficult one,' Gemma replies.

I turn to look at her. She is staring into the distance, eyes wide.

'Do you have any experience of it?' I ask.

She grimaces. 'A close friend of mine. A few years ago.'

'What happened?'

I feel her stir uncomfortably next to me. She turns towards me. 'I don't usually talk about it.' She pauses. 'If it's any consolation, none of us knew she was unhappy. She was always such fun. The life and soul of the party. We were a close group of friends who met through work, on a training course. We all loved her company. We were so very shocked when it happened.'

I squeeze Gemma's hand. 'That's awful.'

'It was,' she says with a sigh. 'Looking back, I think she was manic. When we saw her she was such fun, but she would go through long periods when she didn't want to go out with us. When we rang her mobile, she didn't pick up. Maybe they were her low patches, and then months later she'd reappear, bouncy and enthusiastic.'

'Jack was never like that. He was always cheerful. He never had patches when he went to ground and avoided me.' I pause. 'Look, I'm sure Jack didn't commit suicide. I'm not going to let this drop, even if it takes the rest of my life to prove it.'

'Some people are very good at disguising their true feelings.'

Anger begins to simmer inside me. How dare she comment on Jack's feelings when she hardly knew him? Ralph returns with an ice bucket, chilling a bottle of Chablis, and three glasses. He opens it and pours us each a generous slug.

'Onwards and forwards,' he says as we clink glasses.

He is so cheerful it depresses me. And in that moment beneath moon and stars, I empathise with Gemma's friend. For a second, I'm not sure whether I want to live or die.

I put my glass down on the coffee table. 'I've had enough wine, thanks. I'm off to bed.'

76

Gemma

Thank God Sarah has gone to bed. What did she say? *I'm sure Jack didn't commit suicide. I'm not going to let this drop, even if it takes the rest of my life to prove it.* A dangerous attitude for her to take.

77
Janice

Patrick, Anna and I stagger back from the bar above the piazza already a bit squiffy. Patrick has had quite a few beers, and Anna and I have already necked a bottle of rosé wine. We find Dad canoodling with Gemma on the patio.

Patrick coughs loudly. A staged, artificial cough. 'Hey, how's it going? Anyone up for some food tonight?' His words slur together slightly.

Dad extricates himself from his tarty bit of fluff. 'I thought we could just have some pasta,' he says.

'Again?' Anna asks. 'I'm worried about my figure. Pasta is so fattening.'

'I hope you're not going to grow into a Kate Moss "nothing tastes as good as skinny feels" type,' Patrick says.

She shrugs her shoulders. 'You know I'm not like that. But I'm not hungry anyway, so I'm off to bed.'

I don't look at her. I fix my eyes firmly on the ground. When I am sure she has gone, I stand up straight and raise my eyes.

'I tell you what, I'll cook supper,' I volunteer.

Patrick shrugs. 'Not for me. I'm not hungry now either.' He slips away from the patio to follow his girlfriend. What a wuss of a brother. He needs to keep that girl in check.

I step into the kitchen and open the fridge. It is bulging with food that no one has touched. I heat up a large bowl of tortellini, and pesto sauce, and passata made by the housekeeper who left days ago. I grate some parmesan, and make a herb leaf salad, adding avocado and figs to spice it up.

I lay it out on the terrace dining table, for people to help themselves. 'Come on, you two, come and eat,' I shout.

Dad and Gemma walk across towards me, hand in hand. We sit and eat in silence.

'That was delicious,' Dad says, pushing his plate away. 'Thank you, Janice.'

'How was Mother this evening?' I ask.

'She seemed rather low. Almost suicidal,' Gemma firmly replies.

Interesting, my evil eye thinks.

78
Sarah

Early on Friday morning I hear a knock on my bedroom door. I open it. Gemma stands in front of me, beach-babe ready. Denim shorts, fraying in all the right places to show off as much of her legs and bottom as possible. A bikini top that looks like a lacy Wonderbra. Open-toed shoes with a kitten heel. Toenails painted a vibrant blue.

'Do you fancy a walk after breakfast, to blow away the cobwebs?' she asks.

I hesitate.

She does the hand on the hip thing that young people do for selfies. 'Come on. You can't stay in your room and vegetate forever.'

'Actually, I haven't been in here forever.' My voice sounds waspish and I don't seem able to control it. 'It's just a few days since the death of my partner. Just be tactful. Give me a break,' I continue.

Head on one side, almost pouting, 'Please, Sarah. It would do you good to get out.'

This girl is relentless. 'OK then,' I reluctantly agree. 'Where are we going?'

'On a cliff walk.'

'How do you think that's going to feel for me, right now?'

She looks me straight in the eyes. 'I thought we could pray together,' she says softly.

I frown. 'I didn't know you were religious.'

She shrugs. 'I'm not particularly, but I like to free my mind and think of others. So we could meditate, if you'd prefer?'

I stand in the door of my bedroom looking at my ex-husband's partner trying to be friendly, and I decide to go along. Without you, Jack, I will need friendship more than ever. I mustn't push others away.

'OK then,' I sigh.

79
Janice

Mother, I watch you, eating a chocolate croissant and sipping coffee on the terrace this morning. You had better watch it, or you won't keep your sylph-like figure. I feel like raising my eyes to the sky because then you are off on a cliff walk, apparently. Not that you told me. I only found out because I overheard part of your conversation with Gemma. You are so slim and sylph like that you look almost ethereal. But really you are a tough old stick, who only ever thinks about yourself. I expect you are getting over Jack already, like you got over Patrick and me, when you left.

You spend time with everyone else but me. I'm going to accost you on the cliff path. You will not get away with treating me like this.

80

Sarah

This sun-drenched day is hotter than ever as I walk along the cliff path, to meet Gemma at the view point; the last place you were seen alive. We set off separately from the villa as Gemma had an errand to run in the village. I wasn't quite ready to leave as early as she did. I think she was going to post a letter.

We are going to close our minds to the world and meditate about your life. I stop and take a slug of water, and wipe the sweat from my brow. I was dubious when Gemma first suggested this escapade, but now I have decided it is an uplifting idea. Romantic. Cathartic. She's bringing a vanilla scented candle to burn as we sit and think. I've brought a backpack with a few snacks and a bottle of water. For the first time since you went missing, Jack, I'm walking along with some purpose to my day. For your sake, in your memory, I must continue to use my life usefully. Life left to live will compensate for life that has been taken away.

I hear footsteps behind me.

81
Janice

'Wait up, Mother!'

She turns around. I run to catch up with her; sweating and panting, resentment burning. She stands and waits as I slow down to a walk, and in a few moments I am standing next to her, full of hatred.

'Are you all right?' she asks.

I straighten up; breath slowing now. 'No. I want to know why you're doing this with Gemma and you didn't ask me?'

'Well, actually, Gemma suggested it. We're just going to meditate together about Jack.'

'But why didn't you ask me to join you?' I spit. 'Why didn't you want to do it with me?'

'I just didn't think you would want to come. Please, Janice, I'm trying my best to cope. I'm not thinking clearly right now. I didn't mean to leave you out. Please don't be angry with me,' you beg, eyes prickling with tears.

My emotion swings. My irrational anger ebbs away. Peace spreads in a gentle heat inside me; warm and comforting, like the hot water bottles you gave me to put on a sore stomach when I was a child. 'OK, OK. I'm sorry.'

She steps forwards and hugs me. My body melts into hers.

'You're most welcome. Come and join us.'

I step back. 'It's OK, Mum, I'll leave you two to it. I'll see you back at the villa later.'

I walk away. But when I am about halfway back to the villa my mood darkens. Once again, my anger towards you rises and engulfs me. It is like a rip tide. I cannot contain it. I turn and run back towards you.

82
Gemma

I'm on the cliff path. I catch up with the bitch who has enchanted my partner. The bitch who doesn't believe her fiancé committed suicide and who is on the verge of ruining my plans, my life. She turns around. She smiles a sad, slow smile.

'Gemma. Good to see you. We're almost there. We can walk the final part together.'

She steps towards me and attempts to link arms. I step back and shrug her off.

'I'm not coming with you,' I sneer. 'I don't believe in prayer and meditation and all that shit. I just needed to talk to you in private. Away from everyone else. Away from the villa.'

She frowns. 'But . . . but . . .' she splutters. 'Why?'

'It's Ralph. He's mine. You need to stay away from him.'

She shakes her head. 'But he's just my friend. We need to get on for the sake of the children.'

I stand, feet apart, hands on hips. 'Like hell you're just friends. He's infatuated with you. You must be doing something to encourage him.'

Her bottom lip jerks as if she is about to burst into tears. 'I'm really not. I was totally in love with Jack. Gemma, I promise.'

'Be careful. I'm just warning you. Stay away from my man. If you don't, there will be consequences.'

'We were over years ago. Honestly, Gemma, you've nothing to worry about.'

She is so cool. So sanctimonious. I feel like slapping her. Pushing her. But I step back.

'Enjoy your meditation. See you later.'

I turn around and begin to walk back to the villa. But when I am well on the way back to the villa, I kick myself for missing the perfect opportunity. I turn around. She is not going to steal my man.

83

Sarah

I continue to walk along the cliff path. Janice and Gemma. Worry simmers in the pit of my stomach. Janice's mood swings are getting worse. She has suffered from paranoia for a long time, but now she seems manic. And mania is more difficult to control. I need to make sure she gets help as soon as we get home. And as for Gemma, why is she so vitriolic? Why does she resent me so much?

My body aches for you, Jack. I feel as if you have been cut away from me with a knife. For so many years my life has been spent in a universe that revolves around yours. The minutiae of our lives shared in intimate detail.

I hear footsteps again. And heavy breathing, as if someone is running to catch up with me again. I turn around. She is here. Running towards me.

She catches up with me. She grabs hold of both my shoulders. She pushes me; closer and closer to the cliff edge. I try to stand my ground. I try to push her back, but she's so much younger, so much stronger than me. So much angrier than me. I hold her back for a second. But she's winning again. I have hardly any strength left.

'I hate you, I hate you,' she shouts.

I try to keep my feet firmly on the ground, but she is so strong, so pumped up with adrenalin. Her angry red face is pushed against mine.

I grab onto her T-shirt in an attempt to stay alive. She bangs my fingers with her hand and I feel pain so great I fear my fingers are broken. Pain so great my mind pictures her wearing a knuckle duster. She grabs my hair and pulls it. She lifts her knee and thrusts it into the soft area just beneath my ribs. I'm winded.

I'm falling backwards. Falling. Floating. My life flashing past me like a film montage. Back clinging on to my mother's breast; cuddling her soft pink angora jumper. She smells of wild cyclamen and patchouli oil. My father's face moving towards me on the day I first learnt to swim. Standing in front of me in the water, holding his hand out to me, to encourage me to take a few strokes towards him. His face is smooth and young again. A cheeky crisp moustache bristling across his upper lip.

Janice in my arms as a newborn, turning her head and opening her mouth, rooting towards my nipple. Patrick and Janice both on my lap, one balanced on each leg, when they were four and two. I wanted to stop time back then, wrap them in cotton wool and protect them forever. The picture in my mind changes again. Ralph is holding my hand. I let go and he floats away. And now, Jack, you are moving towards me, stroking my cheek, softly, gently, telling me you'll love me forever. I open my lips to tell you I love you too, but now I am no longer floating. I feel wind rushing past me and I am hurtling downwards faster and faster. I thump against something prickly. The world turns black.

84
Ralph

'Where the fuck has Sarah got to? I haven't seen her all day,' I shout across to the younger generation who are idling around the swimming pool.

Patrick is sitting on the edge at the deep end, resplendent in pink shorts peppered with palm trees and pineapples, drinking an iridescent blue cocktail through a straw. His eyes are fixed on Gemma, who is lying on her back in the pool, on a green plastic inflatable crocodile. She's almost naked apart from three coils of pink string which seem to be masquerading as a swimming costume. Her figure is perfect. Abdominal muscles so flat and toned, I can see the line between them. Tip-tilted breasts with generous cups. Thighs that are curved but not too much. But there is something about her perfection that is boring to me. She always looks the same. Part of a modern battalion, brandishing masculine eyebrows and plastic talons for fingernails.

A little variation entices me. Like you entice me, Sarah, with your face that is strong but delicate, lively with ever-changing expression. Your hair changes colour in the sunlight. It springs to curls when there is moisture in the air, and styles a little differently around your face every single day.

It would solve my problems if Gemma and Patrick ran off together. I wouldn't need to finish with her when we got home. I wouldn't have to cope with her histrionics. Why don't you just start going with Patrick, Gemma? And you wouldn't need to worry; if you married him you'd get a tranche of my wealth in the end. After all, that's mostly what you want me for, isn't it?

Anna is so busy thrashing through the swimming pool like a seal with her stylish front crawl, she can't have noticed where Patrick's eyes are wandering. Janice seems oblivious of everything around her too. She has pulled a chair into the shade in the corner and is glued to her sudoku book.

The young people didn't hear my question, so I move closer. 'Come on, everybody, has anyone seen my ex-wife today?'

Gemma sits up in the belly of the crocodile, but it overbalances and throws her into the water, squealing. She swims doggy paddle towards the side of the pool, carefully keeping her hair and face out of the water. Gemma never wants to do anything to disturb her hair and make-up, because she spends so many hours on her beauty routine. She arrives at the edge of the pool and clings to the side with both hands. Her fake fingernails are pink today.

'We went for a walk earlier, but I haven't seen her since,' she says, fixing me with her puppy-dog look. The one she uses to try and let me know how much she adores me. She pauses. 'I guess Sarah must just be in her room. Or at least that is what I have assumed, all afternoon.'

'Well, she isn't,' I snap. 'She hasn't been around since ten a.m. I've been trying to get in touch with her all day.'

Now that Gemma's body is hidden by the water in the pool, Patrick manages to tear his eyes away from her and zone in on our conversation.

'Did you say Mum's not around?' he asks, taking a sip of his vulgar concoction.

I have to stop myself from laughing nervously at his lack of concern. 'Yes. You've obviously been very worried about her, not to have noticed.'

A tight almost grin. The pseudo grin he gives me when I annoy him. 'Cut the sarcasm, Dad. I was just trying to be considerate. I guessed she wanted to be left alone.'

Anna has stopped swimming. She pulls off her speedo goggles and cap and clings on to the poolside next to Gemma, panting slightly. When she has caught her breath, 'What's up? Are you looking for Sarah? I haven't seen her either.'

I look across at Janice. Her sudoku book abandoned, she is walking across the patio, towards the downstairs toilet; eyes on the ground, shoulders rounded.

Exasperated, I raise my hands in the air. 'Seriously, everybody, I need some help here. Let's all sit down together around the patio dining table and talk about this. Come on. Chop chop.' I pause. 'I'll go and fetch Janice; make sure she comes back from whatever she's up to.'

Five minutes later, all five of us are sitting around the outside table, glasses of water, fetched by my soon-to-be-doctor son, have been placed in front of us as if we are at a conference.

'First things first,' he asks, 'have you checked Mum's room for passport, wallet, phone?'

'Her wallet and phone are gone. But her passport is there,' I tell him.

'That fits in with maybe wanting to go and get a coffee or something in town,' Gemma says, adjusting the pink string coil around her right nipple.

Patrick's eyes fix on her again, and this time Anna notices.

'Why don't you put on a T-shirt?' she suggests. 'You might feel more comfortable.'

Gemma flashes her tooth-whitened smile. 'Comfortable is as comfortable does. I like to look nice.'

Patrick smiles across at her, telling her with his eyes that she looks more than just nice.

'Look, I do not care what anyone looks like right now,' I

bark. 'Do you think I should ring the police?' I continue. 'After everything that has happened, maybe they will investigate earlier this time?'

Gemma taps her claw-like fingernails on the table. They match her bikini strings. Her attention to irrelevant detail is obsessive.

'I don't think you should ring the police yet. It'll be twenty-four hours again before they do anything. Bound to be. Sarah's a grown woman. She can look after herself,' she says.

'But Sarah's riddled with grief. Who knows what she could do, what might happen. Do you really think they would be so prescriptive?' I reply, as I pour myself another glass of water.

'Mother has always liked a lot of time to herself, hasn't she?' Janice chips in, voice sharp edged. 'Maybe we shouldn't panic yet.'

'As long as we panic in time.'

'Calm down, Dad,' Patrick says. 'Janice is quite right. Panicking won't help. Mum won't have gone far. We'll get her back. She's someone who has always needed a lot of time alone. And after what has happened to Jack, she probably needs that alone time more than ever.'

85
Janice

I'm sitting at the table on the patio listening to my father and Patrick continuing to pontificate about what we should do now, to try and find my mother. What time they should ring the police. Whether they should walk the streets. Whether they should jog along the cliff path, calling her name. It is all pointless. I killed her. She has joined her fiancé. They'll never find her alive.

86

Sarah

I open my eyes, the world is misty grey. I blink. I am lying on gorse bushes, which scratch against my skin. Distant shapes and the shadows of darkness surround me. Where am I? Have I just woken from a dream? Above me, a few distant pinpricks of light come into view. Am I dead? Am I paralysed? What has happened to me?

I stretch the muscles in my fingers. They move. I try to move my ankles. My right ankle twists. My left ankle sends a searing stab of pain, through the bones in my leg, burning the edge of my hip, burning into my groin. Wherever I am, whatever has happened, I need an ambulance, quick. I try to pull myself up to sitting to find my mobile phone, but my muscles won't move. I give up. I lie back. I need to sleep.

87

Ralph

'Can't you sleep, Gemma?' I ask as I walk towards her.

She turns towards me and smiles. 'My mind's running in overdrive and the heat is crippling.'

I put my arm around her. 'Mine too. I can't wait to call the police, I'm so worried about Sarah.'

She pulls me towards her and holds me against her, to comfort me. I smell her scent of magnolia and vanilla. I feel her warm arms around me, but all I do is think about you, Sarah. The electricity I feel when you touch me. The resonance of your voice that calms me. The silly little jokes you make that cheer me. Your sensual grin. Your ethereal face. Your silken blonde hair. I know your every expression. Every worry line. Every laughter line. The warmth of your hand in mine. The hand I thought I would hold forever.

I cling on to Gemma and my tears start to fall.

88

Gemma

We are standing together on the patio, the darkness of the night wrapping around us like a cloak. Disco music pumps in the distance – a party must be going on near the beach. You hold me against you, smelling of lies and make-believe. Crying for a woman you will never have. A woman who left you years ago because she didn't love you. Your infatuation with her makes me feel sick.

I wipe your tears away. I pull you towards me and kiss you on the lips. Gently at first, then greedily. But I cannot distract you. Your waterfall of tears refuses to stop.

'I know you did it,' I whisper in your ear, biting it a little; teasing the surface of your skin with my teeth. You step back from me as if you have been poked with an electric cattle prod.

89

Ralph

Friday morning. Still no sign of you, Sarah. It's time to phone the Carabinieri. I am so tired my body feels heavy as I slip my legs out of bed and place them on the cold tiled floor. I stretch myself slowly to standing and yawn. I pad across to the door, pull my silk dressing gown off its hook – the one you bought me many years ago, wrap it around me and pull my iPhone from the charger.

I walk out onto the terrace. It's early but the sun is already high in the sky and the air solid with heat. It presses against me as I stand at the edge of the terrace looking down at the shimmering ocean. Fingers trembling, I dial the police and ask to speak to Luca. A few seconds later, I hear his voice.

'Good morning, Ralph, what can I do to help?'

'Sarah is missing,' I tell him, voice high pitched and panicked.

'We'll come immediately,' he says and puts the phone down.

Fifteen minutes later, Luca, Matteo and two young male officers arrive, in a swathe of uniformed authority. I lead them through the villa and out onto the terrace. They stand in a semicircle, Luca to the far right, Matteo next to him. Two young men to Matteo's left. One with blond hair and brown eyes as round as saucers, the other dark and swarthy like his colleagues. I stand in front of them, so worried about you, Sarah, that I fear I may collapse. I sink into one of the patio dining chairs.

'What's happened this time?' Luca asks, leaning down to stare at me intently, brows lashed together. Matteo stands hands behind his back, leaning forwards and frowning.

'She went on a cliff walk, yesterday morning, and hasn't come back.'

Luca shakes his head and raises his hands in the air. 'Not again.' He sits down and pulls up his chair next to me. 'Who saw her last?' he asks, eyes riddled with concern.

I sigh. 'Gemma, I suppose. They had breakfast at the villa, went for a walk together. Sarah continued without Gemma, and never came back.'

I turn my head away to prevent him from seeing the tears pooling in my eyes.

'My officers, Angelo and Lorenzo, will check the villa to see whether we can find any helpful information. We will send a search party out as soon as possible. Helicopters, everything. We will do everything we can to find Sarah, I promise you.' He pauses. 'And I will contact you the second we have any news.'

I turn to him and manage a weak smile. 'Thank you.'

'Do you have any suspicion or worry about what might have happened?' he continues.

I shake my head.

His face is grave. Funereal. He puts his hand on my arm. 'How was she feeling after the death of her fiancé?' he asks. 'We have a lot of suicides in this town built on a cliff. People come here to kill themselves. It is a beautiful place to die.'

My stomach tightens. That thought has been incubating within me, but I have been trying to push it away. To compartmentalise it. 'She wasn't feeling good,' I reply. 'In fact, she seemed desperate and bereft. I tried my best to comfort her.'

His eyes darken. 'Let us hope your best was enough. Thank you for telling me. At least we all know what we might be dealing with this time.'

90
Gemma

I am snuggled beneath the bedsheets when I hear our bedroom door open. Footsteps stomp inside. I sit up, bedsheet wrapped across my chest, and blink.

Two Carabinieri are standing in front of me; staring. A tall syrupy blond with honey-brown eyes, and a dark-haired razor blade of a man with a thin face, and a nose the shape of a scythe. The syrupy one pulls an identity card from his pocket. He steps towards the bed and waves it beneath my nose. Real or fake? I do not know what it is supposed to look like, so his action means nothing to me. I wave my arm to ask him to take it away.

I point down at my breasts. 'Go away. I need to get dressed.'

'We do not understand,' the dark one says in very broken English.

How stupid are they? How intrusive? Can't they work out I need to put some clothes on? It's pretty obvious. I reach for my iPhone and type my words into Google translate. An electronic voice reads out my instruction to them in Italian. They listen. They nod. They leave.

I put on some clean underwear and fling last night's clothes on top. I hastily brush my hair, and slap on a dab of make-up, mind and pulse racing. There is nothing in here to incriminate me. But what about you, Ralph? Hands trembling, I push my hand behind the wardrobe to check your espadrilles are still there, in the plastic bag from the local supermarket. They are still stuck between the wardrobe and the wall, halfway up, where no one will see or find them.

I pad across the room and open the door to invite my intruders back in, with a steady smile. I watch them fumble through our chests of drawers. Through my piles of lacy black knickers and Wonderbras. Through your Hugo Boss underpants.

They open the wardrobe door and flick through all the clothes on hangers. They pull out all the shoes and put their hands inside every one to check nothing is hidden inside them. Then they focus on the bedside tables, rifling through our papers; our passports, our driving licences. Into the bathroom, opening the cabinet. Nosing through our contraception, our painkillers.

When at last they nod and leave, my pounding heart begins to quieten.

91
Janice

Two Carabinieri step inside my bedroom. I drink in their presence. The sharp smartness of their military uniforms. Their broad-shouldered authority.

'Sarah Kensington is missing,' the tall blond one, who looks a bit like Jason Donovan, says in stilted English.

'I know, she's my mother. And we're all very worried about her.'

'We need to check your room in case she left behind any clue as to her whereabouts,' the darker one adds more fluently.

My body throbs with relief. For a second I thought they had come to arrest me, but I suppose they won't have even started the search for your body yet.

92
Patrick

Anna's body softens towards me. I stroke her breasts as I kiss her, and she murmurs with pleasure. She climbs on top of me, straddling my chest, legs open, one either side of me. Our kissing intensifies.

A knock at the door. Two men burst in.

'Carabinieri,' one of them says, flashing his card towards the bed.

Anna turns bright red and rolls off and away from me.

'Oh my god,' she screams, 'can this holiday get any worse?'

93
Sarah

Cornflower-blue sky above me. Cotton-wool clouds floating slowly past, so close, I feel as if I could stretch out and touch them. Where am I? What has happened to me? Am I in a dream? Am I in an Imax theatre?

I try to sit up, but when I move red hot pain shoots through me. Then I remember last night. Waking up in a misty grey place, on top of gorse bushes, surrounded by the shadows and the shape of darkness. I take a deep breath, fight against the pain and pull myself up to sitting.

It must be morning now. I'm sitting on bushes and rock, two pine trees at my side. The scent of pine reminds me of Christmas. But the warmth of the sun tells me it is far from that time of year. Despite the sun, I feel chilly. I shiver inside, and dust prickly foliage off me.

Falling. I remember falling.

I look up. I see a sheer sheet of rock. It looks to be about forty feet high. Oh my god, I must have fallen off the cliff. But . . . but . . . why am I here? Jack, where are you? Why aren't you here? I think of you, Jack, and I feel empty and sad. Then dread and fear engulf me. And I know something really bad has happened to you. The sound of your name hangs heavily on my mind. Your face moves towards me, telling me you love me, and then it becomes bruised and bleeding, and your shiny eyes become staring and dead. Dead. That's it. You're dead.

We were on holiday in Italy and you died falling off a cliff. In the distance of my mind, I see shadows of other people who came on holiday with us. But I don't know who they are. I cannot see their faces. How did I manage to fall? I do not know. All I know is I need to get home, I need to get your body home, I need to get away from here. My mind is closing down. I am pulled towards the soft, gentle, comfort of sleep.

94
Patrick

'Do you mind waiting outside for a few minutes while we get out of bed and get dressed?' I say to the Carabinieri who have just invaded our room.

One of them nods, the other bows. They are both so stiff they look as if they have been ironed into their uniforms. They leave us.

'The bastards. How dare they disturb us like that,' Anna hisses as she slips out of bed, face like stone.

'Give them a break. They're only doing their job.' I pause. 'I mean, I need them to find my mother.'

Her face softens. 'I know. I'm sorry.'

We pull our clothes on hastily, and clean our teeth.

'Let's go,' I say.

'I'm not quite ready.'

She sits at the dressing table, plugs in the straighteners and begins to fix her hair.

Does it really matter if her hair has a kink? Thankfully, she only bothers to attack a few frizzy bits, over a matter of minutes, and then we step out of the bedroom together. The Carabinieri are pacing along the corridor, and as soon as we leave, they enter. To be fair, it's no wonder Anna is finding all this difficult. And to think this is the first time she has met my family. I need to try harder to be considerate.

'I tell you what, Anna,' I say, 'you go and relax on the terrace. I'll go and buy us some breakfast.'

She smiles and kisses me. 'Thanks.'

I leave the villa. The soft morning sunshine on my back lifts my spirits a little as I walk along, trying to tell myself that Mother is going to be fine. She's twisted her ankle and her phone is out of battery. The slightest of twists that will be right in a jiffy. Or perhaps she just needed a bit of time to herself. And then worry worms through me again. She's had a brain haemorrhage. A stroke. An aneurysm. A heart attack. She's lying in a puddle of blood, with a serious brain injury, after being mugged and raped. Come on. I must face it. There's no non-serious explanation for her absence.

I walk along the passageway. Past the colourful ceramic tiles that announce the names of the entrances to the villas. Across the piazza, in no mood to stop and admire the view today. Into the village, along the main road that runs along the cliff, above the sea, until I reach the bakery.

I join the queue, and stand inhaling the scent of fresh baking. It cuts into me and fills me with sadness. Memories push towards me. Lazy mornings spent chatting with Mother over coffee and croissants. Brisk walks along the river in Twickenham. Late nights drinking red wine and laughing together.

I buy two chocolate croissants and two plain, and scuttle back to the villa. I warm them up for a few minutes in the oven, brew fresh coffee, place it all on a tray and carry it out onto the patio. Anna is lying on a sun lounger, head buried in a physiology textbook. I place my wares on the coffee table beside her. She puts the medical tome down and sits up.

She sighs. 'Patrick, surely you know me well enough by now to realise I'm always watching my weight. I can't eat stuff like that for breakfast. They're made with too much butter and too much sugar. Not a healthy ingredient in sight.'

'As a matter of fact, I do know how to make croissants. I used to make them with Mother,' I say, voice sharp.

I sigh inside. When Anna and I are in London, concentrating on our medical degrees, we understand one another. We are both equally committed to our medical course. We first met in dissection, over a cadaver. And our relationship sprouted from there. We began meeting for coffee to watch operations together on the internet. But we soon started hooking up every evening. When we have qualified, we want to move out of London together, to a pretty rural village, and become GPs. Dating another doctor makes perfect sense because we both fully understand how demanding this career is and what a toll it puts on us. Until recently this relationship has been one of peace and understanding. But now we seem to be in a downhill spiral and I don't know how to reverse out of it.

'Right now, my health is the last thing on my mind,' I say as I take a large bite of croissant. Soft folds of pastry dissolve in my mouth.

'I'm sorry. It's just everything that's happened is making me uptight.'

She kisses me and I melt inside. For a second I fantasise that nobody is missing, nobody is sick, and all Anna and I have to do is look out for one another. Enjoy the freedom we usually have.

95

Ralph

At least we know what we might be dealing with this time.

Luca's words echo in my head. Words said to reassure me, but words that terrify me. He left several hours ago, with his dark-eyed shadow, Matteo, to supervise the search for you. Meanwhile, his overenthusiastic colleagues are ransacking our villa, searching for clues as to your whereabouts. I'm sure they won't find any. Desperate to find you, my love, I have been through it twice with a toothcomb already.

I hear a repetitive whirring beat in the air above me. I look up. A red and white helicopter is hovering above our villa. I watch it soar upwards like a clumsy insect, and progress slowly along the cliff path, tilting and swerving. It bends jerkily and descends sideways towards the sea. Has the pilot seen something? My heart pounds and I feel sick. It climbs again and I exhale loudly with relief.

I smell an overdose of perfume. Kenzo Elephant. Vanilla and ginger. Gemma is here. Tapping me on the shoulder. I turn around. She's dolled up for the day. Painted on slugs for eyebrows, not a hair out of place. Skin-tight beach dress. High-wedged espadrilles; bright blue to match today's fingernails.

'Hello, darling,' she says, and kisses me on the lips.

When she releases me, I turn my head to check where the helicopter has gone. She stands next to me, holding my hand. The sky is clear. I can't see the chopper anywhere; above or below me. And then I hear the thud of blades again. I squint into the sun, shielding my eyes with my hands. It comes into view high up behind the terrace. We watch it dip down to the cliffs to the right of the villa, hovering and diving, jerkily, along the coast. It melts into the distance, and I turn to Gemma.

'I'm so worried. It might be bad news if they find her.'

She gives me a clipped smile. 'Don't be so "glass half empty". It might be good news instead.'

Glass half empty, glass half full. Idioms that have become clichés annoy me so much. My stomach tightens, and I clench my teeth.

'Come on,' she says, dropping my hand, 'let's have breakfast and stop dwelling on it.'

'That's a tall order,' I mutter.

'Breakfast? Or trying to ignore what the helicopter is doing?'

'Both,' I reply.

She tilts her head and smiles. 'Why don't we have a change of scene and go out for breakfast instead?'

I don't smile back. 'Jesus, Gemma, I'm really not in the mood for a change of scene. I need to be here in case the police want to see me.'

Her eyes darken. 'What's up with you, Ralph? Has something happened to your mobile phone? They can contact you wherever we are in the village?'

'What's up with you, Gemma, I thought you had a heart?' I snap back.

Her pale pink skin reddens. She crosses her arms. 'Unlike you, I've got a heart – a big one.'

My temper begins to simmer. Soon it will be boiling. If we were cross with anyone at primary school they used to tell us to count to ten. If anything has happened to you, Sarah, my love, ten *years* won't contain my anger. I close my eyes and count. I open them again to see Gemma standing next to me turning puce.

'How dare you accuse me of not having a heart,' she shouts.

'Then tell me why you're trying to pretend today is normal,' I reply, inhaling too deeply, too quickly.

'Because I don't have a guilty conscience like you do.'

One. Two. Three. Four. Five. Six. Seven. Eight. Nine. Ten. I still want to put my hands around her neck and strangle her. I close my eyes and count again.

I take both her hands and hold her eyes in mine. 'Gemma, you mentioned this last night. Try and explain what you mean,' I say as sweetly as possible. 'We need to be as honest as possible with each other for our relationship to work.'

'I saw you climbing onto the terrace from the scrubland, before lunchtime on Friday. You were trying to cover up where you'd been, weren't you?'

'Are you mad? Of course not,' I shoot back. 'I accidentally dropped the villa keys over the balustrade and jumped over to pick them up. That was all. What on earth did you think I was doing?'

96
Gemma

A pathetic excuse, too long in coming. You're not the sharpest knife in the box, are you, Ralph, if you thought I'd fall for that? I hold you against me, wrapping my arms around you, stroking your back with my hands, massaging you with my fingers.

'I should have guessed it was something like that,' I say, voice like honey.

I push my crotch against the softness of your groin to stimulate your erection. I've got your original espadrilles ingrained with flora from the scrubland, dickhead, not just the cliff path. Forensics will have a field day. Your bitch of an ex-wife got what she deserved. And I've got you where I want you, you prick.

97

Ralph

You hold me, you minx, and then you push your crotch against my soft penis. It springs up hopefully. I know your trick; you won't be wearing any knickers. Or if you are, they will be crotchless. But I am not my penis. Haven't you realised yet, men's parts have minds of their own? They rise and fall whenever they want.

You're playing me about the scrubland. What do you want? To control me? To force me into marriage? Or to blame me for something dreadful that you have done?

98

Sarah

My body jolts awake. Almost immediately, from the light, from the heat, I sense it's around midday. I'm lying on a bed of gorse, a canopy of pine needles sheltering me from burning sunlight, body and face bathed in sweat. The sweat is so sticky it feels like pus has been plastered all over me. My ankle throbs. The inside of my thigh feels as if it is being repeatedly stabbed with a chisel or a hammer. I cannot move my left leg. It must be broken. My fingers throb too. A fragment of memory moves towards me. Something hard smashed against them.

My backpack is lying close to me. I manage to lean across and pull it towards me with my good hand. I unzip it. I grab my mobile to ring for help. No signal. I rummage through the bag. It contains a large bottle of water and squashed KitKats, which have been reduced to chocolate-covered foil and red paper wrappers. I treat myself to a sip of water, knowing how careful I must be to conserve it.

The sound of helicopter blades rotating simmers in the distance. I look out from beneath the tree and see it hovering out at sea. I try to pull myself up, to limp to where the pilot might see me. But my left leg is a dead weight and I can't manage. I wave from sitting and scream and scream. But it is pointless. No one can see me. No one can hear me. The helicopter dissolves in the distance.

I lick the KitKat foil to get some energy. I bump along on my bottom, to get away from the tree. Slowly, painfully, until I'm in a position where someone might see me. The chisel and the hammer drum into my crotch harder and louder with every second. The fingers of my left hand throb and ache. The sun is like a fire in my face. But I push against the heat and the pain, until I reach a sheer drop. I look down on a hundred and fifty metres of vertical rock and feel dizzy and sick. And then I understand with more clarity what has actually happened. I have fallen off the cliff path and landed on a bush-covered ledge. If I hadn't landed on this ledge, I would be dead. But if the helicopter doesn't come back soon, I will die here, slowly and painfully. Oh my god, Jack. I hope you didn't suffer like this.

I sit and wait, but the helicopter doesn't return. My skin feels as if someone has poured boiling water over me. I begin to shiver and know that I have stayed in the sun too long. I watch it slowly drop into the sea, spilling light and colour across the skyline. I should fight my way back into the shade so it can't burn me in the morning, but I do not have the energy. I will have to sleep here and move when I wake. Perhaps I will feel better tomorrow.

I take a few sips of water, and a lick of melted chocolate. Then I lean against my backpack and try to sleep. But sleep doesn't come to me, just blurred images of faces around a cherry-wood table. Fear and dread permeate through me as I remember you are dead. That I need to take your body home. This was supposed to be a holiday. Not a wake.

Memories come flooding back to me. Ralph upset in the piazza. You and Ralph off walking, to bond together. Then you went to get me a present, but never came back. Someone pushing me off the cliff. Finally, I tumble into the vacuum of sleep.

99

Ralph

Friday night. And there's still no news about you, Sarah, my love. They carried out a thorough helicopter search today and found no sign of you. My heart leapt when the phone rang and I could see it was Luca. After all this time, I expected he would have some news. But no. It was a courtesy call to keep me informed that they had made no progress. As I spoke to him, a stone sank in my stomach.

And I cannot get today's conversation with Gemma out of my mind. I don't trust her. What dirt does she think she has got on me? What is she playing at?

I sit on the terrace alone, sipping a large G&T, turning my mind in on itself. She wants my money. She wants to marry me. She doesn't want me in prison. She just doesn't want me to leave her. That's it. I need to hold her close, I need to bind her to me.

100

Ralph

Saturday morning. Radio silence. Still no news. Worry resonating inside me, making me feel weak and ill. I slip out of the villa, walk along the footpath, stopping for a while to watch the builders putting in the foundations of the new build next door to Villa Panorama. Across the piazza where a group of young children are playing tag, their parents standing chatting. Into the local jewellers. The jeweller, an elderly man, with grey hair glazed around his head in a monk's ring, is standing behind the counter.

'*Buongiorno*,' he says.

'*Buongiorno*,' I reply.

'Ohhh, English.'

'That's a sign of how good my Italian is. One word from me and you know where I'm from.'He looks at me blankly. 'I want to look at diamond rings,' I continue, rubbing my wedding finger.

He nods and smiles. 'Special occasion, is it?' he asks.

'Maybe,' I reply, grimly.

He bends down behind the counter, and fumbles and rummages. He reappears holding a large open drawer in his arms, and places it gently on the counter.

'Here you are, sir. Here is my special selection. Can I ask, how much are you thinking of spending?'

His words feel like a trap. Whatever amount I say he'll try to make me spend it, even if that is completely unnecessary.

'I'm flexible about cost,' I mutter as I lean across to look at the rings.

I do not care which ring I choose. In the end I'm not going to marry her, and I'll just have to let her keep it. So I shouldn't waste too much money. But then again, if I don't buy a decent ring I won't look as if I'm committed. And that is what I need to do.

Janice told me she overheard Gemma and Jack arguing on Thursday night when she was walking to her bedroom. She thinks Gemma threw herself at Jack and he rejected her. That would have damaged her pride considerably, but my guess is that the opposite happened. Jack was a randy bugger who cheated on his wife. Maybe he forced himself on Gemma. She has admitted to me that she became violent in the past with a man who forced himself upon her. I smile inside. There's a thought. She pushed Jack off the cliff because he raped her. After all, the man was a heartless monster who cheated on his wife. And now to protect herself from any suspicion, Gemma's trying to insinuate she knows I killed him, with her stupid story about the scrubland. If she really thinks she's going to get away with that she's got another think coming.

But all the same, I think it's wise to keep her close for now. The hassle of defending myself is too great. The police would side with her, against me; stitching me up with a motive of passionate jealousy. So, engagement to Miss Artificiality looms in front of me.

I look in the tray the jeweller has placed in front of me. I see a ring with three large diamonds, like the one I chose for you, Sarah. Do you ever think about the day I asked you to marry me? I took you out to our favourite restaurant, The Petersham, on Richmond Hill. I ordered a bottle of champagne. We hadn't known each other long. I was nervous in case I was rushing you. But as soon as I saw you, I knew you were the one for me.

Everything was perfect that evening. The green velvet dress you wore that clung to your breasts and waist, cut just above the knee; a showcase for your perfect legs. We sat at a table by the window, looking out across patchwork fields, cows grazing, the River Thames snaking by without a house in sight. Countryside with a London postcode.

The champagne we drank as we perused the menu was chilled to just the right temperature. The moment I leant across the table, took your hand in mine and asked you to spend the rest of your life with me. Your azure eyes sparkled with happiness as you said, 'Yes,' and I slipped the ring on your finger.

Where is that ring now? And your wedding band? You took them off eight years ago, didn't you? Are they at your house in Twickenham? Or have you tossed them away, or sold them on eBay, because they didn't mean anything to you? One day, Sarah, you'll have me back. You'll wear my ring again.

I carry on staring at the tray. I decide on a bulky solitaire set in rose gold. Just right for my never-to-be bride.

'I'll clean it for you, sir, and put it in a box.'

I nod my head. 'Thanks.'

I stand looking at the jewellery in the wall displays as I wait. The shop is full of trinkets and treasures; a solid silver owl with diamonds for eyes, gold cufflinks decorated with a mosaic of jet, earrings that drip with rubies and sapphires. A heavy gold charm bracelet with a large gold S embossed with diamonds attached to it.

'This bracelet,' I say pointing to it, 'can I have that too, please.'

I'm buying it for you, Sarah, as a symbol of our continuing love and friendship. Come back soon so that I can give it to you. This time you'll be mine forever.

101

Sarah

I open my eyes, body pulsating with pain, mind clearer today, knowing where I am immediately, as rock and sky spring towards me. Flexing my arm muscles to use all my strength to pull myself up to sitting, sharp pain radiating from my left hand. Pain that makes me wince. I shuffle painfully along on my bottom, to the edge of the cliff, and force myself to look down again. Frightened of heights all my life, I take a deep breath and blink. The view comes into focus, making me feel dizzy and sick. The sheer cliff. The turquoise sea glittering in the soft early morning sunshine. A cruise ship on the horizon. I look to my left. About thirty feet down, there is another ledge, peppered with pine trees.

102

Ralph

I walk back to Villa Panorama, cradling my expensive treasures. Praiano is busy today. Bustling with tourists, their flip-flops clattering along the pavements. Young locals more smartly dressed, out to impress, meeting up in cafés and bars, filling the air with melodic chatter. They all look so light-hearted, not addled with regret and worry like me. Teenagers rattling past on motorbikes. Elderly women wearing black, hobbling along, carrying food shopping.

Back in the villa, silence pushes against me. Gemma, Patrick, Anna and Janice must all be asleep. I make myself an instant coffee and sit on the terrace, peace disturbed by the insistent whine of a pneumatic drill, grinding into my head like toothache. The builders next door. Do they have to make a racket like this on a Saturday morning? It doesn't matter. Nothing matters except you coming back, Sarah.

The scent of vanilla and ginger engulfs me. I turn around. Gemma is here, walking towards me in a white fringed bikini with matching cork wedges. She is wearing large silver gypsy earrings and has clipped her hair up. Big round white-rimmed sunglasses. A fake Bond girl from the sixties.

'Hey,' she says as she bends to kiss me.

I pat the sun lounger next to mine. 'Please, sit down, I need to talk to you.'

'That sounds ominous,'

I force my lips into a smile. 'It isn't meant to.'

A forced smile is returned. 'Good,' she replies.

She sits down slowly, crossing toned legs, leaning forwards in her 'selfie' position. The one she practises in front of the mirror every morning to make sure she is social-media ready.

I swivel round on my sun lounger so that I am opposite her, looking into a face caked in make-up. She thinks her make-up is subtle; Bamboo Beige by Laura Mercier. Expensive, of course. It costs Gemma a lot of money to look as cheap as she does. But when facial skin is all one colour, it cannot look natural.

I lean across and take her hand in mine. I stare into her pale blue eyes, watery and thin against pancake skin and dark brown hair. Eyes that melt into insignificance in comparison to the cornflower blue of yours.

'Gemma, I want to ask you something.'

'Fire away,' she says.

'Please, Gemma, will you marry me?'

103
Gemma

I take a sharp breath. He has asked me to marry him at last.

'Yes,' I reply. 'Yes. Yes. Yes, please.'

He whips out a small black leather box embossed with gold from his pocket. He opens it and pushes it towards me. A pretty solitaire, set in rose gold; my favourite.

'I hope you like it. We can go and exchange it if you don't.'

He slips it on my finger.

'It's beautiful.'

I knew I'd get him eventually. Fortitude and resilience, combined with charm and sexuality, were bound to work in the end.

104

Janice

How many ways, Mother, do I love you? How many ways do I hate you?

I hate you for leaving us. I hate you for living with Jack. I hate you for your smug confidence. Your beauty. Your success. For the way you get on with people so easily. We look similar, but nevertheless people do not accept me the way they accept you. You wrap people around you with warmth until they blend into your life. I am an awkward add on; an appendage to the vibe.

When I was a child and you held me against you, I loved you more than anything in the world. I still treasure that memory. I love our girls' nights out; drinking and chatting. I love it when you take time for me; cook my favourite food, or stay up late waiting for me to come back from a date.

I know I love you. I know I hate you. And most of all, contorted with emotion, I wish I hadn't harmed you.

105

Ralph

She accepted my proposal as quickly as a vulture hones in on a dead body. Faster than a Venus flytrap snapping its jaws around an insect. Her face was jubilant, as she shouted, 'yes.' But not in a happy way. She looked power crazed, as if she had won an Oscar or a battle. I think my fiancée is a megalomaniac.

And my plan is flawed. If I break off the engagement, she will be bitter and damage me. When the time is right, I will have to figure out how to get rid of her permanently, without leaving her free to harm me. To quote Baldrick from *Blackadder*, I will need a very, very cunning plan. When I put my mind to it, I will think of one. I'm just having to tread carefully and take a day at a time right now.

She is standing next to me on the terrace, holding my hand. Or rather gripping me too tightly, making me feel as if I can't move, I can't breathe.

'Why don't you pop to the kitchen and fetch a few bottles of bubbles to share with the others, when we tell them?' I suggest. 'My back's hurting. I need to lie on a sun lounger and stretch it for a moment or two.'

'Poor you.' She blows me a kiss, simpers and then skips off across the terrace.

As she walks away, I tremble inside. I had to propose to her. I had no alternative. I lie back on the sun lounger and try to relax by melting into the Mediterranean heat. Trying to compartmentalise, by placing what I have done and still need to do into a sealed box in my mind.

But something is wrong. I hear shouting in the distance. I jump off the sun lounger and find myself walking across the terrace towards the noise, towards the open windows of the bedrooms. It is coming from Anna and Patrick

'I'm not sure how much longer I can do this,' I hear Patrick shout. Anna's high-pitched scream reverberates around the balcony. I hear sobbing. But it isn't Anna. It's Janice. I'm all too familiar with the sound of my daughter's cries. Janice is crying over you, Sarah, and I am too. Sarah, we need you so much. Please, please, come back soon.

106
Sarah

My heart jumps. A red and white helicopter is hovering in the distance. I close my eyes for a second and pray. Please, please, find me this time. I pull myself up to standing. I shout. I wave. It moves across the sea; nearer and nearer. I hear the repetitive thud of the blades. Hope fires inside me. This is it. I will be free. I will be safe. It stalls for a second and jerks sideways. It glides closer to the water and rises again. Higher and higher. Up towards the cliff top above me. I hear it clearly at first. But then its sound fades as it moves away. Before too long it has completely disappeared.

I sit down, head in my hands with despair. I treat myself to a precious sip of water. Its nectar soothes my mouth and throat for a second. In my wildest fears, I never thought I would die like this. I imagined wasting away of cancer in a hospital bed; my children holding my hand as I passed. Telling me how much they loved me. Isn't that what everyone wants really, to be with their children at the end? Or maybe a quick heart attack, so fast I wouldn't even know about it. A road accident, or a plane crash. Dramatic incidents after which I would be sorely missed. But never did I picture this – dying of starvation, alone, on a cliff ledge, the man who I was about to spend the rest of my life with already dead.

107
Gemma

I walk through the villa carrying two bottles of Louis Roederer champagne, which I just chilled in the freezer for ten minutes, admiring my pretty solitaire as I waited. The ring I have craved for so long. It is such a good job that Sarah met her fate.

Engaged to be married. Soon I'll be Mrs Gemma Kensington. I'll have money and a name with resonance. My heart is singing with happiness. Will it be a small gathering, the sooner the better? Or church bells and choristers; a showy do that takes a year to plan? Whatever, I will have a dress of low-cut, skin-tight satin, with a small train. A bouquet of lilies. And no prosecco, the best champagne; vintage, of course. Available on tap all day. Bridesmaids in pink satin? Maybe. Or maybe that is a little old fashioned. A fantastic honeymoon, of course. A luxury cruise or a safari.

I step onto the terrace at the villa. Patrick, Anna and Janice are sitting in glum silence on the sofa, slumped over mugs of coffee. Anna is wearing baggy blue cotton pyjamas and fluffy slippers. Patrick looks to have pulled on the same clothes as he was wearing yesterday; his face and clothes are crumpled and his hair needs brushing. Janice is wrapped in a white towelling bath robe. Ralph is lying on the sun lounger where I left him. Fast asleep and snoring gently.

'Hey,' I shout. 'Has Ralph told you the news?'

Patrick's body straightens. He looks across at me. 'Have they found Mother? Is that why you've brought the champagne?' he asks.

'No. Not as far as I know.'

His eyes flatten. He shrugs. 'Then what have we got to celebrate?'

I nudge you. 'Ralph, I'm back. Time to tell everyone our news.'

You sit up slowly. We watch you yawn and stretch.

Impatience coagulates in my stomach. 'Hey. Come on, Ralph.'

You cough. 'Gemma and I . . . well . . . I asked her to marry me. We're engaged now.'

I stretch my hand out to show them my ring.

'But . . . but . . .' Patrick splutters. 'What's going on? Why is this happening whilst Mother is missing?'

'And to think I thought congratulations were in order,' I reply with a smile.

'Congratulations,' Janice parrots, voice sharp.

She runs her eyes up and down me, letting me know, yet again, that she thinks I'm tarty. Well, Janice Kensington, tarty is sexy; and men like sexy. Janice is pretty but frumpy and I wouldn't want to be like her in a million years. Look at her sitting there in a fluffy white bath robe. If I had long blonde hair like that, I would choose black silk and lace. If I wasn't in digital marketing, I would be a style consultant. I would do such a good job.

Anna says nothing. She sits and frowns. I suppose she's jealous because she wants to get engaged to Patrick. Doesn't she know that getting engaged is a commitment, not a competition?

'I'll get the glasses. Let's have the champagne,' I say brightly, ignoring the atmosphere around me.

Envy is something I'm going to have to get used to. But I suppose now that I'm so fortunate, having you, having money, it will be easy to rise above it.

108
Sarah

I look over the cliff, down towards the ledge beneath. I see a canopy of trees. Stone pines. Umbrella pines. Can I do it? Dare I? I close my eyes and lean forwards. Should I – could I – make myself jump?

109
Gemma

'Here's to us,' you say as we all clink glasses.

You look so good in your blue polo shirt and white shorts. You haven't shaved yet today and your designer stubble is edgy and interesting.

You take a sip of champagne. 'Patrick has made a very good point. And I am really sorry this is happening under these circumstances, but the sadness we have experienced this week has made me realise I did not want to wait any longer to consolidate our love for one another,' you continue.

My heart sings. I don't think this would have happened if you were still around, Sarah.

'Well, here's to the happy couple,' Patrick says reaching for Anna's hand. Anna stiffens and pushes his hand away. She looks as if she is just about to burst into tears.

'When's the big day?' Janice asks, running her eyes over my body yet again.

I look across at you.

'We haven't had a chance to discuss that yet,' you reply.

Your eyes are flat. Unreadable. I'll talk to you about that later, in our room. But now, after careful consideration, I'm thinking we could tie the knot as soon as we get back. I'm wondering about Chelsea Registry Office. It's in Chelsea Town Hall and I have heard it is an excellent venue. We could have our reception at the Bluebird Restaurant, a short walk down the road. They have two private rooms available for hire. But actually, I'm not sure either of them is big enough. Maybe we should try the Royal Automobile Club on Pall Mall; you are a member. The Great Gallery restaurant has gold filigree on the walls, similar to one of the drawing rooms in Buckingham Palace, that I saw in a photograph. If we have our reception at the RAC Club, I'll feel like royalty.

110

Sarah

I'm falling. Slowly. Faster. Faster and faster. No time to pray. No time to think. This is it. This is the end. I am moving towards death, through a cyclone.

111
Patrick

We step into our bedroom, sunlight streaming in through the window, making me blink. I feel heavy inside. So deflated. All the weird stuff going on between Dad and Gemma. And no one knows where my mother is. It's Saturday now and Mother has been missing for just over two days. Stony faced, Anna flops into the chair in the corner and crosses her legs.

'I can't believe your father is marrying that bimbo,' she announces.

I think of Gemma's generous smile and hourglass figure. 'I'm not sure I would describe her like that.'

Hands on hips, my slender, tasteful, make-up-free girlfriend, who hasn't even slipped out of her pyjamas yet today, asks, 'How would you describe her then?'

I hesitate. I take a deep breath. 'Kind. Attractive. Interesting.'

'OK, OK. That's enough.' Anna puts her head back and laughs. 'I don't think you're a very good judge of character.' She pauses. 'Gemma's a bimbo, that is a fact. But you like her, don't you?'

'I don't dislike her,' I reply, equivocally, stomach tightening at her comment about my character judgement.

'Not half, you don't,' Anna replies, raising her eyes to the sky.

I suppress a sigh. 'She's not brainy like you, but she's fun. Dad deserves a little fun.'

'She's tarty and artificial, not wife material,' my girlfriend snarls.

I shake my head. 'Some men like that look.'

A snarky smile. 'What you are really trying to tell me is that you like the way she looks.'

'I didn't say that.'

Her eyes darken. 'But that's what you meant.'

A sigh escapes from my lips. 'It isn't what I meant.'

'You're always looking at her legs, her breasts. She's like a bitch on heat. You're like an uncastrated dog; panting as you look.'

'That's not very flattering. Do you have a particular breed in mind?'

A short, sharp smile. 'I'll have to think about that.'

'Well, take your time. I'm not ready for your next insult yet.'

She nods her head. 'You are out of luck. It's come to me. You are like a spaniel, naive and always craving attention.'

'OK. That's enough.'

I turn my back on Anna. The heavily embroidered silk quilt rustles beneath me as I flop onto the bed. I close my eyes. Two days since Mother went missing. I'm back in the car when she was driving me to university, our Volvo laden to the gunnels with clothing and books. That first term, frightened about how much I was going to miss her. Not wanting to admit it to anyone. Wondering which one of us would cry first. In the end it was her and not me, but I was so close to blubbering. We were only apart for a few months until the Christmas holidays. How will I cope if I am never able to see her again? I open my eyes and look across at Anna.

She is crying now. I brace myself. I slide off the bed, walk across the room, kneel in front of her and put my hands on her thighs. 'What's the matter?' I ask gently.

'I wish it was me with the engagement ring,' she manages between sobs.

'You don't seem very happy with me at the moment. Surely getting engaged would be a mistake right now?'

She wipes her eyes on her sleeve and swallows. 'Maybe the security of an engagement ring would embolden me; make me feel secure.'

I hold her eyes in mine. 'Security before we are ready would be like a ball and chain. Our relationship needs space to grow and develop. Anyone's relationship needs time to develop if they meet as young as us. We're only twenty, for goodness' sake. We may be about to grow into very different people.'

Her face crumples, and reddens. She is about to cry again. 'Are you saying you don't love me anymore?' she asks, voice thin and weak.

A single tear runs down her right cheek. I brush it away with my fingers.

'No. I'm just saying we should work on our love.' I pause. 'It's so important to both of us.'

112
Sarah

I find myself lying face down in pine needles, stabbing into me, making me cough and choke. I lift my head, and spit them from my mouth. I blow my nose. Searing heat presses against me. My lower body throbs. As the world comes into focus, I realise the tree branch I have landed in is a long way from the ground. If I fall down from here, I will not live. Nausea overcomes me and I vomit, but I have had so little to eat, only bile comes out.

Hands trembling, slowly, slowly, I hold on to the branch and twist my body towards the trunk. I cannot believe it holds my weight. I wrap my legs around the tree trunk, almost passing out from the stabbing pain in my leg. Pain so severe it makes the memory of childbirth pale into insignificance. I let go of the branch with my arms, holding on to the tree trunk with my legs. Inhale. Exhale. Breathe. Breathe. I wrap my arms around the tree. Clinging on tight with arms and legs, I wait a few minutes to compose myself. A few more deep breaths before I slide down, slowly, splintering my hands as I move. At last I collapse in a pile on the rock at the base of the trunk, heart thumping with fear. Have I made any progress? Will a helicopter see me from here? The world turns black again.

113

Gemma

'Good morning,' I say, flashing my best smile. Wrapping my nakedness around you, my soft sensual skin recently massaged with coconut oil.

'What are you doing, Gemma?' you reply, pushing me away. 'The others can see us up here, from the terrace.'

'Does it matter? We're young and in love.'

'It matters to me. You're making an exhibition of yourself. Go and put some clothes on right now.'

Knots twist in my stomach. 'You sound like a bossy dad.'

'Maybe that's because I am one.'

'Your children ought to be more open minded. After all, you've been divorced for long enough.'

I skulk back inside, riddled with disappointment. I scoop my silky black robe from the floor and wrap it around my perfect body. What is the matter with you? Do you have erectile dysfunction already? You are only forty-five. Surely you are a bit too young to need Viagra. I stand looking at myself in the mirror. At my generous breasts and hourglass waist. At my toned, flat stomach and slender, shapely legs. At my chestnut hair cut into a bob that finishes at the best angle to show off the curve of my cheekbones. At my pouty lips dusted with just the right amount of lip gloss. There's nothing wrong with my physical appearance, that's for sure. So what's happened? Have you proposed to me, but despite all my efforts you're still fretting over her?

I sit on the bed, head in my hands. What can I do to make you want me more than you want her? I thought, since you had finally proposed, you had made a clear choice. But when you reject me physically, it makes me unsure of your love. Despite everything. Despite my beautiful ring. Despite how convenient it is for me that Sarah is never coming back.

I stand up and, hands trembling, walk towards the dresser, and begin to rummage through the bottom drawer of the heavy chest where the villa owners keep spare linen. This is where I hid the spliffs I brought with me, in case of emergency. I want to smoke one right now to relax.

Where the fuck are they? There's too much in this drawer. And I was so sure I'd put them in here, carefully wrapped between two cotton sheets. It is rammed so full I can hardly open it. I manage to squeeze my wrist inside and press down, so at least the drawer opens. I begin to pull stuff out. Napkins. Two Christmas tablecloths; white linen embroidered with holly and ivy. I continue rummaging. Sheets. Counterpanes. Pillowcases. My fingers push against something hard. I pull out a rectangular box; black leather, the name of the local jewellers embossed across it in gold filigree. It matches the box my engagement ring came in. My heart lurches with pleasure. Another present for me. You must love me really. Despite your mood swings and selfish behaviour.

I take the lid off the box. A heavy gold bracelet. Wow. It must have cost a fortune. But then as the wife of a wealthy man I will have to become accustomed to dripping with valuable jewellery. I pull it from the box. A large gold 'S' plastered with diamonds hangs from the middle. 'S' for Sarah. It's not for me. It's for her.

You bastard. You prick. You bastard with a prick that doesn't work. Or at least doesn't work for me. You've still got the hots for her, even though she's dead. You've always had the hots for her.

I fly out onto the balcony.

'What is this?' I spit as I throw the bracelet at you. You duck. I miss and it clatters on the terracotta tiles behind you.

'A present for Sarah,' you reply, scowling as you scoop down to pick it up.

You stand up, caressing it in your hands, looking at it fondly. Then you slowly, carefully put it in your trouser pocket.

'Why the fuck have you bought her a present when I am your fiancée?' I shout.

You shrug. 'I just wanted to give her something to keep forever; to cheer her up when she gets back. She was my first wife, remember. We have children together.'

'How could I forget?' I pause. 'You're such a stupid prick, wasting your money on someone who must be dead. Someone who couldn't give a fuck about you.'

114
Ralph

'You love her so much you murdered Jack to try and keep her, didn't you?' Gemma is shouting, spittle flying from the corner of her mouth.

I step towards her. 'How dare you accuse me of that.'

She puts her head back and laughs in my face. 'I saw you sneaking back. What you said about the villa key was a lie.'

'You're such a bitch, threatening to stitch me up to cover up for yourself. I know what you did to Jack. Janice heard you arguing. You killed him, didn't you?'

Gemma is red faced, breathing heavily; incandescent with rage. 'If you saw me on the cliff path, I needed to talk to him. I'd had an argument with him. I needed to apologise.'

'What did you need to apologise for?'

She shakes her head, tears in her eyes. 'None of your business.'

'Well there you go. You killed him.'

'No.'

'Why else couldn't you tell me what happened?' I taunt.

'OK then, you bastard. I'll tell you. You never give me enough attention, so I made a pass at him, the night before he died, to try and make you jealous. He rejected me, and I was upset. I was rude to him and aggressive. So the next morning I went to find him on the cliff path to beg him not to tell you or Sarah about my behaviour. He wasn't very helpful. He said he always tells Sarah everything.'

'Ha. On the cliff path, were you? You're a bitch and a liar. You killed him and you're trying to set me up for it.'

'How dare you speak to me like that? And you had the audacity to pretend you loved me – to ask me to marry you.'

Gemma turns away from me and begins to stomp across the patio.

'Where are you going?' I shout after her.

She turns her head back and glowers at me as she grabs for her suitcase. 'Getting away from you for a while. I'm going travelling while you sort yourself out, you bastard.'

115

Sarah

I'm moving in and out of consciousness. Dreaming of the future. Of my home. Of my bed. My bathtub. Dreaming of the past. Of my wedding to Ralph. Of the pain in my heart on the day I left. Sometimes I think what I see is real. A cloudless sky. A turquoise shimmering sea. Sometimes I am wrapped in your arms, Jack, feeling positive and relaxed, and for a second I think I have died and gone to heaven. But then I scent pine and sea breeze and find myself pressing against rock in a vain attempt to suppress the pain that is slicing through me like a chainsaw blade. And I know that you are dead and my life is practically over.

The world is blurred around the edges. Sunlight searing past me in big yellow floaters. I see an incision in the cliff below me. A thin scraped line through metal-grey rock that continually widens and narrows. My heart leaps with hope. Is it a path? The more I stare, the more the line thins. I blink and it disappears.

116

Patrick

Sunday morning. Three days since Mother went missing. Three days in which Dad has astonished us by getting engaged. Life is a roller-coaster, that's for sure.

Anna and I are walking along the cliff top path, holding hands. I would rather walk freely, it would be easier to keep my balance and not twist my ankle. But Anna insists on holding hands when we do a countryside walk. She says it is romantic.

She turns to me. 'You know, Patrick, this holiday isn't a holiday, it's a hellish nightmare. I've never felt so wretched and uncomfortable in my life.'

'I have noticed.'

'What's *I have noticed* supposed to mean?' she snaps back. 'That you find me difficult?'

I hesitate. 'No. It's just that you're not as relaxed as you normally are. But then how can any of us feel relaxed with what's going on?'

She squeezes my hand. 'If you don't mind, I'm thinking of flying home. I know we're supposed to stay, but I can't.'

I squeeze back. 'I do mind. I'll miss you.'

I pull her towards me and kiss her.

'I love you,' I tell her.

She pulls away, face pinched and pale. Lips thin.

'Well then, prove it. Propose to me and buy me a ring.'

I step back and stand looking at her. 'That's quite an ultimatum. We've discussed this. I need some time to think.'

She bursts into tears. 'If you loved me, you wouldn't need time to think.'

117

Janice

It's the evening after the engagement, but the bride-to-be hasn't treated us to her company tonight. She's in bed with a migraine apparently; and has been all day. Anna too. Migraines must be catching. Even though I spent ages preparing this meal of lobster and prawn risotto, Dad is spooning it into his mouth, eyes glazed. It might as well be tasteless for the amount he is appreciating it. Patrick too looks as if he couldn't care less what he is eating.

And what about me? Guilt hangs around my neck like a brick on a chain. I'm not sure how much longer I can live like this.

118

Patrick

I'm counting the days. It's Monday morning; four days since Mother went missing. Worrying about her is driving me insane. Anna is dressed in her airport clothes, whitewash denim jeans, her favourite faded T-shirt, ankle boots and cardi. Flinging her toilet bag into her suitcase with a thunderous look on her face.

'I'm going,' she says, voice like acid.

I walk towards her and try to hug her, but her body stiffens and she pushes me away. I raise my upturned hands in the air and shrug my shoulders.

'It's you who is driving this. We could relax; take our time. We don't need to split. We're only twenty years old, for God's sake. We've still got three more years at medical school to get through.'

Her eyes darken. 'I'm very well aware of our educational timetable, thank you.' She pauses and pushes her hair back from her eyes. 'I need to split from you. I can't put up with your reticence a second longer.' She shrugs her shoulders in pretence of nonchalance. 'You just don't appreciate me enough. It's draining my confidence.'

She closes her suitcase and clicks the lock. I do not know what else to say to her. I do not want her to leave. But I do not want to get engaged; not yet. Maybe one day. My mind is confused. I'll be sad if she goes. I'll feel trapped if she stays.

'I'll miss you,' I say tentatively.

Her face crumples. She bites her lip to suppress tears. 'By the time you get home I will have moved out of the flat. You've had your chance and you've blown it.'

119

Sarah

The thin, scraped line through the cliff that widens and narrows as I stare at it comes into focus as a path again. It must be a path. Or is it a goat track? The sun blazes into my face; sunglasses lost as soon as I fell means that my eyes are being scalded all the time. But I blink to rest them and stare again. My heart lurches. It is definitely a path of some sort.

I drag my body that is no longer a body but a pain conduit towards it. It is very narrow. Too narrow to bump along on my bottom. It must be a goat track. I haul myself up to standing. The pain that constantly shoots through me increases. One misstep and I will be over the edge. I will have to limp along on what I guess is my broken hip.

Don't look down, I tell myself. If I do, I will panic and faint. I begin to move. Right foot forwards. Dragging my left foot next. A dagger slicing through my groin with every step of my left leg. Three steps in, I'm already exhausted. I need to carry on for you, Jack. I need to get your cold dead body back home to bury you. I will bury you in the churchyard in Whitton, next to Susan. I will throw a red rose into your grave. I will still love you, every day for the rest of my life.

Another step. Another pull of my left leg. Another jolt of searing pain. I need to carry on because I want to see my children again. My life is coming back to me. My son, Patrick. My daughter, Janice. Patrick has dark wavy hair and a broad face. Janice is blonde like me. I want to take Janice in my arms and comfort her. She has always been so vulnerable, so brittle. When she was a toddler she climbed onto my knee and hugged me.

'Mummy, I love you too much,' she said.

And she did, and she does. Which is why she has always been so edgy about me leaving Ralph and loving you, Jack. She wanted to live with me all the time. Should I have sacrificed my individuality and put her first? Maybe I should. But I couldn't. I just couldn't. I suppose the problem, Jack, was that I loved you too much, too.

Because of her mental health issues, I have repeatedly tried to encourage her to see a counsellor or a psychiatrist, but she adamantly refuses. So I always try to listen and talk to her to compensate. I need to get back safely so that I can continue to help my beautiful girl.

I take a few more dragging steps. Pain pulsates and ricochets. And I need to get back to talk to Patrick. I need to take him out to dinner and coax him into chatting about Anna. That is his girlfriend's name, I think. He seems to like her a lot, but they are edgy together.

And Ralph. What about Ralph? My ex-husband who still loves me. The man I have caused so much pain. I wish he didn't dote on me so much. I wish his life had moved on. The sight of him so drunk and upset in the piazza on the first night of this dreadful holiday moves towards me. He is turning into such a piss-head and it is so demeaning. I think back to the sober and sensible but slightly boring chap I married.

We married too young. Aged twenty-one, as soon as we left university. I had no life experience. I gravitated to him because he was handsome and kind. But handsome is as handsome does. It doesn't mean we get along. We were never interested in the same things; not really. And in the end, I couldn't sacrifice my life for his.

But guilt stabs into me as I heave my wounded body along. It is me that has destroyed him. I pinch myself. Like mother, like daughter, if I am going to start reasoning like that. I must stop this immediately.

I stumble on a loose piece of rock and look down by mistake. Blood begins to rush from my head. I brace myself to fall, but the faintness passes almost as quickly as it came. Seconds later I feel normal again, apart from the pain in my leg, and the pain in my heart.

120
Patrick

I'm sitting on the terrace feeling sad that Anna and I didn't make it. Her pinched face as she left will haunt me forever. But how could I spend the rest of my life with someone so pushy? Surely, for a successful relationship, you need to allow each other room to grow and develop? But . . . but . . . Anna is pretty. Anna is hardworking. She will be a passionate, caring doctor. We had so much in common. Am I a fool? Should I have just rolled over and committed? All I know is, despite our recent bickering, I'm going to miss her like hell.

The front door of the villa bangs as it opens and closes. Dad is here, walking towards me carrying a bag from the bakery in his hands. He looks exhausted. Ashen.

He places the bag on the table and sinks into the chair next to mine.

'You're up early,' he says.

'Well, I've had a difficult morning.'

His eyes push into mine, laden with concern.

'Anna and I have split up. She's left in a taxi, to get to Rome airport,' I continue.

He grimaces. 'Split up totally?'

'Yep. She's moving out of the flat and everything.'

He shakes his head. 'Very sorry to hear that, mate.'

'So am I. It's given me quite a shock.'

He pats me on the back. 'Sometimes women are more trouble than they're worth. They have given me more than enough trouble over the years.'

121

Ralph

'Gemma's left too,' I tell Patrick.

He frowns. 'That's weird. When you had just got engaged and everything.'

I shrug. 'Well, she decided to take the opportunity to go travelling while we're here in Italy. As soon as she gets back, we'll plan the wedding.'

'Where's she gone?' he asks.

I take a deep breath. 'She was heading for the ferry station in Amalfi. She fancied to head for Salerno and Rome – she hadn't decided on a set itinerary – she just wanted to go with the flow.'

'Lucky thing.'

122

Janice

Tuesday lunchtime. Our third Tuesday here. Dad has had to extend our booking at the villa and it must be costing him a fortune, but he doesn't seem to care. He has been so successful, money has not been a problem to him for years. Another day where the dry heat scalds across the skyline. Another day when the coastline jumps with boats and tourists and happiness, and yet we have to live through time that has stagnated.

It is so sad that what was supposed to be a special holiday has turned into torture. There is no news. Mother is still missing. Anna and Gemma have left. Gemma has been texting me, sharing her adventure. She's on her way to Rome right now. How I envy them both. I wish I was travelling with them, or even that I was back home right now, moving between Mum's and Dad's homes as usual. Seeing my friends. Going into Kingston-Upon-Thames shopping. Hanging around in Superdrug and Topshop. Volunteering in the local Oxfam shop. I wish we had all never come here in the first place.

Patrick, Dad and I lay lunch out on the patio table. Fresh rolls from the bakery. Mortadella, prosciutto and bruschetta from the delicatessen. A baby leaf salad I have topped with avocados and figs. I'm not hungry. None of us is eating very much. We just step through the motion of putting out food. Sticking to some semblance of routine helps us wade through the day.

I sit down opposite Patrick, who is ashen, with bags under his eyes. He hasn't shaved for days and his stubble is lumpy and slightly ginger. I am not sure who he is more worried about, Mother or Anna. Dad sits at the head of the table, shoulders rounded, staring into space, eyes glazed. He has shaved now, but he isn't bothering to co-ordinate his clothing. I think he is throwing on the same old orange T-shirt every day. He used to do odd jobs around the house in it. It is peppered with holes and I am surprised he brought it on a luxury holiday. Dad is missing Gemma. He keeps texting her. I bet she is having a blast. I question her morality. It wouldn't surprise me if she's shagging her way around Italy's capital. The way she flirted with Patrick was a bit of an eye opener.

'This is unbearable. When will there be some news about your mother?' Dad says as he reaches across to help himself to a piece of bruschetta. 'I haven't even heard the helicopter go up today,' he continues. 'After lunch, I'm going to ring the police and ask them what the fuck's going on.'

'I wouldn't put it like that. It won't help,' Patrick says, grimacing, and pouring himself a glass of water.

Dad frowns. 'You don't need to micromanage me. As if I would say that,' he snaps. 'It is just a way of expressing myself to close family. I'm not a stupid prick.'

I take a bread roll and start buttering it. 'Do you think we should go out looking again?' I ask. 'It makes me feel better when we are doing something to help, even if it's futile. And it helps to pass the time.'

Dad turns to me and sighs. 'I'm not sure I can face it. We've already walked the cliff path three times calling her name, looking behind every pine tree, every bush. Now we need the police to up the ante with the helicopter search.'

'Maybe we need to get the British authorities involved,' Patrick suggests.

'How the hell do you think that is going to work?' Dad replies. 'We are not senior in the army or part of the royal family.' He stands up. 'Fuck it, I'm getting some wine.'

Patrick and I exchange glances. A 'we'd better stop him from drinking if he is about to call the police' look.

He returns brandishing an open bottle of rosé, and three wine glasses.

'Not for me, thanks,' Patrick says, putting his hand across the top of his glass, just as Dad is about to pour.

'Sanctimonious, aren't you? Come on – have a glass. It will relax you.'

Patrick shakes his head. 'It won't help. It won't change the situation. It won't make things any different.'

'I don't want to drink at lunchtime either.' I pause. I stand up and take the bottle. 'In fact, I'll put a stopper in and we can have this tonight. I'll go and make you a cup of herbal tea instead.'

Dad's face darkens. 'No herbal crap, thank you.'

He stands up, grabs the bottle off me and pours a third of it straight into his glass. He begins to drink it in large gulps as if it was water.

Not in the mood to watch Dad getting rat-arsed because he is so stressed. Not wanting to end up having to prop him up and carry him to bed, 'I'm going to have a rest. Call me as soon as there is any news,' I announce.

In the privacy of my room, I close the shutters, and collapse onto the bed, feeling heavy, as if my body is cased in metal. I see you, back on Thursday morning, standing there in front of me on the cliff path, pushing your wind-whipped hair from your face. Wearing your Dior sunglasses. Looking delicious as usual, despite your pain, your grief, your lack of make-up and the pallor of your skin from lack of sleep. You always look good, even when you are worried and upset. I suppose it's your bone structure.

'Please forgive me, Janice. Let me explain why I left; how much I loved Jack.'

If only nothing else had happened after that. I breathe deeply to try and avert a panic attack. As I lie counting to five; in and out, in and out, the heaviness that is pulling me down begins to lift. I feel as if my mind is a biscuit tin, lid shut tight but slowly prising open. I see you once again standing on the cliff path. I feel the sun burning my skin. I see the sea sparkling beneath us, pushing against the steep wall of the cliff. I look up at the steep sharpness of the tree-covered mountain above.

'I never wanted you to leave,' I said, and burst into tears. You stepped towards me to hold me against you. You stroked my hair. You smelt of Rive Gauche, your favourite scent. You smelt of love and reassurance.

'I never stopped loving you,' you said. 'Not for any second of any day.'

I know what I see is the truth. I never laid a finger on you, did I? I contained my anger. My disappointment. I love you too, Mum. So much. Too much. Please, please, come home as soon as you can. I will not complain that you left, ever, ever again.

I will do what you have always suggested; go to a counsellor, go to a psychiatrist. I'll even agree to take their dreaded cocktail of risperidone, diazepam and lithium, if they want me to. I want to get better. Please, come home.

123
Ralph

I feel better after one glass of rosé. Softer around the edges. I pour myself another glass. Thank God Patrick and Janice have left me to my own devices. It's role reversal at its worst when your kids turn into wine police. At least they are both in their bedrooms and not on patrol right now. I neck the next glass and pour myself another. The bottle is empty. I throw it into the recycling bin.

Hours later, Luca and Matteo are here, sitting at the patio table. Looking so smart in their black, designer uniforms. Smart. Serious. Severe. Smelling of authority. Clean shaven, reeking of competing aftershave.

'Thank you for coming,' I say, trying hard not to run my words together. 'I would be most grateful for an update on the whereabouts of my ex-wife, Sarah Kensington. It has been five days since anyone has seen her.'

I watch Luca's lips quiver. He leans forwards. 'We have scoured the cliff path and found nothing. Every day a helicopter has flown along the cliffs, and checked five miles out to sea, too. We have not found a trace.'

'This is terrible news.' I pause. 'I feared this as I hadn't heard from you, but it hurts to hear it.'

Luca leans across the table and puts his hand on my arm.

'We'll keep looking. We are doing everything we can. We need to interview everyone in the villa again, to see whether there are any clues to her whereabouts that we may have overlooked.'

'Patrick, Janice and I are still here.'

Luca raises his eyebrows and stiffens. 'And Gemma Richardson and Anna Jenkins? Where are they?' He moves his hand from my arm.

'Anna has returned to London to move out of their flat. She and Patrick have split up.'

'And Gemma Richardson?'

'She's gone travelling,' I say, limply.

Luca folds his arms. His shoulders widen. He pushes his eyeballs into mine. 'Mr Kensington, I specifically told you to make sure everyone stayed here, until the case is closed.' His voice is cold and clipped. 'Do you not remember me saying that?'

My insides tighten. I should have thought about this. This is a serious mistake. I shake my head. 'You'd already interviewed everyone. We couldn't see the harm in it.'

Luca purses his lips. Matteo doesn't speak, but he has understood. He sits next to Luca, frowning and shaking his head. Matteo's and Luca's eyes meet.

'My instructions are law here in Italy. In Italy we treat the police with respect,' Luca says.

I take a deep breath. 'I can assure you I respect you greatly. I apologise on their behalf. They didn't understand why they weren't allowed to travel. I did try to explain, but they disregarded my comments.' I pause and raise my eyes to the sky. 'The arrogance of youth.'

Luca's eyes soften. 'OK, OK. I see you did not mean to be difficult. We will get in touch with them both. Let's start with Gemma Richardson. Where is she right now?'

'She's in Rome. I heard from her last night.'

'Oh good. So we can send someone to interview her there. Please can I have her mobile number?'

I pull my iPhone from my pocket, to retrieve her details.

124

Sarah

Dragging, limping, bleeding, I reach a small sandy cove at the bottom of the goat track. I collapse in the sand. Sand and sea and rock spin around me. I am falling into a vortex.

I open my eyes to the world again to find a man with a full head of strong grey hair leaning over me. His eyes are bold and brown. His face is heavily tanned and creased in folds. He is talking quickly, rattling on in a language I do not understand. As he leans over me prattling, I realise that one of his front teeth is missing. That is such a shame because, apart from that, he is quite good-looking. He keeps leaning across me and pointing. He has a tattoo of a mermaid on his arm.

'I do not understand,' I tell him.

I stiffen as he bends down further, puts his hands beneath my armpits and tries to lift me up to standing.

'Stop it. Stop it,' I shout as pain explodes all over my body.

He flops down on the ground next to me, and that is when I realise I am sitting in sand. I look around. I am in a sandy cove at the bottom of a cliff.

'Are you English or American?' he asks.

I think I must be one or the other, so I say, 'Yes.'

'My name is Lorenzo. I am *pescatore*. What is your name?'

I open my mouth to reply, but close it again. I just can't remember.

I shake my head. 'I don't know,' I tell him sadly.

This seems so wrong. I don't feel as if I am the sort of person who doesn't know who she is. I feel a confidence inside me that tells me that I usually know what my name is and exactly what I want.

'I am *pescatore*,' he repeats. 'I take you home. You tell me where you live. Where you need to go.'

I am too embarrassed to tell him I can't remember where I live. My leg throbs in pain. 'I think I need to go to hospital, please.'

The world around me is coming into better focus. I see a small rubber dinghy in front of us, attached to a miniature anchor; claws embedded in the sand. And out at sea a fishing boat is bobbing up and down in the bay in front of us. Lorenzo waves to a person on the boat who waves back. A person in a bright yellow jacket. *Pesce* means fish doesn't it? Lorenzo is a fisherman. *Pesce*. Which language? Maybe I am in Italy. But I have no idea who I came with or what I am doing here.

I watch Lorenzo move the rubber dinghy, pushing it into the water, throwing the claw anchor after it so it will stay put. He turns around and walks back to me.

'I lift you to the boat.'

His strong muscled arms, gnarled like ancient tree roots, pick me up as easily as if I were a child. As soon as he moves me the pain in my leg fires up again. I bite my lip to stop myself screaming. I inhale and exhale, deeply, slowly, to try and relax and not let the pain control me. He wades into the sea in his thigh-high boots and places me gently in the middle of the dinghy. He jumps in the stern, lifts the anchor and pulls the cord to start the engine. The engine putters. The small rubber boat struggles through the waves towards the fishing boat. As we get closer, I see she is called *Dexy*. Her name is announced in black lettering painted across a blue hull.

The crew man on the boat is in full view now. He is about thirty years old with straight, shiny brown hair. Lorenzo throws him the dinghy painter, he catches it.

'My son, Mario. He work with me,' Lorenzo explains.

A son. I have a son. I see his face in front of me. But right now I can't remember his name. Mario and Lorenzo are gabbling away together in a resonant sing-song language that reminds me of sunshine and holidays. And sadness and death. Heaviness presses against me and weighs me down. Dread engulfs me and for a second I feel I know someone has died.

Mario chucks something that looks like a sling down to Lorenzo. Lorenzo wraps it beneath my bottom and encourages me to sit in it. He pulls up the straps and climbs up onto the fishing boat. They work together to pull me on board. They untangle me from the sling and I sit in the middle of the decking onboard, panting with pain and exhaustion. They sit together on a wooden bench that is nailed down, looking at me. As if they don't know what to make of me. What to do with me. What is the matter with them? Haven't they seen an Englishwoman before?

English. Yes. England. That is where I am from. I turn my mind in on itself to try and concentrate, but I cannot remember which part. Mario disappears into the cabin and returns with a bottle of water and a lunch box. He thrusts them into my trembling hands. I clumsily manage to twist the top off the water bottle and take a sip. And another sip. I begin to guzzle like a hungry baby. This water is like heavenly elixir. The best thing I have ever drunk in my life. But I have drunk too much, too quickly. My stomach gripes and I bend over to rub it.

'Eat. Eat,' Lorenzo encourages. 'It will settle you.'

I thrust open the lunch box, pull out the pizza slice that is inside and take a bite. The cheese is soft and delicious. Heaven. But one bite is enough. I know after not eating for so long I must take it easy. Then I place the rest of the slice in my pocket, and save it for later.

Father and son begin to gabble to each other. They turn around and gabble at me, jabbering words towards me that I guess must be questions.

I raise my arms in the air and shake my head. 'I'm so sorry I just can't understand you.'

They begin to use English.

'What is your name? Who are you?' Mario asks.

'I have no idea.' I shrug.

'Where are you from?'

'England,' I pause. 'I think.'

Lorenzo pulls a handheld telephone from his pocket. He presses the side and gabbles into that. A robotic voice in this strange language I do not understand, gabbles back.

'We take you to Salerno to hospital there. We will arrive quick, quick.'

But our journey doesn't seem quick. The heavy wooden boat lumbers through the water, rising and falling awkwardly through waves that seem to rotate and lift the hull and swing the bow every few seconds. As my body is thrust around and around and from side to side, I feel sleepy. I feel sick. So sick and tired, I think I will die.

I close my eyes as the boat continues to churn and lumber. I have no idea who I am, or where I am going.

125
Ralph

I am walking along the passageway towards town, on my way to buy a few supplies. I stop to have a look at the building site next door to Villa Panorama. They are only at the stage of foundations and concrete flooring, having just put a self-levelling skin on top of the first layer of concrete. The villa they are building is already advertised in the window of the local estate agents with a computer-generated 3D design picture. It will have five bedrooms, all with en-suites and private balconies, a generous well-equipped kitchen, two large reception rooms and a large patio with a pool. Open plan and perfect without a dank, dark dining room! The owner of the site must be about to make a packet, judging from the estimated price.

It would once have been a dream of mine to own a place in Italy like this. But even if by some miracle you were found alive, Sarah, after everything that has happened, I will never be able to face coming here again. I take one last look at the perfect view from where I am standing, take a deep breath, and walk on towards the general store and the bakery.

126
Sarah

I wake up and open my eyes. I'm comfortable, just the right temperature, not too cold, not too warm. I cannot feel any pain in my groin, or in my leg. I try and roll over, but I cannot move very far as my arms are attached to tubes and wires. I push my chest up to sitting and blink. I am in a white-walled hospital room, attached to a heart monitor.

A nurse in a blue dress is walking towards me. She is smiling. She has neat features and wispy blonde hair. She reminds me of someone, but I'm not sure who. She slides a hospital tray across my lap and places a small paper cup containing tablets in front of me, and a glass of water.

'Take these. They'll help with pain relief.'

I do as I am told. I finish the glass of water. It is fresh and delicious.

'Where am I? What happened?' I ask.

'You were found badly injured, with a broken hip, at the bottom of a cliff. We had to replace your left hip as an emergency, but you are recovering from surgery well.' She pauses and takes the paper cup from my tray. 'It is quite common after a serious accident, but you don't seem to remember anything, not even who you are or why you are in Italy. We are not worried about it. We have given you a brain scan and everything seems normal. There is no permanent damage. We expect your memory will soon come back.'

I frown. 'So I am in Italy?'

'Yes, you were found at the bottom of a cliff, just outside Praiano. Does Praiano mean anything to you?'

I shake my head. 'No.'

'Please, try not to worry. I am sure everything will soon come back. Try and rest. Get some sleep.'

She leaves the room and closes the door softly behind her. I do as she suggests. I fall asleep and dream.

I dream I am about to get married to the man I love. I am wearing a pale pink silk wedding gown and carrying a bouquet of lilies. My engagement ring is a large sapphire surrounded by diamonds. Standing in a beautiful old house that looks like a French chateau. Its windows are decorated with stone arches and elegant shutters. I am looking out onto a sunken garden with a border of dahlias, chrysanthemums, iris, roses and delphiniums as I wait to walk up the aisle. I turn to kiss my husband-to-be, but before I really see his face it fragments in front of me. What is his name? And where has he gone?

I wake up and open my eyes to find myself still in the hospital bed. A man is sitting in a chair by my bed. He is wearing a severe black uniform, and a military hat. He is small with a hooked nose. Concerned brown eyes meet mine.

'Hello. I'm Luca, local Carabinieri,' he says.

He seems vaguely familiar. 'Have we met before?' I ask.

He nods. 'On several occasions, madam.'

I frown. 'I don't remember. Local Carabinieri? So I am in Italy?'

'Yes. You are in hospital in Salerno.'

'Never heard of it.'

'You were found at the bottom of a cliff in Praiano. This is the nearest place with a big hospital.'

'Yes. The nurse told me I was found in Praiano. Never heard of it either.'

He leans closer. 'Do you remember anything about what happened?'

'I think I'm about to get married.'

He bites his lip. 'Well, you were but . . .' He hesitates. 'It didn't quite work out like that.'

'What do you mean?'

'I'll make sure your family are here to see you within a few hours. Then it will all start to come back to you. Do you remember your name, or where you are from?'

I shake my head. 'No. But the nurse told me she thinks I will soon.'

A name presses into my head. 'Jack, I want to see Jack.'

His face stiffens. 'Jack isn't available right now.'

The man in the black uniform begins to move in and out of focus. And then he is sliced out of my vision as if someone is pulling black shutters slowly down in front of my eyes. The machine my body is attached to emits an ear-piercing screech. My body begins to jerk uncontrollably. I hear a voice in the distance shrieking in Italian.

'*Arresto cardiac. Chiamare il medico.*'

And I know I'm having a cardiac arrest.

127
Janice

I am lying on a sun lounger longing to see you, Mother. Longing for you to come home. I'm doing what you have always suggested; going to a counsellor, about my mood swings, about my paranoia. The way I blame myself for death, destruction and chaos that has nothing to do with me. My weird problem of over dwelling on coincidences and counting them as fate. I have booked a series of appointments with a psychiatrist, Dr Ffeffer, on Harley Street, when I return home. Dad is paying. I have already started some sessions with her on Zoom, as a stopgap. And I am doing CBT on Zoom with one of her colleagues, Anabel Bolton. It's going to be a long hard haul, but I feel a little better already.

At least I have acknowledged the truth. I know I didn't kill you. I didn't kill Jack. In fact, I haven't killed anyone. And I do not intend to. From now on I'm going to keep my guilty paranoia in check. My thoughts cannot damage you. My thoughts cannot damage anyone. I have always just about managed to keep my anger under control. But still I've blamed it for real-life damages caused by accidents or others.

I know what happened to Chris's dad now. I just felt responsible for the fact he'd died because I was so jealous of Chris's exam results. I didn't do anything to his car, that was all in my head. I had been so full of hatred for Chris, I felt guilty for my negative feelings. I hated myself. I turned my hatred into a paranoid fear.

My paranoia started with the dog. After you left us, you bought a golden retriever puppy and named him Rufus. Whenever we went to stay, the dog made it quite clear that he preferred Patrick to me. Rufus was not very subtle with his favouritism. He would follow my brother everywhere. As soon as Patrick patted him, he would roll over onto his back, expecting Patrick to rub his tummy. When he did, Rufus purred with pleasure, like a cat. But whenever I tried to stroke him, he'd shy away.

Easter weekend. Our special time with you, Mum. On Good Friday, walking in the Black Mountains, Rufus appeared from behind a bush with a large piece of steak in his mouth. He wolfed it down before we could take it off him. It was towards the end of our walk so we were soon back to our holiday cottage. We found him dead in the hallway an hour later. Stiff as a board, his tongue black and sticking out. It was obvious that he had been poisoned so we rang the police. The police said they thought it was strychnine, and that some of the local farmers still used it on their farms even though it was now illegal. They said they thought they knew who had left it on the public footpath and they wanted us to have Rufus autopsied so that charges could be pressed.

You didn't want to get into a legal battle with a Welsh farmer. So you had the dog buried. We cried and cried for days. You soon bought another puppy, Merlin. Merlin is still alive, doubtless being spoilt by your dog sitter right now. He loves me more than anyone in the world. So I have agonised that Rufus died because he didn't love me and I punished him by killing him. Merlin loves me, so he is still alive. I have cried myself to sleep so many nights over this.

And the coincidences I worry about go on and on. An ex-teacher of mine, who I always disliked, was stabbed to death in a 'random' attack at Archway tube station. I resented you meeting Jack, and he died. I was feeling angry with you, and you have disappeared.

Untangling my issues over Zoom, my mind is becoming clearer. I feel light. I feel free. Come home and I will share my lightness with you.

128

Ralph

We are sitting in our usual position. Luca and Matteo on one side of the dining table, me opposite them. Matteo as still and silent as ever. Luca clasps his hands together and leans forwards; eyes darting and tense.

'We have good news and bad news,' Luca tells me. My body stiffens. 'We have found Sarah. But she is very sick and it is touch and go whether she will survive.' My body reverberates with despair. 'She can't remember who she is, but I recognised her,' he continues.

'What's happened to her?' I ask, voice panicked, heart racing.

'She was found by a local fisherman on a beach at the bottom of a cliff. He brought her to the hospital at Salerno. She was concussed, with no memory. She had broken fingers and a broken hip. The worry is she has now had a cardiac arrest, after all the physical stress her body has experienced. I suggest you and your family go and visit her immediately. Your presence may make all the difference. I have arranged for a police car to drive you there. The driver will be here in five minutes.' He pauses. 'Oh, and I do not want to worry you, but we were not able to get in touch with Gemma. So we are running an investigation to make sure she is safe. Have you heard from her lately?'

'Yes. She's fine. She's staying at the Palazzo Montemartini. I really don't think you need to worry about her. She is living a life of luxury at one of the best hotels in the world.'

129

Sarah

I am not awake. I am not asleep. Not sure if I am alive or dead. People are standing around my bed. I sense their presence, but I can't see them. All I can see is you, Jack, lying dead on a slab in front of me. Your head is bloody and pulverised. You fell off the cliff, but the police told me you committed suicide. Perhaps they will tell me that I attempted suicide too. Because I couldn't live without you.

I see Gemma, air-kissing me on both cheeks, pretending that she is pleased to see me. Her outfit isn't very subtle. Denim shorts that have frayed considerably at the curve of her buttocks. A bikini top that looks like a white lacy Wonderbra. Red lipstick so red it should be used to paint post boxes. Tapering fingernails – turquoise with lines of glitter plastered through them.

She puts her hands on her hips, and shouts. 'Leave Ralph alone, he belongs to me.'

She is pushing me towards the edge of the cliff. I am pushing back, trying to resist. But she is so much younger, so much stronger than me. I hold on to her.

'Please stop this,' I beg.

130

Janice

I sit at your bedside watching your chest rise and fall, breathing softly in a coma. The doctor says that you may wake up any time within the next few hours, the next few weeks. Or not at all. You may remain in a permanent vegetative state. Your fate is in the lap of the gods, apparently. My mind is becoming stronger, but I'm not sure I can cope with a statement like that.

I kiss you softly on the cheek. 'I love you,' I whisper, 'I need you. Please recover from this.'

131
Patrick

I have lost Anna, and now it looks as if we will lose Mother. I need to tighten up my life, learn to appreciate what I have while I have still got it.

132

Ralph

So, Sarah, you must have been depressed and jumped. Jack's death might have killed you, too. I sit at your bedside, tears streaming down my face. Sarah. You are my love. You were my life. What is that quote? *You were the wind beneath my wings*. I used to think it was corny. But it isn't. It's beautiful. It perfectly describes what you have been for me.

TWO DAYS LATER

133

Sarah

I open my eyes and the clouds are gone. I know where I am. I know who I am. I reach across and press the buzzer by my bed. And I know with certainty that it was Gemma who pushed me off the cliff. I see, feel and hear what she said and did, every time I think back. My mind is no longer confused.

The pretty blonde nurse who looks a bit like Janice rushes in. I hear her footsteps dash across the room. She leans over me, smelling of musk and lavender.

'Sarah, can you hear me? If you can, please blink.' Her voice is soft and melodic.

I blink.

There is a flurry of activity. I am surrounded by the medical team. By authority. By strident voices. A tube is removed from my throat. I can think, and now I can speak.

'Please, please,' I say in a strange croaky voice. 'Please, call my family.'

134

Janice

I hug you so tight, Mother. I do not ever want to let you go.

'I love you so much. I've missed you so much. I've been so upset after our argument; blaming myself for your fall,' I say, and burst into tears.

We continue to embrace, clinging together like ivy. Like limpets.

'You didn't do anything to hurt me,' you say. 'You came back to tell me you never wanted me to leave, and burst into tears. We hugged, I reassured you. You had your usual rant for a few minutes and stopped. Then you left, I was fine.'

I take a deep breath. 'I'm working to put this right. I've started CBT for my problem. And I'm going to see a psychiatrist when I get home; I've been speaking to her on Zoom already.'

Your smile is so wide it lights up your pale face. Your eyes sparkle with enthusiasm. 'That's the best news.'

'Come on, Janice, my turn now,' Patrick says, and I just move around a little so that he can squeeze in too.

I do not know how long we lean over the hospital bed holding you.

After a while Dad butts in. 'Hey, you two, I would like some time alone with your mother,' Dad says, tapping us both on the shoulder. 'Why don't you naff off to the canteen for a while. Here's some money for drinks and a snack.'

135

Ralph

I sit by the bed and hold your hand. It is rough with calluses after your five-day ordeal. Your usually pale, almost translucent skin is red and blistered from the sun, lips like parchment. Your blonde hair looks fairer than ever. The doctors say it is a miracle that you are alive. They are going to write up your case in a medical journal. Very few people have survived such a big fall, even when broken by trees and bushes. So much to say. So much to talk about. Where should I start?

'How are you feeling?' I try.

'Comfortable,' you croak. The intubation tube has left your throat sore. 'They have looked after me so well in here. They have stopped the pain.'

'Was it very terrible?'

Your sapphire eyes pool with tears. You bite your lip and nod your head. 'Yes. But I knew I had to survive. I knew I needed to take Jack's body home.'

My stomach tightens. Jack. Always Jack. Your deceit of so many years hurts so much. That bastard. He got what he deserved.

I fight the knots in my stomach and manage to push my anger down into a sealed compartment. 'We'll come through all this. I'll always be here for you,' I say, voice cool as ice.

You squeeze my hand. You smile your perfect elfin smile. 'You always have been, Ralph. I appreciate that so much.'

My heart melts. I smile back at you. Then, 'Why did you do it?' I ask.

You widen your eyes. 'Do what?'

'Jump.'

You shake your head. 'You're joking, aren't you? You didn't really think I would jump?'

I frown in surprise. 'What happened then?'

'Your girlfriend, Gemma, pushed me.' An electric current flashes through me.

Did she? Did the bitch do this?

'The memory of what Gemma did has come back to me so clearly,' you continue. 'I remember everything. Down to the last detail. I even remember what she was wearing. I need to tell the police as soon as possible. I'm not safe while she's around.'

The electric current tightens around my heart, around my head.

'She's not around. She's gone travelling. You do not need to worry about her right now.'

I grind my back teeth together and clench my fists.

'It was awful, Ralph.' Your voice is breaking. Your eyes fill with tears. 'She told me to leave you alone because you belong to her and then she pushed me off the edge. I begged her to stop. It was a cold-blooded attempt to murder me. No mercy.' You pause. 'She was so strong. So determined.'

I sit beside you on the bed and hold you against my chest. I massage your back to soothe you. My poor dear girl. I never wanted you to suffer like this.

'I never want to see her again,' you continue.

'You won't. I'll finish the relationship; I was going to anyway. She was never the right woman for me. She will never harm you again. I promise.'

Your body stiffens. 'How can you promise? You don't control her. I must tell the police, as soon as possible. They'll arrest her.

She will be charged. Even if you finish with her, what's to stop her coming back to kill me?'

I pull away from you and sit holding my eyes in yours. 'When you get back to the villa there is a lot I need to explain.' I pause. 'Please promise me you won't tell the police, not yet. If you do, our family is in deep, deep trouble. If you care about our family, please, please respect me about this.'

136
Sarah

My family have left to return to the villa, and now that they have gone, I feel so very tired. I wrap myself in the crisp cotton hospital sheets and will for sleep to give me release. But Ralph's words haunt me. *Please promise me you won't tell the police, not yet. If you do our family is in deep, deep trouble.* What has happened? Has Janice done something awful? Has Patrick? Has my mind become confused? Did someone else push me off the cliff?

137
Patrick

Back at the villa, sitting on the terrace, inhaling the scent of jasmine and bougainvillea, looking down at the jewelled sea. So pleased to know that Mum is recovering well. Soon I will be able to leave this nightmare behind and fly home to another one. Anna texted me this morning to say she has moved out of our flat. What has happened between us? Where did we go wrong? I really thought that Anna and I would last.

138
Sarah

Luca and Matteo are hovering around my bedside like birds of prey; their uniforms so sombre and funereal, they remind me of a pair of ravens. I push my torso further up the pillow so that I can see them better. Luca's chair is on my left, Matteo on my right. I look past them, out of the hospital window. It isn't exactly a room with a view. All I can see is the metallic glare of the cars in the car park. But then, I don't want a view. I don't want to look at the sea.

'What happened, Sarah? How did you fall off the cliff?' Luca asks, leaning towards me.

I shrug my shoulders. 'I can't remember. I must have slipped.'

He smiles a knowing smile. 'That was rather careless, wasn't it? It's a long way to slip. Are you sure you didn't have any help?'

I take a deep breath. 'Do you mean was I pushed?'

He nods. 'That's exactly what I mean.'

I grimace. I so want to tell him. But Ralph said our family will be in deep, deep trouble if I speak. I trust Ralph implicitly. He has always been there for me, for our family.

I take a deep breath and lean back on my pillows. 'I don't remember anything at the minute. Maybe I fainted. I just don't remember. The first thing I knew was finding myself awake on a ledge, in serious pain. Pain clouds your memory, you know. And so does intense heat.'

Luca makes a few notes in his pad. His pen scrapes across the paper in a swathe of flowery writing.

'Did you see anyone else on the cliff path before you fell?' he asks.

'No.'

'Had you arranged to meet anyone?'

My mind is screaming to say Gemma. But my mouth replies with a short, sharp, 'No.'

'We're asking everyone who was staying in the villa if they remember anything. Anna Jenkins has been contacted. She didn't have anything to add. She was in bed with Patrick when you fell. But we still haven't managed to speak to Gemma Richardson. Do you remember whether she had arranged to meet you?'

'No. And I don't think she would have. I'd only just met her, and she hardly knew me.'

'We are finding it really odd that we can't get in touch with her. Do you have any idea where she is?'

'She's gone travelling, hasn't she?'

Luca's mouth twitches. 'Perhaps.'

139
Ralph

I pick you up in a car I have managed to hire. The area is so rammed with tourists that the vehicle I have managed to get for the day is overpriced and expensive. I've paid through the nose for a Smart car, which seems to have the strength and safety of a tin can. I hope I don't give it even the slightest bump. It would just split in half.

Your favourite nurse, who you insist reminds you of Janice, and who, it just so happens speaks excellent English, helps you to the car, carrying the day bag I brought in for you. You hold her arm and walk slowly using your stick. You slide into the front seat, keeping your left leg straight out in front of you.

'Thank you so much for everything you have done for me, Francesca.' You beam at her, before shutting the car door. Or rather the thin metal plate that purports to be a door.

I start the engine and we begin to worm our way out of the car park.

'Thank you for driving me back, Ralph.'

'It's my pleasure.'

'Please, Ralph, I can't bear to look at the sea. Please can we go via the inland route?'

'Of course. The roads will be straighter, more comfortable.' I turn left out of the hospital and left again.

'I can't believe Jack's dead. At the moment it just feels as if he's gone away for a while and will be back soon. I'm half expecting him to be at the villa when we arrive.'

I turn to glance at you. You are sitting with your head back and your eyes closed, tears running down your face. You cry the whole journey back. As I lift you from the car and carry you down the steps to the piazza. As I lift you across the piazza, a group of widows dressed in black watching us. As I stumble along the path to the villa, past the building site next door. You cry and cry. Will your crying ever stop?

140

Sarah

I can't stop crying, Jack. I can't hold it together. I had to fight to survive. I so wanted to because I wanted to honour your life and make something of what is left of mine. But the actuality of leaving hospital, longing to be with you but not able to see you again, has unleashed a whirlwind of emotion. It came from nowhere. One minute I was in the car, thanking Francesca, thanking Ralph, and then it hit me. Bowled me over in a sudden hurricane of despair. The despair clings to me like a sticky fog and I can't move through it.

Ralph has parked the car on the main road and he is carrying me down to the villa, across the piazza, past a group of gnarled old women wearing widow's weeds. They have lost their husbands too. They watch us with kind, worried eyes. Do they remember how it feels? I cling on to Ralph. His closeness, his familiarity, soothes me a little, as I lean my head against his chest. He smells of the sandalwood soap he always uses. The soap the children always buy him at Christmas.

We arrive at the villa. Ralph still holding me in his arms and stretching to press the doorbell. The door opens and Patrick and Janice are standing in the hallway.

'Move. Move. My back is killing me, let me get her to the sofa.'

My children step aside. Ralph deposits me on a sofa at the side of the dark old-fashioned dining room, in the middle of the house. Leaning over me and setting me down as delicately as if I was precious china. I arrange myself as comfortably as possible. Ralph fluffs up a large, embroidered cushion and puts it behind my back.

'Can I get you anything?' he asks.

'No, thanks.'

Patrick and Janice have followed us into the dining room and are waiting to greet me. Patrick steps forward first. He looks tired and I know he hasn't been sleeping. He leans down and gives me a bear hug.

'Love you, Mum.'

His words make me want to cry all over again, but I bite my lip to suppress tears. Janice is hovering at his side.

'Come on, bro. My turn.'

He steps aside and Janice envelops me in her arms, wrapping me in the cheeky designer scent of the sea she always wears. 'Love you more,' she says.

'She couldn't do, it's not possible,' Patrick announces.

Being love bombed is too much for me right now. I start to cry again.

'Are you crying because you're happy to be home, or because you're sad about Jack?' Patrick asks.

'Both, I think.'

He steps towards Janice and me. Our group hug would put the cast of *Friends* to shame.

141

Ralph

You cried in the car all the way back to the villa. I have broken my back carrying you down here and as soon as Patrick and Janice welcome you, you begin to cry again.

'Should I carry you to your room so that you can have a rest?' I almost snap.

You wipe your eyes. 'They taught me to cope with stairs at the hospital. I need to get used to them. So, yes, I would like to go to my room and rest, but I can manage alone.'

You push yourself up to standing with the help of your stick and begin walking slowly across the room.

142
Sarah

I cope with going up the stairs exactly as the physiotherapist at the hospital taught me. I hold on to the banister and use my good leg first. When my good leg is bearing my weight on the upper step, I lift my operated leg to join it. Good leg, bad leg – alternately, all the way up.

I walk slowly across the landing, open my bedroom door, and, carefully placing my bottom on the side of the bed, lift my legs up and lie back on the bed. I rummage in my pocket for my phone and tap to call the funeral director who is looking after your body until we fly home.

'Please, please, can I come and visit Jack Rutherford?'

'Yes, madam, we have finished embalming his body – you can visit whenever it suits. Someone is here on duty twenty-four-seven.'

Ralph borrows a wheelchair from the local doctor's surgery and pushes me to the funeral home.

'I'll wait for you in the lobby,' he says as the mortuary assistant arrives to collect me to visit you. His eyes melt into mine, soft with sympathy. 'Good luck.'

I leave the wheelchair behind. I only need it for long distances, it's not as if I can't walk at all. I lean on my stick as I walk along slowly with the mortuary assistant. He is a stocky man with a bulbous nose and straight black hair. His mouth is slightly indented like a pencil line in putty.

We step into the morgue. The undertakers morgue, not the police morgue this time. Once again it looks like a catering hub lined with wall-to-wall freezers. But they are not freezers. They are cool compartments containing the bodies of people others miss and love.

Every death affects so many others. I stand in the midst of stainless steel and try to contemplate how many people's lives are completely ruined by one person's death. Each death is a cascade of unhappiness. The fine line between life and death is the part of the human condition that makes us so vulnerable. The constant murmur in the back of our minds that we and all those we love will die eventually. Death is life's only certainty. To compensate we wrap routine and organisation around us, to make us feel safe. To fool us into thinking life is permanent. To make it seem as permanent as possible.

We spend our lives trying to protect ourselves from death. But we cannot protect ourselves forever. And I am standing here in the middle of a nightmare I have always dreaded. A nightmare that makes me question whether life is actually worth living. If there really is a kind god out there, why can't we stay with the people we love forever? Some people believe we will all be together in the afterlife. Surely, after so many centuries of death, by now, if that was true, we would have some proof of it? Or at least a very clear sign? And so I can't buy that theory. I will never rely on hope that everything is perfect in the afterlife. Life is life. Death is death. Time is now.

The funeral director is opening a cupboard. He slides out a steel shelf on which a body lies, draped in a white cover.

'Shall I lift the cover, or would you prefer to do it?' he asks.

'I'll do it.'

'Do you want me to leave you with your loved one, alone?'

I nod my head. He bows politely and leaves. I walk towards you and stand a while, not daring to lift the sheet. I feel so sick and faint. But I need to see you again. I need to accept that you have gone. I push my hand to the edge of the sheet and hold it in my fingers. I force myself to keep my eyes open as I pull the sheet away.

The embalmer has tidied you up. Washed the blood from your face. Covered your bruises with make-up. You do not look as crushed as you did when I had to identify your body. But you do not look like yourself anymore. I lean down and kiss your cold, cold lips. Your cold cheeks. The top of your head where you were getting a bald patch. One last touch of your lips.

'Goodbye, my love.'

143

Ralph

I'm sitting in the lobby at the undertakers, waiting for you to come out of the mortuary. Everything is white and peaceful. A shiny marble floor. Marble tiles on the walls. A glass coffee table with marble pillars for legs decorated with an abundance of lilies. I'm sitting in a white leather armchair, opposite a large, white leather settee. A receptionist, dressed in a smart white blouse, wearing large pearl earrings, sits behind a marble desk, typing into a computer. From time to time, she answers the phone, but I cannot hear what she is saying as she's behind a large sound-proof glass screen. Piped classical music fills the air, heavily biased towards strings. The air smells of lavender and vanilla.

You appear at last from behind a section of marble wall that suddenly opens. You walk slowly towards me, carefully balancing each step and leaning heavily on your stick. Paler than pale. You are losing weight, aren't you? You are wearing a black linen dress. Black doesn't suit you. It is a colour too heavy for your almost translucent skin. You need warm colours and pale shades. You look so fragile, I just want to hold you and protect you.

But I need to wait. Grief is a process. You need to step through it. I have been reading all about it so that I know how to help you. There are five stages of grief and they follow a general pattern, but can overlap and intermingle. Denial. Anger. Bargaining. Depression. And finally, acceptance. It is when you reach acceptance that I'll be able to step in.

144
Janice

I've been sorting out the food again; lunchtime today I am serving meatballs and tortellini. No one else has the time or energy to sort out the catering. Patrick is busy swotting for an exam a few days after we get back. We fly back on Thursday, so he has left it quite late to revise. But then he has always been such a brainbox, so I guess he'll be all right.

Mum is totally wrapped up with planning Jack's funeral; I know she has arranged for an organist to play one of his favourites at the beginning and end of the service. Toccata and Fugue in D minor by JS Bach. She has seemed very animated about that. And she's writing a poem about his life to read when it's her turn to speak.

And Dad? Well Dad is in a constant daydream. He is hardly eating and is drinking heavily – a bottle of rosé and a few stiff G&Ts every night. And a glass or two at lunch as well. In the day he sometimes disappears to his bedroom to move other people's money around on his computer, but most of his time is spent lounging on a sun lounger on the patio, fast asleep or staring into space.

Lunch. San Pellegrino. Freshly squeezed lemonade. Rosé wine for Dad. Spicy Italian meatballs with tortellini. And another of my exotic baby leaf salads. I've popped a bit of chorizo and feta cheese in for a change.

I sip the lemonade. Not bad. Not too bitter. Not too sweet. It has come out nicely this time. 'So how's Gemma, Dad? How is her trip going?'

Dad takes a gulp of wine. 'She's having a ball. Keeping me updated. Staying in a posh hotel in Rome.'

'Well, when are you two getting married? Will it be a short engagement?'

Dad looks over at Mum shiftily.

Mother's head stiffens. She widens her eyes in surprise. 'I didn't know congratulations were in order, Ralph. Why didn't you tell me?' She shakes her head, softly, sadly. 'I'd have thought you would have mentioned it.'

She bursts into tears and leaves the table. We hear the repetitive thud of her stick going upstairs. Dad follows her.

Patrick and I exchange glances and sit in silence, picking at our food.

145
Ralph

'Please let me come in, I need to explain.'

The bedroom door opens slowly. You stand in front of me wearing your pale pink towelling dressing gown. I sigh inside. You are red faced. You've been crying again.

You walk into the middle of the room and sit down on your dressing table chair, round shouldered and diminished.

'Are you really this upset that I'm engaged to Gemma?' I ask, hoping this means you have some feelings for me deep down.

You shake your head and purse your lips. 'Yes. Of course I am. She tried to kill me. Or haven't you remembered that? You are engaged to the person I need to report to the police.' You pause. 'And you've been stopping me from doing that. Is it because you are so in love with her that you can't accept she's done anything wrong?'

I almost put my head back and laugh, but I stop myself. If only you knew, Sarah. 'That's a bit rich coming from you. What about you not telling me about Jack, for all these years?'

Your eyes darken. 'I had a good reason. What's yours?' you snap.

'It's important that you trust me.' I sit on the edge of the bed and lean towards you. 'And I didn't tell you about my engagement because it's a sham and I have no intention of going through with it.'

You narrow your sapphire eyes. 'How ridiculous is that. Do you expect me to believe this nonsense?'

'I do because it's true.' I shrug. 'I hoped if I got engaged to Gemma, you'd be jealous and want me back.'

You take a sharp breath. Your chin juts out as it does when you are angry. 'That's a tasteless comment, isn't it – talking about conniving to get me back when I am in agony grieving the man I love.' You pause. 'We've not been together for years, why would I want you now?'

'You wanted me in the first place. I was your first husband. The only husband you've ever had,' I remind you. Pretending your comment hasn't hurt me by stretching my lips into what I hope is a warm friendly smile. 'You seemed rather keen on me to begin with.'

You shake your head, slowly, sadly. 'Before I realised I'd made a mistake. We were never truly in tune with one another. Most divorces are instigated by people who marry too young, before they are sufficiently mature. Then they grow up and grow apart.'

'Is that how you saw us?'

'Yes.' You pause and take a deep breath. 'And if you remember, I told you that when I left.' You shake your head. 'I tried to be honest with you.'

Your words burn into me like gun shot. I know you said it once but, because we stayed such close friends, I never believed you. I pinch myself and take a breath. I don't think you mean what you say now. You are just being cruel because you are in the throes of grieving. If you hadn't met Jack you would have never left me, and now that Jack is dead you will come back. I need to believe in myself, to hang on to that hope.

You scowl at me, and your chin juts again. 'And what has any of this got to do with not going to the police?' Your voice is sharp and insistent.

I hold your sad blue eyes in mine. 'How long have you known me?' I ask

You sigh. 'It feels like forever.'

'And do you trust me?'

Your face softens. 'In the past, and for as long as I can remember, I would have trusted you with my life.'

I step towards you and put my hands on your shoulders. 'Then trust me on this, now.'

You sigh again, louder and longer this time. You shake your head and shrug. 'I'll have to talk to the police before I fly back for Jack's funeral. I will leave it until then. But that is the best I can do.'

'Thank you.'

'And I can assure you, Ralph, I am most uncomfortable with this.'

146
Sarah

Jack's funeral is the day after tomorrow. His parents and sister are coming. And Susan's mother. I've planned it all from here, heart in shreds, almost permanently in tears. Tomorrow we fly home; all of us. Patrick, Janice, me and Ralph. Gemma still hasn't returned from her travels; but she will have to return soon, to receive the justice that is coming to her. I'm organised. Already packed, except for the last few essentials that I need today. At last it's time to call the police to tell the truth about what happened to me. They will find her, and Gemma will finally get the punishment she deserves. I pick up my iPhone, about to dial, but my bedroom door flies open and Ralph marches in.

'What's going on?' he asks, voice sharp.

I step away from him. 'I'm about to call the police.'

He moves towards me and puts his hand on my arm. He snatches my phone from me and holds it high above my head, far too far for me to reach.

'Please, don't,' he pleads. 'Please wait for me to explain.'

Anger and fear boil inside me. 'What's going on, Ralph? Why couldn't you explain in the first place?'

He places my phone in his trouser pocket. 'We need to sit down and talk.'

I have a cold feeling in the pit of my stomach. Ralph sits on the bed with an expression on his face that I have never seen before. I sit on the dressing table chair opposite him.

'You were right, Jack didn't commit suicide. Gemma murdered him.'

I close my eyes. I feel as if I am about to faint even though I am sitting on the bed. This must be a dream. A nightmare. But when I open my eyes Ralph is still sitting on the bed opposite me, his face still contorted into the strange expression I have never seen before, even though I've known him for twenty-five years. And I know this isn't a dream.

'How do you know she killed Jack? Did she tell you? If you know she killed Jack, why didn't you tell the police?' I splutter.

Slowly, slowly, he shakes his head. 'She admitted she killed Jack. He didn't jump. She pushed him off the cliff. But she told me why. And I didn't go to the police . . . in order to protect him. If they find out what Jack did to her, he'll be disgraced.'

A stone coagulates in my stomach. My body feels heavy. 'What do you mean, what Jack did to her?' I ask, voice coming out as a whisper.

'I'm so sorry to shatter your illusions about him, but . . . Jack raped Gemma.'

The room begins to spin around me. 'Raped her? No. That isn't possible. He didn't have an aggressive bone in his body.'

I rush to the en-suite, the room spinning faster and faster, feeling flushed and sick. I put my head down the toilet bowl, body so hot I feel as if I am on fire. I vomit. I retch at the stench of the vomit and am sick again. I cling on to the toilet bowl until my body heat diminishes. Until the spinning stops. But . . . but . . . that wasn't Jack. Gemma is a liar. A murderer and a liar. I begin to shiver, teeth chattering.

After a while, I stop shivering. I manage to stand up and flush the toilet, wash my hands and clean my teeth. I splash my face with cold water to revive myself. But then the monstrous nature of what Ralph said comes back to me. Gemma raped. Your sperm inside her? Your sperm inside her and that is why you are dead? I wretch. I vomit again.

Ralph knocks on the bathroom door. 'Are you all right?' he asks.

'Of course I'm not all right,' I shout through the door. 'I don't think I'll ever be all right again.'

147

Ralph

The BA flight is rammed. I didn't expect it to be so full mid-week. Business people in dark suits. A noisy school trip accompanied by teachers who look exhausted already. Sarah, I'm so proud of you. So glad you were proud enough not to kowtow to the police.

It wouldn't have been fair to Jack's memory and pride, would it? It would have spoilt his funeral, which you have worked so hard to arrange. And it's going to be such a beautiful tribute. I think you will feel much better when it's over. Funerals are so cathartic, aren't they?

148

Sarah

I wake up back in my Edwardian pile on the Embankment, Twickenham. Egyptian cotton sheets smooth against my skin. I yawn and stretch. I sit up in bed and the bedroom comes into focus. The marble fireplace. The antique sofa. Our possessions push towards me, bristling with familiarity. The photograph of us on our first holiday together; our trip along the Nile. The coral we probably shouldn't have taken from the beach on the Caribbean. The Art Nouveau mirror we picked up in a junk shop, that I keep on my dressing table, next to my perfume and face cream.

I feel empty. I begin to tremble. Could you have betrayed my trust in you and raped someone? Psychology experts say that rape is aggressive, not sexual. I never thought you were unfaithful to me. I trusted you completely. Being near you made me feel safe and warm. You were always my safe place. But did I just never know the real you? The aggressive you? Now I am grieving twice; for the man I knew, and the man I didn't. Was I right not to tell the police? Am I right to protect you? I still love you enough to want to do that. Even though the thought of you raping Gemma makes me feel ill, I have to give you the benefit of the doubt. The side of you that I always saw would have never behaved like that.

Patrick, Janice and Ralph are all here. They stayed overnight, to keep me company. Janice tucked me into bed last night and kissed my cheek. They are coming to your funeral with me, thank goodness. Thank goodness for my family. Janice seems calmer since I returned from the dead. As if she really appreciates me at last. The counselling she's having is really helping. All the years I have spent trying to encourage her to ask for help, she has finally taken the bull by the horns herself. My darling, brave girl. You never had children, did you? That must have been a great sadness for you.

I force myself to get out of bed, limbs already tired and heavy before the day begins. I feel perpetually exhausted right now, because I'm depressed. It is reactive depression, so in the end I hope it will go. I'm depressed because my life is empty, not because I'm ill. Years will pass. My interests may grow.

I shower and put on my black dress from Hobbs; the one you always liked. I take two diazepam tablets. Patrick managed to obtain a private prescription from one of his professors, to help me through the day. They say it's addictive. Perhaps I'll need it for the rest of my life. I can't imagine ever feeling normal again. I'm not sure I can manage without help.

By the time I step into the kitchen I feel loose and floppy. As if I will float numbly through the day. Patrick, Janice and Ralph are in the kitchen sitting around the old pine table, drinking coffee and crunching toast, suited and booted for the day. Dark suits. Black ties. Nothing frivolous. Nothing colourful.

'Can I get you anything to eat, Mother?' Patrick asks. 'Cereal? Toast? Boiled eggs? Bagels? Muffins?'

I shake my head. 'No, thanks.'

'Perhaps you should have something?' Ralph interjects.

'I really can't manage to eat.'

After what seems like hours, the hearse and the funeral car arrive; waiting outside our house like black shiny beacons of distress and unhappiness. We travel inside the funeral car and follow the hearse to the local church. I sit looking out of the front of the car, watching the hearse containing the stiff carcass that is all that remains of you, and I feel distant, as if this is not really happening.

We arrive at the church. It is a pretty church built in pale stone, with a gothic clock tower. Small stone crosses dotted across the apex of the roof. You used to attend this church with Susan, didn't you? Before she was too ill to go. It is a grey day. We step out of the car. It isn't raining, but the air is damp, as if it is about to drizzle at any moment. The moisture in the air seeps out onto my hair, onto my shoulders, I feel damp as I float into the church on Ralph's arm; Patrick and Janice behind us.

Jack's family, whom I have never met but recognise from photographs, are sitting at the very front, to the right-hand side of the aisle. His mother, his father, his sister. And Susan's mother, a widow, whom I also recognise from photographs, is sitting to the left. Our family sit a couple of rows behind her.

I turn my head and watch the church filling up. You were the head of the local school, so people arrive in droves. Teachers. Parents. Pupils. Ex-pupils. Friends from church. The church is full and yet still more people arrive. They are crushed together at the back of the church in front of the tower. They line the sides and stand squashing towards the pews.

The music begins. Toccata in Fugue by JS Bach. The pallbearers step along the aisle in time to the heavy beat of the organ. Through the numbness of the diazepam my heart still breaks in two as I witness the start of your last journey. I close my eyes. I cannot bear to watch a second longer.

When I open my eyes, the oak coffin draped with a cloth bearing the school colours is standing in front of the altar, between the choir stalls. And the choir have arrived from the vestry, angelic in their frilly high-necked cassocks with kind, sincere faces.

The vicar stands in the front of the church, wearing his white robes, reserved for celebration days, weddings and funerals. If only I could press a button and swap celebrations.

'It is with great sadness that we are here today to grieve our friend and church member, Jack Rutherford, so few months after the loss of his wife, Susan. So often when a couple love each other as intensely as Susan and Jack did, the death of one is followed all too quickly by the death of the other.'

My stomach tightens. This is going to be more difficult than I even imagined. Does everyone think you jumped off the cliff because you couldn't bear to be without Susan, when you were about to be the happiest you had ever been with me? Despite the fact I was your next of kin, and we were about to be married. Despite the fact all your relatives know I organised the funeral. I take a deep breath. It doesn't matter. Nothing matters except for the fact you're not here. Our relationship was for us. Or at least I always thought it was.

The service rolls on in front of me. We stand up. We sing a hymn 'Now Thank We All Our God'. Your sister, Helen, a stout woman with short wavy hair, is invited to the front by the vicar. She reads your favourite poem from childhood – *The Owl and the Pussy-Cat*. It was both of our favourite poem from childhood, wasn't it? I swallow hard to hold back tears.

Another hymn – 'Almighty, Invisible, God Only Wise'. If God was so wise would he have allowed you to be taken away from me? The words, *Almighty invisible God is not there,* resonate in my mind.

Your father, a former teacher too, who at eighty-two looks exactly like the senior citizen you might have become, is standing at the microphone now, smart in grey and black tweed, and a black trilby hat. He taps the mic for a sound check; a professional even in the throes of grief. He talks about your passion to be a teacher. Your love of your school. Your wife. His words float away from me into the distance. Somewhere in the distance I hear myself cry.

Another hymn, by now I don't know or care which hymn anyone is singing. The grinding religious caterwauling ends. The vicar is introducing me. Ralph is nudging me. I shake my head to warn the vicar that I am too overcome to step to the front and read the poem I wrote to you. The vicar steps towards me and leans into our pew.

'Is it too much for you?' he whispers.

I nod my head and bite my lip to suppress tears. Ralph holds my hand more tightly. The service moves on to the last hymn.

Toccata in Fugue again. You are carried out in state by six pallbearers. The congregation follows the stately procession as it winds its way down the aisle, out to the left of the church, towards the burial ground. The grinding drizzle has now become heavy rain. Ralph opens his umbrella and puts his arm around me to shelter me.

We gather around the open grave. The silence in the air so thick it could be cut with a knife. I stand looking at the ground, at my feet dressed in black patent leather, at the grass and mud beneath.

'To everything there is a season, and a time to every purpose on earth. A time to be born and a time to die. Here in this last act, in sorrow but without fear, in love and appreciation, we commit Jack Rutherford to his natural end.'

The vicar's words float around me as I stand holding Ralph's hand. If I wasn't holding his hand, I would collapse.

Your coffin is lowered next to Susan's grave. Earth is scattered. Your mother bows her head and throws a red rose on top of the oak casket. My body crumples against Ralph's as I watch it land with a thud.

149

Ralph

You lean against me as we walk away from the burial. I have my arm around you. I smell your Rive Gauche scent. Taste the closeness of your breath. Jack is safely buried. No more questions. No more answers. My heart sings with love. We can be together as a family now.

150
Sarah

York House, Twickenham. Do you remember? How could you forget? It is where we were about to get married. A French-style chateau, built by a courtier of King Charles I, in the seventeenth century, somehow bequeathed to Richmond borough council. We stand in a panelled room looking out onto formal gardens that rival the summer borders at Wisley; lilies, roses, delphiniums, dahlias, pinks. But instead of our marriage celebration, it is your wake. And instead of pale pink silk and happiness, I am swathed in black linen and misery.

Smartly dressed staff, black themed and funeral appropriate, are standing at the entrance bearing trays of Chablis, merlot and fruit juice. Cups of tea are being served from an urn in the corner. A simple fare of sandwiches, crisps and quiche, cupcakes and biscuits, has been laid out on the side. People are huddled together in groups, heads down chatting, voices quiet. So many people. Pupils, teachers, church congregation, friends, family and two policemen. Ralph, Patrick, Janice and I are standing together, between the tea urn and the sandwiches, sipping glasses of wine. The merlot tastes rough, heavy on my tongue.

'The service went well, don't you think?' Ralph beams.

'I suppose so. Personally, I would rather we were somewhere else. Anywhere else, actually,' I reply.

'That goes without saying. Of course it would be better if it wasn't necessary,' he replies. 'I was just making conversation.'

I bite my lip, put my hand on his arm and squeeze it. 'I know. I'm sorry. Thank you for being here.'

Someone taps me on the shoulder. I turn around. It is your mother, Jack. Her sharply cut white hair frames her strong face. She is wearing a black suit and a lilac blouse. Amethyst earrings. Amethyst is her birth stone, isn't it? Lilac is her favourite colour. After seeing so many photographs and watching her at the funeral, I know exactly who she is.

'I'm Jack's mother, Annette,' she tells me.

'So I gathered.' I shake her hand. 'It's good to meet you, I'm Sarah.'

She beams at me. 'That wasn't hard to guess.' She looks embarrassed and grimaces. 'I know this sounds awkward, but until Jack died, I didn't realise you were his next of kin. After Susan died, Jack's father and I sort of assumed we were.' She pauses. I look into eyes so like Jack's I can hardly bear it. 'You were in a relationship with my son? About to get married?'

I take a deep breath. 'Jack and I had been close friends for years. We met through his school. I teach there. And we had recently become partners. We didn't want to upset you, or Susan's family, so soon after Susan's death.' I pause. I swallow back tears. 'But yes, we were in love. And about to announce our engagement to you all.'

'You poor darling girl,' she says. 'If only.'

She takes me in her arms and holds me tight. So very tight. She smells of sadness and Opium perfume.

151

Ralph

I am standing watching you, Sarah, fraternising with Jack's mother. looking into each other's eyes. Laughing. Smiling. Crying. Hugging. So tightly. Oh, so very tight. Don't get too involved with this woman. We are a family again. After so many years, you must get ready to come home to us.

152

Sarah

Your wake is over. Ralph, Patrick, Janice and I are stepping out of York House to walk to my house a few minutes away in central Twickenham. It's raining really hard now. A pelting sheet of grey shrouds the world in front of us. We shelter beneath the stone porch of the entrance.

The two officers I noticed at your wake, Jack, are walking up the entrance steps towards us. They must be friends of yours. The man has blondish – almost brown – hair, a short pudding-basin haircut, and golden skin. The woman has shoulder-length, slightly red hair, cut in a bob. She has a sharp nose and pert round lips. Something about her reminds me of the supermodel Lily Cole.

I stand watching them walking towards us in the rain and I wonder, Jack, how you knew them. Are they ex-pupils? Why were they at the wake in uniform? Were they educational officers who used to visit our school? If they were, I don't remember them, but then my mind is all over the place at the moment.

They move closer and closer. Perhaps they have left something at the venue. We step to one side to allow them to pass into the building. They change course and veer towards us. The man stands in front of Ralph.

'Ralph Kensington, I am arresting you on suspicion of the murders of Jack Rutherford and Gemma Richardson. You do not have to say anything. But it may harm your defence if you do not mention when questioned something which you may later rely on in court. Anything you do say may be given in evidence.'

Ralph stands in front of the police office looking stupefied.

'A request has been received that you be extradited to stand trial in Italy, and pending the determination of that application, you will be held in custody.'

He slips his arms behind Ralph's back and cuffs him. All the blood rushes from my head. I put my right hand onto the wall of York House to steady myself. Sirens wail. Two police cars come screeching around the corner and slide to a stop. I watch the male police officer bundle Ralph into the first one. Ralph struggles against him, but with his hands cuffed behind his back, there is nothing he can do to escape.

Flower-faced Lily Cole steps towards the rest of us; Patrick, Janice and me. 'My name is DS Joanne Covington,' she says. 'Please, may we talk?'

'Of course.'

'Do you want to come to the police station? Or could I come to your house? That would be more private.'

153
Ralph

The prick of a police officer bundles me into the back of a police car roughly, as if I am a dead piece of meat, not a human being.

'What's all this about, you dick?' I snarl. 'You're dealing with the wrong person if you think it's all right to behave like this.'

He sits next to me in the back of the car, eyeballing me.

'Are you threatening me?' he asks.

The driver starts the engine.

'I explained when I arrested you,' the prick continues. 'I'll go through it again when we reach the custody suite.'

154
Sarah

'If you don't mind, it's been a long day, so I'd like to go home. We can talk there,' I tell DS Covington.

Almost as soon as we get in the police car it's time to get out. Deposited outside 2 Lebanon Park, with Patrick, Janice and DS Covington; legs weak, body trembling. As I fumble and rummage for my keys from the bowels of my outsized handbag, Janice stands next to me and whispers from the corner of her mouth, 'What's going on? Why the hell have they arrested *Dad*?'

'I've no idea,' I reply. 'I suspect we are about to find out.'

I open the door and we step into my hallway.

'I'll put the kettle on. I expect everyone could do with a cuppa,' Patrick announces, and disappears into the kitchen. 'It might help keep us calm.'

Janice, DS Covington and I walk into the living room. I flop into the kid leather Chesterfield. Janice sits next to me and takes my hand in hers. DS Covington perches on the armchair opposite us.

'I'm so sorry to be bothering you, today of all days, when you have just buried your fiancé. But it's important. Let's wait until your son comes in with the tea, so I can explain what's happened to you all at the same time.'

We sit in silence. I look down at the deep pile cream carpet.

Patrick steps into the room with a tray of tea. He pours us all a mug, and hands them out. He sits in the armchair by the mantelpiece next to DS Covington. She takes a sip of tea, puts her mug on the mat on the coffee table in front of her, and crosses her shapely legs.

'Let me explain. Ralph Kensington has been arrested today on suspicion of the murders of Jack Rutherford and Gemma Richardson. We expect he will be extradited to Italy to face trial.'

'This is a terrible shock.' I shake my head in disbelief. 'We didn't even know Gemma was dead. We thought she was travelling,' I say, body trembling. 'And Ralph wouldn't have been cruel enough to kill my fiancé. He loves me far too much for that. He's a kind man, not a monster.'

'It can't be true. My father's not a murderer! He's never been violent. I've never even seen him squash an ant.' Patrick's eyes are dark with anger. 'Someone else must have killed them. Gemma was travelling. Dad wasn't even with her.'

Janice says nothing, but her eyes well with tears.

'Sadly, I can assure you the Italian police have plenty of evidence against him for the crimes. If they hadn't, they wouldn't be able to request extradition. Gemma's body has been found close to the villa. I expect Mr Kensington will be in Italy in less than a fortnight. He'll be held in custody until then. These crimes are far too serious for bail to be considered.'

We sit in stupefied silence, a silence so deep that the ticking of the clock on the mantelpiece sounds like a gong.

After a while DS Covington asks, 'Would you like me to arrange for a family liaison officer to visit?'

I cannot believe this is happening. I put my head back and scream.

155
Ralph

Frogmarched into the custody suite by the prick of a police officer who is obviously wearing fake tan – the key to his honeyed good looks. He introduces me to a custody officer, who is wearing a blue cotton uniform. First, I am hand searched, and my jacket, tie, shoes, belt, watch and iPhone are removed. Then I am passed through a scanning machine as if I'm a piece of luggage. A mugshot is taken. I'm fingerprinted. A swab of my DNA is taken with what looks like a cotton bud.

'One last thing,' the custody officer says, 'do you have your own legal representation, or do you want me to call the duty solicitor?'

I give a nonchalant shrug. 'I'm bemused as to why I need legal representation, given the fact I haven't committed a crime. But if it is on offer, I'll take the duty solicitor – thanks.'

Re-cuffed, far too tightly, I am escorted to a holding cell.

They call it a holding cell but actually it is more like a plastic bubble with a shelf moulded into one wall to be used as a bed. A frog-eyed video camera is mounted high above me, monitoring me twenty-four-seven, even when I go to the plastic toilet in the corner. Deliberately intimidating. Deliberately claustrophobic.

But I will not let the bastards grind me down. This won't take long. They've got nothing on me. I'll be back home with you very soon, Sarah, my sweet.

I lie on the plastic shelf reliving the day. The relief I felt as Jack's body was lowered into the ground. The warmth that spread through me as our family stood at the top of the steps of York House at the end of the wake, about to walk to your house together, Sarah. The one you bought with our divorce settlement. Imagine the mansion we will be able to live in when we sell both houses and move back in together. This business with the police is a temporary blip.

Bored of waiting, I fall asleep and slip into a dream. Arriving at the Villa Panorama, this time it is just the four of us; you, me, Patrick and Janice. No appendages. No hangers on. Just the way it should be. Sarah, you step into the master bedroom with me.

You move towards me and hug me. 'Happy birthday, darling.' You kiss me. A real snog of a kiss. The sort of snog that with us always used to lead to sex.

But you pull away and beam at me with a smile in your eyes.

'I can't wait a second longer to give you your birthday present.' You open your handbag. You pull out a small rectangular gift-wrapped present resplendent with ribbons and bows. 'Here you are,' you say, pressing it into my hands and kissing me again.

I rip away the paper to reveal a small leather box engraved in gold filigree with the name of the local jewellers in Praiano. Déjà vu. You gave me these cufflinks before, in real life. I open the box knowing what I will find; silver cufflinks engraved with my initials.

In my dream – for somehow I know it is a dream, even though I am moving through it as if it's real – I open the box. It's is empty except for maggots. Maggots, wriggling and squirming and swarming inside. I put back my head and scream. 'What's the matter with you, Sarah?' I shout.

The sound of my voice wakes me, and I sit up and bang my head on the plastic ceiling above it. Not wanting to go to sleep again, I slip from my plastic cocoon and begin to pace.

After hours and hours of pacing, or at least that is what it feels like as I have no way of telling the time, the cell door opens. A custody officer steps inside. He is tall, thin and pointy, with dark blue eyes.

'Come with me,' he instructs. 'It's time to go to the interview room.'

He leads me there along a pale, plastic corridor. He opens the door and I step inside a small room with no windows to find a woman wearing civilian clothes; dark suit and cerise-pink blouse, sitting, waiting. She looks up as we enter.

'Ralph Kensington, I presume?' she asks.

I nod.

'How do you do, I'm Jasmine Norrington, your duty solicitor.' She turns her head to the pointy custody officer. 'Can we have the room, please?' she demands.

'Of course. I'll leave you for ten minutes. And then I'll return with my assistant to carry out the interview.'

We watch him close the door behind him. 'What's going on, Mr Kensington?' she asks. 'Tell me the truth here. Could they have sufficient evidence to convict you?'

'No way. I haven't done anything.'

'Well then, you're fine. As long as you are being honest, you are fine. They won't have enough evidence to request your extradition. They are just trying this on to try and frighten you.'

'But . . . but . . . why would they want to do that?'

'Needing to try and boost their conviction figures. Picking on anyone and anything they can find.'

There is a knock on the door. It opens and a police officer steps inside.

'How do you do? I'm DI Robert Stephenson,' he says. 'And my DS is about to join us.'

Even as he speaks a subtle redhead enters the room. Hair in

a severe cut. Large green eyes. 'DS Covington reporting for duty,' she says with a thin, tight-lipped smile.

DS Covington and DI Stephenson sit down opposite my duty solicitor, Jasmine Norrington, and me.

DI Stephenson leans forwards towards me. 'Let me explain what's happening here. The Italian authorities have applied for permission to extradite you to Italy to face a double murder charge. They are accusing you of murdering Jack Rutherford and Gemma Richardson.'

'Gemma's dead? I thought I must have misheard earlier,' I say with a gasp. 'That's dreadful news. I need time to grieve. It is ridiculous to accuse me of murder.'

'The Italian police have persuasive evidence. Some downloaded from Gemma's phone, which they found abandoned in a hotel in Rome, links you to Jack's murder. And they have now found Gemma's body with further evidence linked to you.'

'Whatever you say, we will be opposing the extradition application, in the hearing at Westminster Magistrates Court next week,' Jasmine Norrington announces, eyes hard, mouth in a line.

156
Sarah

The police are allowing me one visit to Ralph in the custody suite. One short, sharp visit, in case he is extradited next week. Since your funeral, Jack, and Ralph's arrest, I haven't been able to think very clearly and I have hardly been able to eat. Term has started. I have forced myself to go back into school, to teach on a part-time basis. I can't bear to walk past your old office. I enter via the side entrance so that I do not have to see the temporary head sitting at your desk. I sit head down during assembly and try not to listen too hard. It hurts me to hear her thin straggly voice addressing the students after the intensity and resonance of yours. It hurts me to hear her limp comments after the jaunty wit of yours. I have applied for a transfer, to any other secondary school in the borough. I need a fresh start. Orleans Park Twickenham are considering me.

But the temporary head at Twickenham School Whitton, despite not having your inspirational qualities, is kind enough. She has given me a half day off to visit Ralph in prison. So here I am, being taken into the custody suite by DS Covington, pushing my handbag and coat through an X-ray machine, stomach in knots.

DS Covington and I walk along the corridor, towards the meeting room. We stand outside. She stands in front of me. She is elegant with an aquiline nose that makes her seem a little haughty, and she looks down it a little as she speaks.

'Before you go in, there are a few things I need to tell you.' She takes a breath. 'If you feel threatened, there's a button you can press. It's beneath the table, on the side you will be sitting at, to your immediate right. If you press it a silent alarm will sound and one of us will come in immediately,' she continues. 'Your conversation is private. But we will be watching, from the other side of the window. If he does anything that looks threatening, we'll be straight in, without you even needing to press the button. We'll have you well covered, I can assure you.'

'I'm not scared. I know he won't hurt me.'

'He's been accused of double murder. Take my advice – don't be complacent. There is no smoke without fire.' She smiles at me, and knocks on the door. She presses a security code and the door slides open. 'Off you go. Good luck.'

I step inside the room. The door closes behind me. Ralph is sitting on a plastic chair, drumming his fingers on the plastic table in front of him. His fingernails are bitten to the quick. He has bags beneath his eyes and I know he hasn't been sleeping. He is wearing clothes that I have never seen before; blue trousers and a shapeless blue T-shirt. They must belong to the custody suite.

'Hello,' I say, and give him an awkward smile as I sit down opposite him.

'Hi,' he replies, holding my eyes in his. 'Thanks for coming.'

I sigh inside. 'I can hardly say it's my pleasure. Everything that has happened to us all lately is awful.'

He pushes his hair back from his eyes. It needs a good cut. It needs a wash. 'Think yourself lucky. Try being in here.' A wry smile flickers for a second, across his lips. 'And just in case you were thinking of giving me a passionate bear hug, we're not allowed to touch and we're being watched.'

I do not smile back. 'I know. I was told.' I pause. 'Our conversation is private though, I think.'

He looks towards the camera in the corner. 'They do not have the sound on, but I bet they are trying to lip read – aren't you?' He leans further in towards the camera. 'Aren't you?' he repeats over exaggerating the movement of his lips.

'Why would they do that?' I ask.

He grimaces and leans towards me, hands shielding his mouth. 'I guess they're trying to catch me out.'

I lean away from him. 'Why do they need to try and catch you out? Haven't you already told them the truth? What's happening? Why have you been arrested? What have they discovered about you?'

He sighs. A long, deep, tired sigh. 'It's ridiculous. They say they have enough evidence to convict me of the murders of Jack and Gemma. It must all be fabricated. The Italian legal system is a fragmented mess. Look at the chaos over the Amanda Knox case.'

My eyes widen. 'If the evidence is flimsy and fabricated, surely extradition will be refused at the hearing next week?'

'That's what my barrister thinks.' He pauses. 'They'll conclude that Jack committed suicide, and will know nothing about Gemma and the rape.' His eyes shine with determination. 'They'll realise that someone, other than me, must have killed Gemma and so I will not be extradited.' He puts his hands out in front of him, flat palmed, and cuts them across one another. 'End of.' A pause. 'And no one, except you, me and Gemma, will ever know what Jack did.' He looks across at me, eyes wide and empathetic. 'I'm so sorry that it turned out you had such a difficult fiancé.'

I never found you difficult. I am broken without you. His words burn into me. He leans across the plastic table and tries to take both my hands in his. I pull away from him and stand up.

DS Covington bursts into the meeting room accompanied by two custody officers dressed in blue.

'Interview terminated. Take the prisoner back to his cell.'

157

Ralph

The police van taking me to Westminster Magistrates Court is like a cattle truck. I am sitting, cuffed, hands behind my back, on a bench in a moving cell, with a window so high I cannot see out of it. The van screeches to a halt. The brakes must need oiling.

The door to my cattle truck cell is opened and I am manhandled out by two loutish guards. One has BO and a beer belly that makes him look pregnant. The other dandruff, and a death tattoo; a serpent from the bowels of hell. I am dragged down the steps from the van. Pulled up the steps at the back of court through the prisoner's entrance. I'm body searched, X-rayed and escorted to a holding cell to await the hearing.

The holding cell contains a small plastic bench-seat welded to the ground. No toilet. No bed. No windows. Anger pulsates inside me. How dare they treat me like this. I close my eyes and picture a landscape of tree-covered mountains and deep cool fjords in an attempt to relax. I breathe deeply and picture I am hiking along a forest path.

I'm hopeful this is the end of it. My barrister is optimistic of a good outcome and so am I. The Italian authorities must be bluffing. They cannot really have anything to tie me to Gemma's body. How could they? And everybody knows that Jack was suicidal after losing his wife.

Hours go by. Despite forests and fjords, my body falls into sleepy despondency. And by the time the door to my cell opens I feel diminished and barely alive. A female guard with rugby-player shoulders and sapphire eyes steps inside. She smells of embrocation. Its aroma of stale menthol fills the cell and makes me cough.

'Are you all right?' she asks.

'I suppose so,' I reply.

She leads me to the court room along a myriad of corridors, enveloping me with her musty aroma. She takes me to sit next to my barrister, Jane Somerville. She is towards the end of the middle-aged spectrum with strong, solid grey hair. She looks up, nods at me and then continues to read the papers in front of her.

The court clerk, a portly, ruddy young man, stands. 'Court rise,' he shouts.

We all stand. The judge enters the room. He is skinny with a thin face and a long nose. He is wearing large, silver-rimmed glasses that make him look a bit like Joe 90. Jane arranges her papers on the desk, and sits watching him attentively. The judge sits. We all copy him.

'Italian extradition application against Ralph Kensington,' the clerk announces loudly.

'Mr Rees, I understand you are acting for the Italian authorities in this matter?' the judge asks.

Mr Rees stands up from his seat in the far-left corner of the court. He is broad and beamy with floppy Etonian hair and small round glasses. He pushes his glasses back hard against the bridge of his nose. He leans forwards and gathers his papers from the desk in front of him. He stands, feet apart, shoulders wide, takes a deep breath and starts.

'Can I check you received documents A, B and C, your Honour?' he asks the judge.

The judge nods. 'Yes, thank you, Mr Rees.'

He turns to my barrister. 'And, Ms Somerville, for the defendant?'

Jane Somerville stands up. 'Yes, thank you. I've read and digested all the information.' She sits down hurriedly.

'Would you like me to run you through all the points, your Honour?'

'That won't be necessary, Mr Rees. I found your written summary most helpful.'

Mr Rees nods. 'Then I have no further points or questions. All the evidence against Mr Kensington is clearly detailed in the paperwork.' He sits down, face closed; tight lipped.

Worry begins to simmer inside me. Why don't they just spit out what they think they know about me so that Jane Somerville can argue the toss? Do I really have to go all the way to Italy to explain myself?

The judge is staring at my barrister.

'Ms Somerville, you are acting for Ralph Kensington. I will hear you now,' the judge says.

Jane Somerville stands and pushes her thick grey hair from her eyes. She holds her papers in front of her. They are quivering a little. I suppose even experienced barristers are nervous sometimes.

'I submit that Ralph Kensington should not be extradited to Italy due to lack of proof that he has committed any crime.' Her voice is husky and manly, her vowels elongated. 'The autopsy concluded that Jack Rutherford committed suicide,' she continues. 'Gemma Richardson's body has been too damaged by its cement casing to give sufficient proof of her cause of death.' She takes a breath. 'Ralph Kensington is a kind man. And a family man. He had invited his family on a special holiday to celebrate his birthday. He had just asked Gemma to marry him. It is clear he has been devastated by her demise.

I wish to request that our state respects this man's personal rights and keeps him here.'

The judge nods his head. 'Thank you very much, Ms Somerville; clearly and succinctly put.'

Jane sits down and looks across at me, pleased with herself, eyes shining into mine. She nods her head at me, chin jutting with confidence.

I watch the judge flick through the papers in front of him, a frown passing briefly across his face. He stands and the court rises. I stand waiting; hopefully, expectant of release.

He coughs to clear his throat. 'This is a serious case, with dire consequences if the perpetrator of such dreadful crimes goes unchecked.' He pauses and looks straight at me. 'Extradition request for Ralph Kensington to be tried in Italy is granted.'

158

Janice

Mother, Patrick and I are sitting in the river garden at the White Swan pub in Twickenham, surrounded by overflowing baskets of yellow and purple winter pansies. Sharing a bottle of Fleurie. The river is meandering past, flashing to silver in the autumn sunshine. The yacht club is out racing; sails slicing through the wind as they slip down the river. A pair of single sculls power past, long lazy strokes gliding through the metallic water. The river birds squawk.

The leaves are dying and their swansong forms a cascade of gold and russet; falling from the trees that line the riverbank.

'So Dad's being extradited today,' Mum says, topping up our glasses. 'I expect he will be on a plane as we speak. How are you coping with that?'

'To tell you the truth, I have compartmentalised what's happened,' Patrick replies. 'I've put it in a box in the corner of my mind and I only get it out to consider it from time to time.' He pauses. 'I know it's cowardly, but it's the only way I can cope with my life.'

I don't reply. I sip my wine and watch two swans glide towards the stony beach. I don't want to upset Patrick and Mother, but I am beginning to fear that Father is guilty; the British government would not have allowed him to be extradited lightly.

'What about you, Mum?' I eventually ask.

'These days I don't think, I just concentrate on breathing,' she replies, with tears in her eyes.

159
Sarah

It is my school lunchbreak. I have started a new job at the comprehensive in the centre of Twickenham, Orleans Park. It's very convenient and it only takes me two minutes to walk there. I accepted a demotion to speed my exit from Twickenham School Whitton. I am no longer a head of English. I am simply a teacher of A-level English; steeped in war poetry, Shakespeare and Dickens. I could no longer bear to be at the school you had been head of for so long, and not see you there, beaming at me in the corridor. Sitting next to me in the canteen at lunchtime. So as of yesterday, I am covering maternity leave for a young woman at the rival local comprehensive. It is a change. An effort to move my life forwards.

I'm sitting on a bench on the Embankment in Twickenham, eating an M&S prawn sandwich and sipping a bottle of mineral water, watching the Thames slip slowly by. The sun paints the surface of the river to a burnished dirty gold. The benches that line the river are all occupied with students and office workers, jackets buttoned up tightly, devouring their lunchtime snacks in an air of intimate silence.

An elderly lady, blanketed in layers of jumpers, stands by the slipway feeding bread to the ducks and swans, which have gathered around the water at her feet, jostling for position. A cabin cruiser putters past. It is a chilly day, deep into autumn.

I sit and watch the young people on the benches and think of you, Jack. About how much I loved you. About how difficult it is for me to accept that you raped Gemma. I close my eyes and try to picture that last evening we spent together just outside Amalfi. Sitting eating fresh pizza and drinking wine. Trying to pretend we were relaxed when actually we were worried the effect the news of our relationship would have on all of those around us. Ralph making an embarrassing speech, an inappropriate eulogy to me, before announcing our engagement. The way he asked me to come for 'a romantic moonlit walk'.

I went, Jack, because I wanted to appease him; to reassure him of our friendship. Looking back I realise I had looked across the table and seen your hand on Gemma's arm as you chatted to her over dinner. Your eyes met as you passed her the salad. Was there a spark? Did she encourage you, and then reject you? I imagine you holding her down, tearing her clothes off. Did I only ever meet part of your needs? Were you a different person when you were with me?

No. You were always so helpful, so kind, so supportive. A rapist is a power-crazy thug. My mind yet again returns to the last night we spent together in Praiano. After all the trouble with Ralph, and you helped me guide him back to the villa, and we made love. Do you remember, Jack? Our bodies would melt together and it always seemed so right. So natural.

I sit here today watching the autumn breeze ripple across the metallic grey river and know, no one will ever touch me like that again. I shiver and tighten the buttons on my coat. I reach into my pocket and pull out the letter I received this morning. I rip open the envelope. It is from the Italian authorities. I have been subpoenaed as a witness in Ralph's trial. I am due in court in Amalfi two weeks today.

Dreading this, I walk back slowly along the riverbank, leaning on my stick. Back towards my new school. Past the sandpit, the sides of which have been built to look like the prow of a ship, jutting out into the river. A group of toddlers are sitting making sandcastles, their mothers standing together at the edge, heads back laughing.

Past the fountain decorated with giant marble carvings of Renaissance-style naked ladies, so incongruous in this town centre rippling with modern life. I look at my watch. Only fifteen minutes before afternoon school begins.

I begin to walk slowly along the riverbank, past the ferry that takes people over to Ham. Looking to the left across the park at the newly painted Marble Hill House; where a king's mistress once lived. I turn left into the park past the ancient walnut tree. Walking along slowly and thinking. Remembering Gemma pushing me. I tried to stand my ground. I tried to push her back, but she was so much stronger, so much younger than me. I grabbed on to her T-shirt, but she banged my fingers with something that felt hard and metallic. She pulled my hair. She held me. She kicked me in my diaphragm and pushed me off the ledge. I remember the desperate sensation of falling. Falling and floating down to my death, my life moving past me like a film montage. Wind rushed past me. I hurtled downwards faster and faster. I thumped against the ground and the world turned black.

So you raped her and she killed you? How does it add up? Why did she want both of us dead? What was wrong with Gemma? Why was she so unhinged? Will I ever be able to move on from this?

160
Ralph

The prison is a hellhole. Overcrowded and in need of renovation. I am in a cell with two other men and there is not even enough floor space for us all to get out of our beds at the same time.

The morning alarm sounds. My cellmate, Enzo, slips out of his bunk first. I don't speak a word of Italian. My cellmates don't speak a word of English. That's good. At least I don't need to communicate with them. Enzo, a big brutish man with arm and leg muscles the shape of boat fenders, pulls on his trousers with a grunt.

I push my head out from under my blanket and try not to watch. If I catch his eye, he glares back, grits his teeth and tightens his fist, so I never look. I push my eyes steadily down to the floor, as I do every morning. On the floor I see dust, dirt and the dead spider I squashed yesterday. In the corner, I see the remains of its web.

I hear the creaking of the bunk as my second cellmate, Mario, gets up next. He is scraggy and lined. In prison for possessing heroin; just a small amount. They lock you up for years for the smallest misdemeanour over here. Mario looks like Keith Richards, with facial furrows so deep in his skin I imagine I could plant potatoes in them. Again, I must not look, I must not stare. I sigh. Another day of suppressed anger and boredom. When it is my turn I slip out of bed and pull on my tracksuit bottoms and my T-shirt. At least I am allowed to wear my own clothes, the ones that Janice sent over. We do not wash today. There's one shower for thirty-six prisoners here, so we all only shower once a week. And the water is always freezing cold. Because hygiene is so poor, sometimes the cell becomes rather high; feral. If it gets too bad the guards force us to wash by pouring water we have collected from the tap in the kitchen over our most smelly body parts and catch the water in the toilet. For my pride, I try not to let myself get too rancid. The problem is the nose is the most adaptive sensory organ so after a few days we can't smell ourselves.

It's breakfast time. There is nothing as sophisticated as a canteen in this gaol. We cook in our cells. The kitchen area also contains the toilet, which is quite disgusting. It's my turn to cook today. We're having omelettes this morning. Just as I start to cook, Enzo pushes past me and urinates. His flow is strong and urine splashes onto my leg. I wince and try to ignore the strong stench of ammonia. He finishes and pushes roughly past me without flushing the toilet. I bite my lip and try to ignore the stench. Breathe. Breathe. The stench of piss won't kill me, I tell myself.

I crack the eggs and whip them and add a little salt and pepper. I fry Enzo's first and step out of the kitchenette to hand it to him. Because there is no mess area in this prison, we eat sitting on our bunks. This prison is inhumane. Nothing to do. No gym. No library. No luxury of prison jobs to help train prisoners and keep them amused. In this place life stops. We only spend four hours in every twenty-four outside our cells. We have two lots of two hours in the yard, with nothing to do but pace. At least it's autumn. In the summer it's so brutally hot some prisoners do not even leave their cells at all.

'*E bruciato*,' – it's burnt – Enzo shouts.

He turns to me and punches me, full throttle on the chin. I almost collapse, but I put my hand on the bunk to steady myself and manage to stay upright. I taste the salt of blood in my mouth and gag. I rush to the toilet and spit into Enzo's urine. A tooth comes out in the bowl. I feel into my mouth with my finger. It is the second molar from the back at the right. I'll need to try and gargle with salt water to prevent it from becoming infected.

I swallow the next flow of blood, pull myself together, and begin to whip the eggs for Mario's omelette. I fry it more carefully this time. I hand it to him; it is still a little brown at the edges as the electric ring only has one temperature and that is too hot. But Mario is my easy cellmate. He smiles.

'*Grazie.*'

A guard is standing outside the railings that act as walls to our cell. Our cell is not a cell but a cage. This cell is not private. The guards can see us through the railings any time they walk past. Maybe with cellmates like Enzo that's a good thing. At least a guard might notice if he was slaughtering me.

The guard standing there is a blond man of about thirty; he looks a bit like Sting did in his youth. He's one of the kinder guards who's never struck me or shouted at me.

'*Ralph Kensington, vieni con me.*'

I'm picking up enough Italian to know that means come with me.

So I slip along the narrow space between the bunks to get to him. Enzo sticks his leg out and trips me up. I land head first, my forehead thumping against the bars of the cell. I reel back and rub my head with my hand. When I look at my hand I see it's sticky with blood. Enzo puts his head back and laughs. I see the gaps in his teeth. Half of them are missing. The guard shouts at Enzo and he shouts back. I do not understand what is passing between them, but it doesn't sound friendly.

The guard opens the cell door and I step out. He locks it again with a rusty key. This prison needed refurbishing fifty years ago. I have the same problem with the guards as I do with the prisoners. They do not speak English. I do not speak Italian.

The young guard checks my forehead and nods at me, as if he is trying to tell me it's OK. He leads me along the corridor in silence. He takes me to a small stone-walled room where my lawyer is waiting.

My lawyer's name is Antonio Russo. He studied law at the university of Bologna. He is wearing a dapper suit and pointed shoes. He has Al Pacino good looks. I was lucky to get hold of him. An ex-colleague found him; tracked him down for me. I'm not welcome back at my investment bank, Heart and Simmonds, now. I've been made redundant. Antonio Russo is costing me a lot of money. But it will be worth every penny if I can get out of this shit hole. And then, when I've been exonerated, I'll get another job.

'Good morning, Ralph,' Antonio says in perfect English. 'Please sit.'

I sit on the plastic chair opposite him.

'How are you keeping?' he asks, flashing me a tooth-whitened smile.

Bruised, battered and tired, I look at him and shrug my shoulders.

'I've come to let you know your trial starts in two weeks,' he continues. 'Is there anything further you would like to explain?'

I shake my head slowly. 'I can assure you, Mr Russo, I've told you everything I know.'

'I certainly hope you have,' he says with a smile. He leans towards me and holds my gaze. 'I want to explain to you that a criminal trial here is rather different from one in the UK.'

I shrug. 'I can cope with that. Spill the beans,' I say.

He takes a sip of water from the plastic cup in front of him. I notice his carefully clipped fingernails. 'There's no jury in the British sense. Instead they have six lay judges who've been elected and work full time. So there's not all the chop and change of the UK system; swearing in different juries every few weeks.' He pauses. 'Instead, the lay judges will decide whether you are guilty or innocent. Two professional judges run the case. They can interrupt the trial at any stage and ask whatever questions they deem necessary. If you are found guilty, they will sentence you.'

Listening to the court procedure is making me feel agitated.

'The equivalent barrister to the prosecution barrister in the UK is the *pubblico ministero*. He or she will be the person who cross-examines you, but don't be surprised if the judges chip in,' Antonio continues.

I watch him take another sip of water. 'I don't suppose I could have a cup?' I ask.

'Oh, sorry, of course.'

He presses a buzzer on the table in front of him and a guard appears.

'*Un'altr tazza e un po'd'acqua per favore*,' he asks.

The guard disappears and returns a few minutes later with another plastic cup and a plastic jug of water. I pour myself a cup and take a sip. It is tepid and tastes of chlorine. What I would give for a beer, a glass of wine or a G&T.

'Be polite. Be succinct. Be honest. That's the best way to keep on the right side of the judges,' Antonio continues.

'What do you think my chances are?' I ask, voice plaintive.

'If everything you have told me is true, fifty-fifty. But you can appeal. In Italy there are very strong rights of appeal. But it's a slow process. Sometimes the appeal process takes as long as twenty years.'

'And during that time, I'd be stuck in here?'

He leans across the table and puts his hand on mine. 'Come on, Ralph. One stage at a time. Let's not go there yet.'

161
Sarah

Our plane lands at Naples airport on a cloudy October day, and we disembark. We wait at the baggage console, surrounded by the enthusiastic rattle of the Italian language. Italian men are so flamboyant and talkative. Always flirting or gossiping. All too often waving their arms and hands in the air as they speak. And the women always sound as if they are scolding, shaking their heads at their partners.

Janice turns to look at me, eyes bursting with emotion.

'Are you all right, Mum?' she asks.

'Don't ask. I don't know where to start to reply. I told you in Twickenham, at least I'm breathing and moving. That's better than poor Jack. And you?'

She smiles a sad, slow smile. 'I'm OK at the moment. It's all the risperidone I've been gobbling. And the endless CBT sessions.'

Patrick stands apart, phoning the taxi driver we pre-booked, trying to find out where we should meet him. I look across at my son, pressed to his iPhone, standing there, seemingly ten years older since Anna left him. Thin and tired. All the excitement that once was there seems to have been drained by his medical course. I know he said he was compartmentalising, but when he takes the lid off the box, will it explode?

Our cases eventually thump along the baggage belt. We collect them and drag them slowly through customs, eyeballed by two overweight and austere officials as we walk past.

We move through the airport to the taxi rank.

The drive to Praiano is a sullen trip. Our driver, Gino, doesn't try to make small talk. Silence settles, apart from the subliminal buzz of the rock-ballad driven radio station he is listening to in the front. And the occasional clatter of the rosary beads hanging from the dashboard, every time he turns, or breaks suddenly.

We see Mount Vesuvius, jutting and proud, to the left, as the taxi thunders along the toll road; shuddering inside as even after all these years I still think about what happened at Herculaneum and Pompeii; all those people and animals instantly dead and preserved for perpetuity in ash.

Later, as on our last journey here, the driver stops to show us the view of Sorrento. A picturesque town, nestled against the cliff and tumbling towards the sea, looked down on from the road above. My heart trembles as I look. Last time, Jack, I had you with me.

We leave the view of Sorrento behind and move inland. We turn onto the magnificent and famous coast road that rolls along the cliffs towards Amalfi. As the view is unleashed beneath me, misery engulfs me. Last time, Jack, you and I were full of hope and expectation. Last time my wedding dress was hanging in my wardrobe in Twickenham. My engagement ring waiting for me in my safe. This time, without you, I look down to admire the engagement ring you gave me. A sapphire surrounded by a cluster of diamonds. The lonely ring that will never sit next to your wedding band. I will treasure it; wear it to the end of my days.

This picture postcard view with its dramatic cliffs, verdant pines and turquoise sequinned sea is so stunning it cuts into me and fills me with regret. Regret so painful I have to close my eyes and concentrate to breathe. I close my eyes and fall again.

Faster and faster. Until I'm shot like a cannonball into deep water and I'm drowning in the sea. I can't think. I can't breathe.

Janice nudges me. 'Mum, we're here.'

I open my eyes. Patrick is fumbling in his pocket for his wallet. He plucks out eighty euros in crisp new twenty euro notes and pays the driver. We get out of the car. The taxi driver, who looks like a cross between Elvis Costello and Phil Silvers, bangs our luggage onto the pavement in front of us, accepts his fare with a nod, and shoots off to his next ride as quickly as he can manage. No smiles. No small talk.

Our hotel is 'boutique', according to booking.com. We look up at a small white villa, with blue shutters. Pots of geraniums brightening up the windowsills.

We step inside into the reception area. A small, panelled room with a wooden chandelier in the middle of the ceiling, which emits a frail yellow light, almost as fragile as candlelight. My eyes blink as they get used to the darkness; after the flood of sunshine outside. The receptionist is a lanky girl wearing a thin black linen dress. A delicate gold cross around her neck. Three pinprick gold studs in each ear. An oil painting of *Madonna and Child* hangs on the wall behind her. She checks us in and hands us three keys attached to heavy wooden tags; the size of bricks. Too heavy to keep in a pocket. She points to some hooks on the wall behind her and makes it obvious that every time we go out, we need to hand them back.

With his father incarcerated, Patrick now seems to consider himself head of the family.

'Let's settle in our rooms and meet here in an hour to go and find somewhere to eat,' he instructs.

Janice and I exchange a glance and nod in agreement – not that I want to meet in an hour. Not that I want anything to eat.

We grunt our cases up to our rooms as there is no lift. My room is very small and decorated with oak panelling like the hallway. A bed and a wardrobe; two side tables with lamps on. That's it. Its advantage is that there is no balcony. No view towards the sea. That's good. I do not want to be reminded of anything that happened last time we were here. I flop across the floral embroidered bedspread that smells of lavender.

I text Patrick. *Scrap dinner for me. I need to be on my own to think.*

OK, Mum. See you tomorrow. Meet you in the restaurant at 7:30 a.m. for breakfast.

I lie on my bed and close my eyes. All I want to do is sleep.

I am woken by the cry of a rooster and sunlight streaming past shutters that were left open last night. I fell asleep before I got undressed. Sweat plasters my clothes against my skin as I rise from the bed and walk towards the window.

The rooster is strutting in the scruffy paved yard behind. A shabby creature with a dull crown and bib, feathers old and mouldy. Weaving between five brown hens who are ignoring him, pecking at the ground for grain. An aged rooster, once a proud cockerel. I feel sorry for him. He looks as if life has knocked the stuffing out of him. I know that feeling.

I turn away from the window and peel off my sweaty clothes. I step into the tepid shower, rubbing my skin hard, as if I were sanding it; closing my eyes, wishing I could wash my problems away. After dressing carefully in the Hobbs dress I wore for your funeral, and spending ages camouflaging my sad face with make-up, I walk downstairs for breakfast.

Janice and Patrick are sitting at a table in the corner of the restaurant, heads together. As soon as they see me they spring apart.

'What's going on? You look like you're plotting something.'

Janice leans across the table and takes my hand. 'We were just worrying about you. How are you feeling?'

'Never better,' I snap.

162

Janice

You have just snapped at me because you are stretched and tense. There was a time when I would have gone off on one if you snapped at me. But my treatment is helping me now. You don't mean it, do you? Travelling here is so difficult for all of us, but especially for you. Patrick and I have to face shattered illusions about the character of our father, but you have to face the possibility that your first husband, and father of your children, has killed the man who was to be your second husband. The love of your life. Your past and your future have both been fragmented.

I wave my hand to get the waitress's attention. She walks briskly to our table.

'*Cappucino, signora, per mia madre, per favore.*'

163

Patrick

Mother sips her cappuccino, but she doesn't want any breakfast. She really needs to put on some weight. She is fragile; thin as a stick. Soon after I ask the receptionist to order a taxi to take us to court, she steps into the restaurant to tell us it has arrived, flashing me a smile. She has a neat face. For a second she reminds me of Anna and pain tears across my stomach.

We sit in silence as the taxi winds its way along the coast road. I sit in the front with the driver; a short squat swarthy man, who drives carefully, eyes fixed to the road. Mother and Janice hold hands in the back. Mother's eyes are closed. Janice is moving her lips; silently chanting. She looks like a mediaeval witch.

We arrive at the courthouse; a characterful old building with an elaborate stone frontage. A look-at-me building in the centre of town. We step inside into the generous marble-floored hallway where our bags and our bodies are X-rayed. I have been studying a crash course in Italian. I go to the reception desk to find out which court we are in. I guide Janice and Mother to court five, where a young man in a dark, tightly tailored suit is sitting on a bench in the corridor outside. As soon as he sees us, he jumps up and walks towards us.

'Hi, I'm Marco, Antonio Russo's assistant. Are you the Kensington family?'

164
Sarah

Inside the Corte d'Assise in Amalfi, feeling sick and dizzy. The young lawyer, Marco, steps towards me and shakes my hand.

'Sarah, I presume?'

'Yes.'

'I'll wait with you, until you are called. Until the clerk comes to fetch you.'

'Thanks.'

Patrick and Janice step towards the court room door, on their way in to listen.

Marco rushes across and blocks their pathway. 'Don't go in. You must wait outside in case you are called as witnesses. You might be needed. And witnesses need to give evidence without knowing what evidence has already been given.'

'OK, OK,' Patrick says. 'We'll go and get a cappuccino or something.'

Their heels click on the stone floor as they disappear down the corridor, leaving me sitting next to Marco on the bench outside court. The bench is formed from wooden slats, which press against my bottom, flattening my muscle, crushing against my bone. I wriggle uncomfortably.

I feel distant, as if I am sitting in a bubble. As if I can see the world but not touch it. My body feels weak; wrists and ankles soft like jelly. I hold my right hand out in front of me. My fingers are trembling. I close my eyes. This will soon be over. Everything passes, even this. Breathe. Breathe.

When I open my eyes again a clerk is at the door to the court, calling us in. Marco stands up, I follow him. I walk towards the clerk, shadowing Marco, taking a deep breath to compose myself.

Into the court room. The first person I see is Ralph, sitting at the front of the court, on the left, as I walk past with the clerk towards a place on the right. He is handcuffed with a prison guard either side of him, wearing a brown suit that I have never seen before. It's far more 'country bumpkin' than what he would usually wear, and it doesn't suit him. The heavy tweed pattern makes him look unsophisticated and old. So different without his Brooks Brothers suit and his Molton Brown haircut. His face has become lined. His eyes look like pinpricks. Perhaps it's fear. Perhaps it's lack of sleep. He nods at me and smiles. I tremble inside. Does he really hope that what I'm going to say will help him?

Despite the ornate ageless style of the building's exterior, this room is small and modern, with new wooden flooring. Lines of modern desks with state-of-the-art microphones and lighting. The clerk shows me to a desk right in front of the two trial judges, who are sitting together at the front in high-backed, wooden, throne-like chairs. They are wearing black flappy ceremonial robes and blouses with Vivienne Westwood new romantic cascading frills. They look as if they should be in a fashion shoot. The judge to the left is about fifty with steel-grey hair and small round glasses. The other is much younger, with black hair and strong eyebrows. His solid, square, handsome face makes me think of Alec Baldwin.

The silence of the court presses against me as I sit down and take a deep breath to compose myself. I look around again.

A young woman with short brown hair stands next to the older judge. She has a neat, slim figure and is wearing a tasteful blue linen dress that clings to her body in all the right places. To the left sit the six lay judges; also robed and frothy with frills. But they are adorned with silk sashes.

The older, grey-haired judge looks across at me and addresses me in Italian. I don't understand a word. Nerves jangle in my stomach.

'Are you Sarah Kensington?' the young woman, who I now realise must be the translator, asks. I nod my head. 'Please stand,' she instructs.

The grey judge spouts gobbledygook. 'Does the defence have any questions for Ms Kensington?' the translator asks.

A young man with *Vogue*-style good looks stands up, pushes his flamboyant fringe from his eyes, and answers in the negative. He must be Antonio Russo, Ralph's lawyer. I have spoken to him on the phone.

'*Chiamare il pubblico ministero*,' the grey judge's voice chimes slowly, accentuating every syllable. It rings around the court room like a death knell.

'Call the public prosecutor,' the translator echoes.

The prosecutor is sat to my left. He unfolds his limbs from his chair and stands up, revealing how tall he is. A man who seems to be all cheekbones and haunting eyes, as if the skin on his face has been stretched straight across his bones with no tissue beneath it. The translator steps forward and stands next to him.

The *pubblico ministero* rattles words towards me, words that leave his mouth as fast as machine-gun fire.

'The autopsy report on your fiancé, Jack Rutherford's, body concluded that he committed suicide. Did you believe that?' the translator repeats in English.

I shake my head. 'No. We were about to get married. He seemed so happy. I couldn't accept it, and I didn't believe for one minute.' I pause. 'But then about a month ago, Ralph told me what really happened.'

A long tirade in Italian as the judges confer.

'Is this information in your witness statement?' the translator asks me.

'No. I gave my witness statement to the police shortly after Jack's death. This information was given to me much later.'

The judges continue to talk to one another. The judges confer with the *pubblico ministero*. The Italian begins to fade and all I can hear is the voice of the translator.

'You may continue. Please explain what you found out,' she demands.

'That Gemma killed my fiancé, because . . . because . . .' I stall, looking at the ground. I feel like crying. I didn't want the police to know this. I do not believe it. But I cannot lie in court.

'Because?' the translator pushes.

'She was bitter, because he raped her.'

The lay judges gasp. The older grey judge is red-faced with surprise.

'Why did you not tell the police this in the first place?'

'I didn't know it when they first interviewed me. Ralph only told me the day before Jack's funeral, and I was just so worried it would damage Jack's reputation, he was so very valued by our local community, so I kept quiet.'

'Did you believe it?'

'I found it hard to. It doesn't fit with my impression of my fiancé's personality.'

'What about Gemma? What did you think happened to her?'

'She went travelling to Rome. I know the police were having a little bit of trouble finding her.' I pause. 'I was really shocked when Ralph was arrested for her murder, after the police found her body. After all, I mean, I lived with Ralph for years.'

The *pubblico ministero* pulls my attention away from the translator. He is giving a loud-voiced lecture in Italian. The translator is listening intently, head on one side.

'Did he ever show signs of violence when you were with him?' she asks.

I look across at Ralph. He is sitting, hands together in his lap, body stiff, staring fixedly at the ground. Blood rushes from my head, but I hold on to my chair and manage to steady myself without fainting.

'He did punch my fiancé in the face, shortly after I told him we were engaged.'

The *pubblico ministero* is tapping his fingers together. 'When was this?'

'The night before Jack disappeared.'

The *pubblico ministero* pushes his dark eyes into mine, forcing me to look at him.

'Why didn't you tell the police?' the translator asks.

I shake my head slowly and swallow. 'I just thought it was natural disappointment. I didn't think he meant serious harm. And anyway, he was inebriated so it was a very weak punch.'

'Do you think punching another person is normal behaviour?'

'No . . .Yes.' I hesitate. 'I mean, not really.'

'Explain what you mean exactly, please. No, yes, is not an answer.'

'I mean, in certain circumstances lashing out is normal. Ralph had been pushed to extremes by my deceit; by the way I didn't tell him about my new relationship when I left him.'

Italian hammers between the judges. The *pubblico ministero* steps forward and joins in. He turns and holds my gaze, again. 'You have misled the police by withholding information. That's all, Mrs Kensington.'

Tears begin to well in my eyes. 'In my wildest dreams I didn't think being touchy when I first told him I was in a new relationship would lead to murder. He was my husband for fifteen years. The father of my children. Why would I think that?'

I am trembling. I am crying. Blood roars in my ears.

165

Janice

Mother steps out of court in floods of tears. She falls into mine and Patrick's arms, trembling like a leaf. She clings on to us like ivy. Father, what have you done to her? What have you done to us?

166

Ralph

I'm sitting in a holding cell in the Corte d'Assise, waiting to be called into court. Today is the pivotal day of the trial. The day I'm being cross-examined by the *pubblico ministero*, so I'm sitting here trying to pump myself up. Trying to feel confident and bullish. Pacing about, widening my shoulders. Breathing deeply. Following all the advice I heard in a TED talk. I must think positive. I must look to the future. Thinking positive is so important. But, Sarah, when I saw your distress as they questioned you, it broke my heart in two.

I will make it up to you. I promise. When I get out of here, I will take you travelling to all the places you wanted to go to with him; Australia, New Zealand, Thailand, Cambodia. I'll add Petra and Jordan to the list, too. And what about a safari in South Africa? Alsatian dog? No problem. I will do whatever you want.

As I sit picturing a fluffy Alsatian puppy in my arms, a guard arrives to take me to court. He is a hefty man with long, greasy hair. He grunts at me in Italian and leads me up from the basement into court.

Everything in the room fades as I look across at my family sitting in a row, ashen and silent. Patrick and Janice sit on either side of you, holding your hands. Resolve to get out of here tightens inside me. I must stay totally on the ball, for your sake. For Patrick. For Janice.

The rest of the room comes into focus again. Antonio Russo and his assistant Marco are poring over court papers and chatting, faces grave.

The court translator hovers next to the throned judges. She is very seventies looking. Short, severe hair. Pretty, with a perfect figure. Sexy cool, not sexy feminine. Large gypsy hoops dangling from her ears. The lay judge jury sit waiting silently in their fancy-dress costumes. The hatchet man they call the *pubblico ministero*, who looks like Rufus Sewell gone wrong, is staring straight ahead, tapping his fingers on his desk. The older judge rises from his throne to speak. The sharpness of his voice blasts into my mind like a pneumatic drill. The translator smooths the skirt of her dress, over her pear-shaped hips.

'May the defendant, Ralph Kensington, please stand. I call the *pubblico ministero* to cross-examine him,' she requests.

Rufus Sewell stretches his lanky frame from his seat, and begins to speak.

'We will start by discussing the death of Jack Rutherford,' the translator begins. 'You will be aware that we found notes on Gemma Richardson's phone, which suggest that if anything were to happen to her, she had information for the police. Can you explain why she feared something may happen to her? And why, at that time, she suspected you had already murdered someone?'

I take a deep breath. 'Yes. It's quite simple. She was insecure and unstable. Fantasising about issues that weren't there.'

Translator. *Pubblico ministero*. Translator again.

'In that case, why did you ask her to marry you?' she asks.

'I only found out how unstable Gemma was after her death.'

The incessant Italian is fading from my mind. All I can hear is English. The court is receding into a misty distance. All I can see is the translator's neat-featured face.

'We'll talk about Gemma Richardson's death later. First we are addressing the death of Jack Rutherford. Gemma Richardson has declared, on notes we discovered on her phone, that she saw you climbing over the balustrade of Villa Panorama, just before twelve noon on the day Jack went missing, looking around surreptitiously. What were you doing?'

'That's easy to explain, I had dropped the villa key over the edge of the balustrade. I jumped over to pick it up.'

'So you weren't trying to conceal the direction you were coming from?'

'Of course not. No.'

'Don't lie, Mr Kensington, we know you killed Jack Rutherford.'

The older judge shouts, '*Interrogatorio inappropriato*.' His shouts are so loud once again Italian cuts into my mind like a knife.

'*Scusate*,' the *pubblico ministero* replies.

To avoid confusion, I need to try harder to push the Italian away.

'What about the espadrilles you were wearing?'

I shrug. 'What about them?'

'Forensics collected from their soles alongside dated proof show you walked from the cliff path to the back of the villa, over scrubland, on the day Jack went missing. What were you doing?'

'I've already told you, I was picking up the key I'd dropped.'

Are they bluffing? Did Gemma really take my espadrilles, when I thought I had lost them? Is that the forensic evidence she hinted at having found? Or are they back in my bedroom in London with the other stuff I had to pack quickly when I left, and the prosecution are bluffing to force me to confess?

The translator pauses, and takes a sip of water from the table to her right.

'As you have heard during the trial,' she continues, 'we have spoken to your son, daughter and ex-wife. It is well known throughout your family and friends that you were still very smitten with your ex-wife and were shocked and jealous when you were told of her engagement. You had motive. Did you kill Jack Rutherford in a jealous rage?'

Both judges reprimand the *pubblico ministero*. I do not need to understand Italian to understand that. Rufus Sewell just looks across at the lay judge jury and widens his saucers for eyes.

'I didn't kill Jack Rutherford,' I shout through gritted teeth. 'Why would I do something like that to the woman I love?'

'So you do still love her then? Your family are correct.'

My head spins into the memory.

I see him in front of me. Remembering the way he tried to get away from me. The way he put his hand on my arm.

'Thanks for the chat, mate. I'd better go. I'm off to the village to get a present for Sarah. I'll see you back at the villa. Let's continue our conversation there,' he said.

I held his gaze. 'Please, don't go yet,' I begged. 'It is far more private talking here.'

'OK. I can stay a bit longer.' He paused, put his head on one side and smiled at me. 'Your life will move on. I'm sure you'll meet someone special soon.'

What a condescending prick. I closed my eyes and thought of Gemma. Her face floated in front of me, stained with too much lipstick and fake tan. She was too young. Too unsophisticated. Anyone with any common sense could see she wasn't the one for me. His words rotated in my mind. Sycophantic. Condescending. Hypocritical. I could not let him get away with treating me like this.

'I had met someone very special. You poached her, you dick,' I said.

'That's not fair. It wasn't quite like that.'

'Well, what was it like?' I asked, fantasising about strangling him slowly. Pushing the air from his windpipe, fingers tightening. Watching his face go red then blue. Watching him trying to gasp for breath but not able to inhale any. The imaginary image faded and he smiled slowly.

'As I said, we got to know each other gradually. It was through the school play, actually. That was when we realised just how much we had in common.'

'Is Twickenham School a sort of RADA for adulterers?' I spat.

He looked so sad. 'Come on, Ralph, be serious. Let's try and communicate properly.' He paused. 'You are practical, interested in figures and numbers. Sarah has eclectic taste; reading anything from magical realism to historical fiction. The most well-read person I've ever met. You don't even like books . . .'

Indignation exploded inside me. 'So fucking what?' I shouted.

What the hell was wrong with the maniac that you had become attached to? Why did he think how many books you read a week mattered? I supposed he was an intellectual snob – after all, he was a school head.

'Who the fuck do you think you are? The reading police? We talked about her favourite book the day we met,' I shouted, and then I exaggerated. 'Sarah continued to make love to me long after she left me. Did she tell you that, you prick?'

Slowly, slowly, his face went ashen. 'She didn't tell me that because it didn't happen.'

I smiled a saccharin smile, and then I made up a date and lied. 'Go on then. Tell me where she was on Friday the sixteenth of May. Three months ago.'

His eyes narrowed. 'I don't know. She's not a prisoner. I don't keep tabs on her.'

'Let me tell you, she was on her back, legs open in my sitting room, begging me to get inside her.'

He grew paler still, whiter than white. 'You're a liar,' he hissed.

I stood up. 'How dare you call me that. I'm not a liar. You're a gullible idiot. If she loves you so much, why is she still shagging me? Has been for years. Or are you cool with that? Maybe you are one of those guys who thinks there is no overlap between sex and feelings?'

He pulled himself up from the bench in front of me. We faced off, eyeball to eyeball.

'Did she need me because even when you first met you were already too old to get it up?' I taunted.

He clenched his fist and pushed it hard and fast into my face. I was out of it for a bit. When I came round, he was hovering over me; fussing.

'Leave me alone, you violent bastard. I hate you for stealing my wife.'

'You've been unconscious. It's all right. You're just coming round,' he said in a soothing sympathetic voice as if he was pretending to be the Angel Gabriel. 'Come on, Ralph, are you OK? Can you try to sit up? I need to know whether to call an ambulance,' he simpered.

'If we call an ambulance it'll be for you not me,' I said with a snarl. 'You are the weed and the wuss.'

I pushed my torso up with my arms. He made a big thing of sighing with relief as if he thought he had really hurt me.

'Good. Good. Take it easy and rest and then we can see whether you can stand,' he said.

'Of course I can fucking stand,' I barked. 'Mr Fucking Fusspot.' I put my head back and laughed. 'Are you feeling guilty that you hit me because you found out that the woman you love is a whore?'

'Sarah is not a whore.' His face contorted with pain.

'Ha ha, why does she sleep with me then, when she feels like it? Isn't sleeping with two men at the same time rather promiscuous? I wonder how many other men she is banging.' I was proud of myself for emphasising the word banging with devilry in my voice. 'Don't you worry about STDs?'

'Ralph, come on, let's stop arguing. Let's go back to the villa and calm down,' he started up again.

'I don't want to stop arguing. I just want to kill you,' I told him.

The wuss looked terrified. But he tightened his fist, pulled his arm back and thrust it into my face again. Then the coward turned tail and ran. That was the second time he had pounded me. I wasn't going to put up with any more of that. I caught up with him, and wrapped my arms around him. His body seemed to crumple in my arms. I crunched my right fist into his left cheek. His body stiffened and he retaliated by thrusting his knee into my crotch.

Crotch on fire, body on fire, my resentment, my hatred, rose inside me. I couldn't push it down. I couldn't control it. My headbutt, neatly done, grounded him. Flat on his back. Unconscious. Sun beating down on him. Cicadas serenading him. I rolled him towards the edge of the cliff. My back ached. I straightened up to rub it, and stood looking down at him. His closed eyelids flickered. At this point he was still alive. Was he dreaming? Mouth open. Dribble leaking. Oh, Sarah, I looked down at him at this point, confounded as to how you could have run off with this aggressive man. After all, he had started the violence.

Rolling him was difficult. Although slim, he was muscle bound and heavy. I struggled to navigate his body over the stony rock. At last, I reached a grassy crevice at the edge of the cliff. I grabbed his ankles and pulled him further along to where three lonely pine trees hid us from any passers-by on the path. I sighed as I dropped his feet to the ground. His head lolled to one side, but he didn't stir. It was approaching midday by then, the sun was high, and the earth seemed to be sweating. My heart pounded in my chest.

I stepped to the cliff edge and peered over. Rock cascaded into the sea like a tumultuous mountain. Sheer. Deathly. Shocking. The height made my head spin and my stomach rotate. I sat down and put my head in my hands. My head began to slow down. If I pushed him off the edge, I figured no one would ever know. It would look like suicide. And then I would have you, Sarah, to myself again. As I stood above him, watching him lying unconscious, the hatred I felt for him welled inside me. I pictured him lying next to you in bed, caressing you.

And then I saw you walking towards me the first day we met in Bristol. You smiled at me with your sapphire eyes. My mind contorted and you were walking down the aisle towards me on our wedding day. The jealousy inside me scalded me as I felt the early heat of your love, your kiss. As I saw you exhausted in the delivery room, holding our babies close to your chest, something snapped inside me and I knew no one else could ever have you.

I rolled the already dead weight of his body to the edge of the cliff. I struggled to pull him up to standing. Then I lifted him as far as I could and threw him over the cliff. He was so heavy it wasn't much of a throw. He tumbled, hitting the cliff face with his head, then somersaulting down, bumping and banging as he fell. He went sideways into the water. Perhaps he was already dead. Perhaps he drowned. I knew only forensics would tell me now.

'Mr Kensington, are you all right?' the translator is asking. 'Do you need a drink of water? Do you need a recess? You look as if you're about to collapse.'

'I'm fine to continue,' I say through gritted teeth.

167
Sarah

My heart rips apart as I sit in court watching Ralph. He looks so wounded and forlorn. So vulnerable. So familiar. It is clear from the way the judge is questioning him that the judge thinks he killed Jack and Gemma. But he's never been a monster. He loved me. He loved our children. Would he be capable of such cruelty? Of murdering the man I love? Of murdering a young woman? But if I believe him, Jack, I have to assume that you are a rapist; a power-crazy misogynist. Or that you were unhappy with me and committed suicide.

One of the men in my life has been hiding a terrible secret. But which one? And why?

168
Ralph

I'm sweating. I'm shaking.

'If you are sure you don't need a short recess, we'll continue and address the death of Gemma Richardson. Is that OK?'

I nod my head. 'Yes.'

'How do you explain the CCTV footage of you carrying what appeared to be a body past the security camera protecting Villa Bella next door to Villa Panorama, the night before she "went travelling"?'

'You must be mistaken. It wasn't me. I guess your footage just isn't very clear.'

'And that her body has been recovered from beneath the cement floor that had been laid earlier that day?'

'I have no comment other than that I didn't kill Gemma.'

But my memory moves towards me once more.

'What are you doing?' she bleated as I threw her onto the bed.

She continued mumbling and muttering, but it was too late. I did not care what she did or said. She was threatening to discredit me. The bitch could not live. She bit my arm. Her teeth broke my skin. I held her arms above her head, and kicked her in the chin with my knee. That knocked the wind out of her. I kicked her in the chin again. I didn't expect it to be this easy. I tightened my fingers around her neck and she lost consciousness immediately, after only a bit of a struggle . . . She died quickly. Sweetly. She can't have suffered much.

When it was over I lay next to her body in bed and pulled the covers over her, just leaving the top of her head exposed. My pounding heart was slowing. My white-hot anger beginning to cool. I knew there was nothing I could have done to save her. She had to go. She was a danger to my wellbeing, and to that of my family. I told everyone she was ill with a migraine while I worried over what to do with her body.

I had to wait until the evening to do something about it. I tucked her up in bed to make it look as if she was sleeping, and locked the door to our bedroom. That night I lay next to her body, still thinking about my best course of action, the thin curtains bleeding light from the terrace. The crisp sharp light of the full moon. The beat from the distant nightclub grew louder in my restless mind as time passed. Gemma's open eyes fixed on me and accused me. I tried to close them, but it was impossible because of rigor mortis.

Instead of just leaving her in bed for longer, I panicked. I got out of bed and emptied the wardrobe, placing its contents under the bed. I rolled her off the edge of the bed. She fell onto the floor with a thud. I waited with bated breath in case anyone heard and came to see if I was all right. My heart was pounding so much I felt it beating against my eardrums. Five minutes passed. No one appeared. I took a deep breath, put my hands beneath her armpits and dragged her backwards towards the wardrobe. Squashing her inside was a real business. But somehow I managed, pressing her arms and legs awkwardly into a position where I could close the door.

I flopped back into bed, exhausted, panting and hot. Where, where could I bury her body? Where should I tell people she had gone? Her migraine couldn't last forever. I was sweating. I was panicking. Sleeping was impossible. I slipped out of bed and crept carefully down into the kitchen. I poured myself a glass of water and sat on the patio looking up at the full moon. Restlessness gyrated inside me like giant butterfly wings.

I left the villa and walked along the passageway towards town, slowly creeping along, desperate not to draw attention to myself. I reached the building site next door and my stomach rotated. Could this be my opportunity? I went to take a look. I opened the gate and stumbled towards the new foundations, switching on the torch on my iPhone to guide me. Wet concrete. Perfect.

Back to the villa I crept. Slowly, slowly, lifting her out of the wardrobe. She was so heavy as I lifted her that I thought I was getting a hernia, I gritted my teeth and staggered to the building site with Gemma across my shoulders. Panting and puffing, struggling for air. I rolled and kicked her body into the wet concrete. I pushed it down with the end of the rake that the builders had left, thrusting and prodding to dig her in far enough, until my arms ached. I smoothed it over carefully. I knew that by morning it would have set. Relief flooded through me. I really thought I had got away with this.

CCTV. Who would have thought of that, on a building site in a secure location? I will carry on denying this. What I said to the *pubblico ministero* may well be correct. The CCTV will be too blurry to be of any significance. It is often of such poor quality.

'Did you take Gemma's phone to the ferry port in Amalfi?' the translator asks.

'No.'

'Did you plant it in a young traveller's backpack to make it look as if she was alive and on the move?'

'Of course not. No.'

As if anyone would have recognised or remembered me. Six a.m., just as the sun was beginning to rise up across the silky ocean, I left the villa and walked to the bus stop carrying a beach bag and towel, dressed in shorts and a T-shirt. Just another tourist on the move. Just another tourist on the way to the ferry port. The bus stop was surrounded by an Italian version of a queue; heaving, chattering and thrusting. I stood to one side, head down. I did not want to catch anyone's eye.

As we all know, only too well, the bus journey from Praiano is one of the most beautiful journeys in the world. The road winds along the majesty of the cliff, buildings and trees clinging on like limpets. The sea a most exquisite turquoise, glittering beneath. The road is so narrow that the bus seems almost too large to fit on it when it turns corners. The uninitiated take a sharp intake of breath at every bend. Even the roadside flowers blaze with beauty; bougainvillea, lilies, orchids, geranium and hibiscus. The tourists sit wide eyed in wonderment. The locals continue their rattling chatter. It was a perfectly possible journey for Gemma to be making as I sat cradling her phone in my pocket.

Yes, it is true, I disembarked at Molo Pennello; the ferry port, but I challenge the bastards to prove it. I sat in the café and bought an espresso; head down, pretending to study a ferry timetable, but surreptitiously looking for an opportunity. Two young women were sitting in the corner by the toilets. A similar age to Gemma. Wearing espadrilles and denim shorts. One in a yellow lacy T-shirt. One in a black Rolling Stones T-shirt with big red lips blazoned across it. One taller and slimmer with short blonde curly hair. The other with generous breasts and an ocean of chestnut hair tumbling down her back. Rucksacks placed at the side of their table as they sat drinking Coke Zero and tucking into slices of pizza.

I walked past the young women to go to the bathroom and tripped over their rucksacks. Flopping over on top of them, I slipped Gemma's phone into a side pocket of the one closest to my right hand.

I stood up and dusted myself off. 'So sorry,' I said as I read their luggage labels.

Roma tours. On their way to Rome via Salerno and Sorrento. I so hoped Gemma's phone would enjoy the trip. And, you bastard *pubblico ministero*, they never fucking realised what was happening. Anger towards the prosecution pulsates inside me. It can't be true. They can't have found these women; and they wouldn't be able to identify me anyway. They only saw my face for one second.

The *pubblico ministero* is speaking again. The translator is looking at him and nodding. She turns to me.

'Let's move on.' She takes another sip of water. 'Did you keep Gemma's credit cards and use them to pay prostitutes to stay in posh hotels so that the police would assume that was where Gemma was?'

'No. As if I would have the wherewithal to do that.'

How did they manage to figure that? The police were getting suspicious that she didn't answer her calls, even though I had managed to send people fake texts. So I knew I needed to sell Gemma's credit card details to a crook in Rome, as quickly as possible. A crook who wanted to stay in top hotels. I thought a top-end prostitute would be perfect. I grabbed a bottle of chilled rosé from the kitchen and hibernated in my bedroom with my computer. I'm a smart guy. I know a thing or two about the dark net and it's easier to negotiate than people imagine.

Two hours, and another bottle of rosé, later, I had achieved my objective. Mafia prostitute codename Chiara B had bought Gemma's card. Chiara B was going to use it to carry out some top-end business at the Rome Cavalieri hotel and the Palazzo Montemartini over the next week. And then she was off to the sumptuous Helvetia and Bristol hotel in Florence. All in Gemma's name. Fantastic hotels with designer spas. Serving designer food that looks like a work of art. They have designer swimming pools with marble pillars and floors. Ornate beds decorated with gold filigree. I thought that when the police came to find Gemma and found Chiara B using Gemma's card, they would not know how she obtained it. They most certainly wouldn't be able to point the finger at me. The dark net makes sure everyone's tracks are invisible, doesn't it? The *pubblico ministero* is making this up to try and trap me into a confession. The only way forward is to carry on with my denial.

I look across the court room and see my barrister sitting as still as a statue, face immobile. But you, Sarah, are sitting with tears streaming down your face. A sliver of guilt pierces through me. Perhaps I shouldn't have lied to you about the morals of your man. I could have just killed him and left it at that.

169
Janice

Dad's trial is over. We're waiting for the judgement. Mother hardly ever leaves her tiny room in the boutique hotel. Neither does Patrick. He's trying to keep up with his medical course online. I'm studying for my A-levels online too. But I manage to take off more time than him.

All this worry about Dad is not aiding my concentration. I'm trying to plough through *Bleak House* by Charles Dickens because I need to write an essay on it. I must admit I'm finding it heavy going. I'm longing to curl up with a cosy crime or a romance.

I'm walking the streets of Amalfi, thinking back to the first morning of our holiday, when unbeknown to us, Jack had already 'fallen' off the cliff. The morning I went shopping with Anna and Patrick, worrying over my relationship with my mother, no idea in my head that there was any problem with Dad. How can he be denying everything when there is so much evidence against him?

I stand at the top of the sweeping stone steps that lead up to the cathedral in Amalfi, and once again admire the quirky mix of its architecture. I turn and look down on the square below. It's the tail end of the season now. A smattering of tourists are sitting outside in the pavement cafés, wearing light jumpers and jackets. Drinking coffee and hot chocolate. Eating pastries and pizza and pasta. Less gelato. Fewer cold beers. I look down on the fountain, at the innocent cherubs who surround it.

I step inside the cathedral. My footsteps echo across black and white marble. I look up and wonder at the beauty of the frescoes. I sit down on a long wooden pew and put my head in my hands. Last summer I came in here and my heart ached for my mother. Now when I think of my father, my heart turns to lead.

170

Sarah

I'm sitting in court waiting to hear Ralph's judgement. Patrick and Janice sit either side of me and I hold tightly on to both their hands. Our palms are damp with sweat. The two lead judges enter the court, dressed up to the nines in their black robes with gold epaulettes and ruffled eighteenth-century shirts. The lay judges follow them in a slow sombre procession; all adorned with silk sashes; striped red, white and green. The colours of the Italian flag, but in the opposite order. I do not know what it represents.

I hold my breath as guards lead Ralph in. My hands tighten around my children's. He stands at the front of the court, to our left, surrounded by eight guards. Ralph is smartly dressed in a suit and a freshly ironed shirt. His hair is brushed to shine. But he is ashen with dark bags beneath his eyes. As I wait for the judgement, I do not know what to believe. I do not know how I feel about him.

The lay judge jury sit down. The older lead judge remains standing. The translator enters court and stands right next to him. She is dressed in a simple black dress today, and has swapped her flamboyant hoop earrings for pearl studs. Tasteful. Elegant. Silence settles across the court room.

The judge speaks. The translator continues.

'The jury find Ralph Kensington . . . guilty of the murder of Jack Rutherford and Gemma Richardson.'

I take a sharp breath. Ralph's body crumples and is straightened by the guards around him.

'I sentence him to life imprisonment.'

171

Ralph

The guards escort me out of court and herd me into a compartment in a van. The compartment is like a prison cell with no windows. Life imprisonment. Life over. I'll have to appeal. They won't get away with this.

172

Sarah

Patrick, Janice and I step outside the courthouse, blinking in the sharp afternoon sunlight. After so many days incarcerated in court, it seems strange to see a world going on around us as if nothing earth shattering has happened. Traffic buzzing past. People ambling along the pavement laden with shopping. A pair of young lovers, hand in hand. An elderly couple, arms entwined, leaning on their sticks.

The taxi Patrick has ordered pulls up. We open the doors and climb inside. The driver, who is about forty and completely bald, nods in greeting, starts the engine and sets off. We sit in silence. He turns the radio up. Classic rock blasts out. Nostalgia for my teenage years fills the air. I'm back listening to music at impromptu parties that sprang up when people's parents were out; snogging, smoking, drinking cider, our whole life ahead of us. And later, listening to Radio 2 with you, Jack. Reminiscing about all the music we used to love; Nirvana, Oasis, Aerosmith.

The taxi pulls up outside the hotel. I lean forward and pay the driver. We slip out and feeling weak and depleted now, I stagger into the hallway.

'Let's have a drink in the bar,' Patrick suggests.

'I feel so tired. I think I'll just go and lie down,' I reply.

Janice puts her hands on my shoulders. 'Come on, Mum. Let's have a drink. Let's talk.'

My children take me by the arms and lead me to the bar. It is small and dark, with no windows, lined with wood panelling. At least it doesn't have a view of the cliffs.

'What would you like, Mum? A double tequila on the rocks?' Patrick suggests.

I pull a face. 'No, thanks.'

'Well, you need something stronger than a Diet Coke.'

'Let's have some red wine,' I suggest.

Patrick orders a bottle of Barolo and some bread and olives.

We sit at a small round table in the far corner of the bar. Patrick pours the wine. He takes a sip.

'So, OK, where do we go from here?' he asks.

I take a sip of red wine. I cannot reply. How do we cope with a father and ex-husband who is a convicted murderer? I cannot even bear to say the words out loud. This isn't me. This isn't us. It's not our family. It is a nightmare that must be happening to someone else.

'Mum, how are you going to cope with the loss of Jack?' There is a pause. 'And for that matter, how am I going to cope with the loss of Anna?'

'Anna isn't dead. At least you have a chance of getting her back if you want to,' Janice snaps.

'I suppose we'll cope a day at a time,' I say limply, taking another slug of wine. 'Like everyone else.'

'That's right, Mother,' Janice replies. 'Life is life. Life is what we see. Life is what we get.'

Not quite sure what Janice means, I have another sip of wine and nod my head.

173

Ralph

Back in prison, I am frogmarched by two guards into a new area. When I left for court this morning, I was in the remand section, now I am taken to the convicted area. I am shoved unceremoniously into a very similar cell to the one I was in before. Again, it's not so much a cell as a cage. The walls are not walls but metal bars. The cell is a similar layout and size to the previous one, but instead of three prisoners inside, now we are five.

Thrown roughly inside, I land on the floor. I pull myself up to standing and find myself face to face with a bruiser of a man with a shaved head and missing front teeth.

'*Buongiorno*. Me, Flavio,' he says.

'Ralph,' I reply.

He takes my right hand in his and crushes it until I wince in pain.

'You English *merda*,' he says and spits on the ground in front of me.

It doesn't take a language whizz to realise that *merda* means shit. It doesn't take a body-language expert to realise that I'm not welcome in here.

He points to a bunk on top of two others, with hardly enough room for a body to fit between the mattress and the ceiling. 'For you.'

'How do I get up there?' I ask.

Flavio doesn't reply. I guess he doesn't understand my question. I'll figure out how to climb up there later.

The other three are sitting on the lower bunks glowering at me. A youngster in his twenties with large brown eyes and chestnut hair. A man of about forty with dreadlocks. Another bruiser who could be Flavio's brother for his looks. Shaved head. Missing teeth. I suppose the dentistry isn't much good in here.

Flavio points at me. 'Tonight, you cook,' he shouts.

I step into the kitchen and toilet area, and my stomach churns. The toilet is in the corner of the kitchen as in my previous cell. This time it is full of diarrhoea. Flies hover around the bowl. I bend down and flush the toilet, but no water comes out. I look around for somewhere to wash my hands but I can't see a basin, so I rub my hands on my jeans and hope for the best.

I step across to the work surface where the ingredients for today's supper are waiting in a brown paper bag. A loaf of bread. Eight plum tomatoes. A red onion and some garlic. My stomach tightens. What should I make?

Tomato soup. That is all I can think of. So I fry the garlic, onions and tomatoes then add some bottled water that I have found on the shelf above the cooker. Finally, I add some salt and pepper, and simmer my concoction for ten minutes. I cut us a generous slice of bread each and toast it. I serve it and step into the cell with each portion to give it to my cellmates. Then I step into the cell with mine. Before I can sit down to eat, Flavio shouts, '*Merda*,' and pours his soup on the floor. One by one, the others do the same.

I push past them and shout through the cell bars for a guard. No one comes. I shout and shout. I need to see my lawyer as soon as possible. I need to arrange my first appeal.

174
Sarah

I stumble into bed after too much red wine, wishing I was stumbling into your arms, my dearest Jack, memories of the gentleness of your touch cascading through my mind. The softness of your kiss. The warmth of your body lying close to mine. And then I picture the indignation on Ralph's face when he told me what you did to Gemma. He must have been lying. He has lied about so much; and I am back feeling the pain of Gemma beating me up and pushing me off the cliff.

I love you, Jack. I miss you so much. I wish you could fold me in your arms and tell me the truth. The truth I want to hear. That you didn't lay a finger on her.

175
Ralph

I'm sitting in a meeting room with stone walls that sweat with damp. My lawyer, Antonio Russo, is sitting opposite me; dressed down today in blue chinos and a Ralph Lauren shirt. He taps his fingers on the plastic table in between us. As usual his nails are perfectly manicured; cuticles like half-moons.

He sips water from the paper cup in front of him. 'You wanted to see me; how can I help you?' he asks.

'I wanted to discuss my first appeal.'

He shakes his head. His silky black hair slides across his forehead. He pushes it out of his eyes.

'You are entitled to appeal; three times. But the evidence against you is so overwhelming, you don't have any chance of winning.' I look into his dark eyes. 'You've been caught red handed; with both CCTV and forensic evidence. You've lied to the court. You lied to me, your lawyer.' He lifts his hands in the air, palms upright, and shakes them. 'I told you I needed to know the truth.'

'I told you the truth and I want to appeal.'

He shrugs. 'Each appeal takes years and costs a lot of money. I know you're a wealthy man, but I can assure you it will bleed your family dry.'

'Weren't Amanda Knox and Raffaele Sollecito exonerated because of contaminated evidence? What if my espadrilles were contaminated in the lab?'

His lips stiffen. 'Unlike you, they were stitched up. I've already had the forensics double checked. At no time in your evidence did you suggest you ever climbed away from the cliff path through shrubbery and brushland. Forensics show you did.'

'So I just have to sit back and accept I'll die in gaol?'

'That's right. I'm afraid that is my opinion, yes.'

I clench my fist beneath the table. I want to hit him and dishevel his perfect Al Pacino face. I take a deep breath and relax my fingers. Damaging my lawyer's bone structure isn't going to help my case, but it might mean I'll be put in solitary and that might be better than having to share with Flavio and friends. Should I? Shouldn't I? I decide against it and let my fingers relax.

176
Sarah

'I'm flying home tomorrow. I've come to say goodbye, Ralph.' The visiting room smells rancid. What must the rest of this place be like? I look across at Ralph, wearing an old pair of jeans and a faded T-shirt. A belter of a bruise on his right cheek. Someone must have really gone for him. Double murderers must be regarded as free game in a place like this. I shudder at the thought of what his life has become.

His eyes darken. 'Well, that's very nice of you. It's goodbye and good riddance, I expect.'

I sigh. 'Ralph, let's not go there.'

He leans towards me as if he is taunting me. 'Go where?' he asks.

I swallow to stop myself from crying. 'Into the past. I can't cope with any detail of it. I just need to hold it together and try and move forwards.' I pause. 'Patrick wants to know whether you are going to appeal?'

'Why doesn't the little bastard come and see me and ask himself?'

I shake my head. 'He can't face it.' I pause. 'And he's flying home with me tomorrow. Janice is staying a bit longer. She's coming to see you as soon as she is allowed a visit. Patrick is coming home to support me. And he needs to get back to his medical course. He asked me to ask you about the case.'

A frown ripples across his forehead. 'My lawyer has told me he thinks appealing is a waste of money. There's too much evidence against me.'

My stomach tightens. 'If you can't appeal, it must be true that you're guilty,' I push.

He leans back in his chair and forces a smile. A smile so artificial it might as well be a frown. A contorted expression that quickly fades. 'What do you think?'

'I find it hard to believe you would have done anything as awful as killing my fiancé and your girlfriend. But if I don't believe it, it means Jack was either unhappy with me and suicidal, or a rapist.' I pause. 'None of the scenarios are very pleasant, are they?'

Ralph tries to smile again. This time he almost succeeds. The corners of his lips flicker upwards. 'You have to make a choice; him or me.'

He reaches across the table and puts his hand on mine. I pull my hand away as if I have been burnt. 'Is that what you want? Me to have to make a choice?'

'Maybe. Work it out for yourself. You know I've always wanted you. What do you think happened?'

The knots in my stomach tighten. Despair washes over me like a tidal wave. He is so strange. So damaged. So different from the person I thought I knew. I should never have come to see him.

'Please, Ralph. Please. I am so contorted by this. I don't care who did what anymore. I just want to know the truth – no more legalistic games.'

177

Ralph

I take pity on you. You deserve to know the truth. Not just a version of the truth banged out between lawyers in court. I look around before speaking, and lower my voice.

'It wasn't Gemma. The court was right. I did kill him. In a jealous rage. I loved you too much, Sarah, and I couldn't cope with the fact that just when I had thought I was on the verge of getting you back, you were marrying him.' You sit with your head in your hands. You hold your knees into your stomach and rock your body forwards and backwards. I stand up to try to comfort you.

'Don't come near me. Don't touch me,' you hiss.

I step back and sit down again. My life is over. What have I done to the woman I love?

'Please, forgive me, Sarah,' I beg.

You don't reply. You breathe deeply and swallow your sobs.

'And what about Gemma?' you ask.

'I killed her, too. To stop her telling the police about me. I lied to you about Jack raping Gemma, he never did any such thing. It was a contortion of the truth. She had been raped by someone else, years ago, and that person had died a few days later, which she felt was retribution. Her experience, which she had discussed with me, gave me the idea for the lie. Those are the best lies. The ones that are closest to the truth.' I pause for breath and take a sip of water from the plastic cup in front of me.

'You bastard. How could you do this? Kill my fiancé? Kill your girlfriend? And if that isn't enough, make out that the man I love committed a hideous crime?'

You are trembling, and I cannot bear to look at you. I look at the floor as I continue.

'I guess she made a pass at him that night, the night we arrived, while we were at the piazza, and he rejected her. Janice told me she heard them arguing as she went to bed. In the morning I caught Gemma mumbling in her sleep. *Jack, don't you want me? Don't you want me?* She loved flirting with other men to try and get my attention. Didn't you see the way she was always trying it on with Patrick? And she was so very jealous of my feelings for you. So I just took the fact that there had been an unpleasant incident between them and contorted it into a convenient lie, to try and protect myself.'

I stop speaking and look across at you. Your face is still, motionless. I have never seen such a ghostly lack of expression on your face. You look like a different person. Shell shocked. Diminished.

'You are a monster, not a man. How could you do this to me?'

'I lied to you because I wanted you to be with me, which you wouldn't if you knew I had killed Jack,' I continue. 'I love you too much. That's why all this happened in the first place. I only ever wanted you. Please, please, forgive me?' I beg.

'Ralph, I will never forgive you. Real love isn't selfish like this.'

178

Sarah

Back home, kneeling by your grave. I lean forwards and gently place twelve red roses on your tombstone, tears rolling down my face.

Oh Jack, I'm so sorry I ever believed you didn't want to be with me and committed suicide. I'm so sorry I ever even entertained the thought you raped Gemma. I feel unworthy of your love. Unclean. As if I have betrayed you and been unfaithful. The mainstay of a relationship is trust, and I haven't given you enough.

I promise you, Jack, that even though I am leaden with grief for you I am going to endeavour to make the best of the time I have left. For your sake. In your memory. As I am blessed to have more time, I will make sure I use it wisely.

I will do everything I can to love and support Janice and Patrick. I will continue with my commitment to teaching English. A good teacher, helping young people, can exert their influence like ripples on a pond. Ripples of energy that keep on encouraging ideas for years to come. You always said that, Jack. That was why you were such a good head and so very loved. Because you cared about your pupils' futures.

I am going to visit the home where Susan died and take an interest in people like her who are suffering. I am going to use the rest of my life fighting for greater good.

179

Patrick

Anna is observing on a ward at the Bristol Royal Hospital for Children. I found out from a friend of a friend of hers. I asked a nurse in the department which rota she was on and when she would finish her shift. I'm about to surprise her with the largest bunch of flowers I could carry. Lilies, roses and delphinium. I'm sitting in the waiting area for parents, just outside the ward.

I hear footsteps along the corridor. I look up, hopefully. It is her, looking brisk, neat and efficient, with a stethoscope around her neck. I spring up and walk towards her. Her face lights up when she sees me. I press the flowers into her arms.

'Anna, please come home. I love you so much.'

180

Janice

Father, you are a danger. A menace to society. I do not want you to live. I look you in the eye as I hand you the small peeling knife I have smuggled past security. You asked me for help to kill yourself, and I've given it. I always told you I had the evil eye. My counselling is really helping, so I'm using it well this time. You're right, you are a bad man. You don't deserve to live. Use the knife quickly. Dig it in deep.

Acknowledgements

I would like to thank all the usual suspects; my wonderful agent Ger Nichol, my editor Lucy Frederick and the team at Avon Harper Collins, and my dutiful husband and first reader Richard Gillis QC. The idea for writing this book came to me on a very special holiday in Praiano with a group of friends from the Cayman Islands. Just to say they are great fun and a far cry from the main characters in this book.

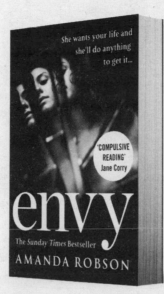

A new couple moves in next door. Nothing will ever be the same again . . .

'Dark, gripping, brutal. I loved every minute'

JACKIE KABLER

(Author of *The Perfect Couple*)